Praise for *And They Lived Happily Ever After*

"This richly emotional rom-com is electric enough to kickstart even the most cynical heart. Achingly real, unexpectedly whimsical, and wholly original."
—Talia Hibbert, *New York Times* bestselling author of *Act Your Age, Eve Brown*

"Therese Beharrie's lovely *And They Lived Happily Ever After* is a warm, witty book that sensitively explores how anxiety and grief can make life and relationships more difficult, and does so with boundless empathy for all its characters. As Beharrie makes comfortingly clear, you can be anxious or conflicted and still be loved for exactly who you are. A little magic along the way doesn't hurt, either—which is handy, since I happily fell under this touching story's spell."
—Olivia Dade, author of *Spoiler Alert*

AND they LIVED Happily EVER After

Therese Beharrie

ZEBRA BOOKS
Kensington Publishing Corp.
www.kensingtonbooks.com

ZEBRA BOOKS are published by
Kensington Publishing Corp.
119 West 40th Street
New York, NY 10018

All Kensington titles, imprints, and distributed lines are available at special quantity discounts for bulk purchases for sales promotion, premiums, fund-raising, educational, or institutional use.

Special book excerpts or customized printings can also be created to fit specific needs. For details, write or phone the office of the Kensington Sales Manager: Attn.: Sales Department. Kensington Publishing Corp., 119 West 40th Street, New York, NY 10018. Phone: 1-800-221-2647.

First Zebra Trade Printing: December 2021

ISBN-13: 978-1-4201-5338-5
ISBN-13: 978-1-4201-5339-2 (ebook)

10 9 8 7 6 5 4 3 2 1

Printed in the United States of America

For my babies. You've brought more joy and love to my world
than I could ever imagine.
For my husband, because I've never been anxious about you.
And for every person struggling with an anxiety disorder.
I see you.

Author's Note

While this book is ultimately a hopeful and joyful love story, please be aware that it portrays an anxiety disorder with on-page panic attacks. It also deals with themes about foster care and adoption, and mentions deceased parents. If you find any of these triggering, please put your mental health first.

PROLOGUE

Since Gaia Anders turned eighteen, her life had changed pretty dramatically. She was no longer in high school, and she was no longer in foster care.

She was *free*.

It had only taken sixteen years—she'd been in the system since she was two—but she was finally waking up in her own bed.

She did a little wriggle, her body acting of its own accord, as if it wanted to celebrate that she was, indeed, waking up in the first bed she'd ever owned. Sure, it was secondhand and a little lumpy and might have been used for activities she'd rather not dwell on, but it was *hers*. She had bought it with the money from her student loan, which just about covered her university tuition and half the rent of a small flat a trek away from where her classes would be when things started in a few weeks.

Also, the bed. Which made the fact that she had almost nothing else in her room, and would likely have nothing else in her room for a while, worth it.

She went through her morning routine, enjoying the silence she hadn't experienced much in her life. Her roommate was staying over at her boyfriend Seth's place, an occurrence she hoped happened often so she could enjoy many more silences. And appliances. Apparently Joss's parents wanted her to have a toaster and kettle amongst other things. Wild.

Fortunately, Joss didn't seem to think it was suspicious that Gaia had moved in without those provisions, but it was early days. Most of which she'd spent with her boyfriend. But that wasn't a problem for now, was it?

Gaia grabbed her coffee and toast and settled on the couch that also belonged to Joss. Her eyes rested on the notebook she'd left sprawled on Joss's table the night before. She had been too beat to take it with her to her room, and since she was alone anyway, she didn't see the harm.

Except now she was wondering if she hadn't taken it with her so she didn't have to be reminded about the other way her life had changed since she'd turned eighteen.

There was definitely an element of denial to her new... Well, she wasn't sure what they were. What should she call having dreams that almost exactly resembled the content of whatever she wrote during the day?

She could put it off as simply that, dreams, but her dreams had never been this vivid. Before she turned eighteen, she could hardly remember them. She only remembered a vague pressure on her chest, remnants of emotions she didn't care to examine. Now, she could not only remember, but they were outlined in the notebooks she wrote her stories in. Every word, every detail came to life whenever she fell asleep.

Last night, that had been her billionaire hero, Carlton Gaines. It had been the impact of the bed against her body as he lay her down to consummate their arranged marriage. It had been his face, somehow both gorgeous and enigmatic, a combination of every feature she found attractive. Straight thick dark hair. Green eyes. Defined cheekbones, a strong chin, lips that could convey emotions with the slightest movement. His body was sculpted, too, though he spent every waking moment working. She may have sprinkled some romance magic on him to achieve that.

There was a part of her that believed it was romance magic causing these dreams, too. It couldn't be a coincidence that the evenings of the days she wrote, her dreams were filled with the scenes she'd put to paper. She became her female main character. She experienced everything through her heroine's eyes, witnessed the other characters adjusting, *responding* to her, even if she didn't follow the script she'd written that day.

Like when Carlton had been reassuring her during the wedding night seduction. The heroine, and thus Gaia, was supposed to nod wordlessly and allow him to *go all the way*. But at some point, Gaia realized the fact that she said things like *go all the way* to avoid the s-word meant perhaps she wasn't ready to *go all the way*—despite what her technically-still-a-horny-teenager hormones fooled her into thinking.

She'd refused to sleep with Carlton. And she'd watched as his package went from *whoomp! there it is*, to *womp womp*.

He'd stomped off irritably, something she hadn't written but was apparently consistent with his character, since that was how he responded.

Gaia waited to see if she could resist the desire to check whether Carlton's new response had appeared in her notebook. She couldn't. She read through the pages she'd written the day before, and, as had happened the other times things had changed in her dreams, she found the new details in black and white, *in her handwriting*, right in front of her.

It was entirely possible that she was sleep-writing, but . . . what were the chances of that happening when it had never happened before?

What were the chances that on the days she didn't write, she went back to being pre-eighteen Gaia, who couldn't remember her dreams for shit?

But . . . magic? What were the chances of *that*?

CHAPTER 1

Twelve years later

"You brought a book to a *party*?"

"Yes," Gaia said, her spine straightening at her best friend's indignant tone. "The deal was that I needed to be here. There was nothing in the terms about socializing."

"You're right," Seth Scott said seriously. "I'll call everyone right now and tell them to bring their favorite book. We can all not socialize and read instead."

"Really?" Excitement bubbled up inside her—until she saw the look Seth gave her. "Of course not really. I knew you were joking. Ha ha!"

She waved a hand to emphasize how little the prospect meant to her. But . . .

Did reading parties really exist?

"You're salivating, Gaia."

"Okay, but think about it. If we all brought our favorite books, it would *facilitate* conversation. An automatic icebreaker. 'Why do you like this book, Lizzy?'" She directed the question to Seth's partner, who was standing next to the refreshment table watching them with a smile. "'Is it because it offers an interesting representation of societal differences in modern day South Africa?'"

"'Why do you like *Coming Together,* Gaia?'" Seth said, imitating her tone. "'Is it because it's about mutual physical enjoyment?'"

"Why are you like this?" Gaia asked, shifting her grip on her romance novel so Seth couldn't see the title. It wasn't as blatant as *Coming Together,* but it *was* an erotic romance and she didn't need to give him ammunition. He could continue shooting blanks.

She smirked, and made a note to use that on him some other time.

"It's the truth."

"Yes," she allowed. "Romance novels definitely highlight both partners' physical enjoyment as important." She looked at Lizzy. "I'm sorry, Liz. I've been trying to get him to read romance for years now. You deserve more than a selfish lover."

"Hey!" Seth said as Lizzy laughed. "You know that's not true."

"How would I know, Seth?" Gaia said. "I'm one of the lucky ones who hasn't suffered through a night with you."

"I wasn't talking to you," he snapped. Lizzy laughed again. He glared at her. "You think this is funny?"

"Oh, no, I'm not getting involved."

"Smart," Gaia told Lizzy, whose sharp eyes sparkled.

"I have my moments."

"You're a corrosive influence in my relationship," Seth said.

"I'm the reason you can be in a relationship," Gaia retorted. "Should I remind you of the toxic habits you had before I became your friend?"

"Yes, do," Lizzy said at the same time Seth said, "No."

There was a short pause. Gaia smiled. This was fun. Teasing her best friend, talking about the old days. Seth was the only person she truly felt comfortable with—outside of the characters in the romance novels she wrote. If she told Seth about her abilities, as she'd settled on calling them, there was a chance he would stop nagging her to spend time with other people. There was also a chance he would book her in for psychological evaluation. That possibility kept her from telling him about it in the years they'd been friends.

No, she would have to resign herself to satisfying Seth through socialization in the real world. With strangers who would ask personal questions about her life. The thought had her heart beating hard against her chest. It joined the vibration that had been there since the beginning of the week when she realized she'd have to act on the promise she'd made to Seth over a month ago.

"Joking aside, Gai," Seth said suddenly, concern clear in his voice. "Socialize. Please."

She swallowed. The doorbell rang. Still, they looked at one another.

"I . . . will," she replied eventually.

"Good."

He gave her one last look before disappearing into the passage to open the door. Lizzy followed, but not before offering Gaia a sympathetic smile. Gaia stared after them for a beat. Then she plotted her escape.

There was the balcony on the right of Seth's small living room. She could go down the fire escape. But voices sounded from the passage, and her legs felt unsteady. She'd denied it when Seth had accused her of being afraid, but she'd forgotten what it was like to interact with real people. *Unpredictable* people. The way her insides were squirming made her think Seth was right. As was the fact that she was on the verge of freaking out.

Now she was walking. Out of the living room, down the passage to the back of Seth's flat. There were no exits there, and since the flat wasn't big, she could still hear people.

An opportunity presented itself when she ducked into Seth's bedroom and closed the door behind her. She hugged her book tight to her body and took a deep breath. This was fine. She was fine. She'd wait here until more people came and they could distract one another. Distraction meant she could slip in, talk to someone who didn't seem frightening, smile, laugh loudly enough that people noticed she was there and having fun. After, she'd leave. It would take an hour at most. She could catch up on some reading now *and* lay Seth's concerns to rest later. Nice and easy.

There's a world outside of your books, Gaia. You can't live inside them.

Gaia bit her lip. She didn't want to feel guilty for living inside her books. Seth just didn't understand how *safe* it was.

A movement from the doorway between Seth's bedroom and bathroom caught her attention. She froze.

What was a half-naked man doing in Seth's room?

"Gaia?"

It took her a second, but the voice sounded familiar. She blinked. Recognized the face.

"Jacob?"

She didn't need him to confirm; she knew who it was. Except he didn't look like the person she'd met twelve years before. Or even seen eight years before, at the funeral of Seth and Jacob's mother. He wasn't gangly or awkward. His braces were gone. And was that a V leading to his—

She whirled around. "*Jacob.* You're a *kid.* Put on some clothes!"

"Nice to see you again, Gaia," he said with laughter in his voice. Even that had changed. Gone was the uncertainty he'd spoken with years before. Now, it was all smooth and silky, like melted chocolate. She imagined climbing into a bath of it, letting it cover her body before he licked—

"Are you getting dressed?" she asked sharply, annoyed. At

him, mostly, because his voice was sexy, as was his torso, and she did not need either of those thoughts living in her head with how she was feeling.

"You know," he replied over a shuffling sound she assumed meant he was putting on pants. Or maybe underpants. She didn't know what was under his towel. She could imagine, but that would be wrong because Seth was her best friend and Jacob was his younger brother and that basically meant Jacob was her younger brother. "After a decade of not seeing one another, I expected a warmer greeting."

"You were standing in a towel. If I gave you a warmer greeting, I'd be arrested for messing with an underage kid."

He laughed. The sound traveled over the small space of the room, landing on her skin, dancing seductively. It was . . . strange, even though she'd written about it countless times. She'd even lived it in her dreams. Still, she'd never thought she could *actually* be turned on by someone's laugh in real life.

"I'm two years younger than you. Unless I'm doing the math wrong, and I'm not, I haven't been underage for a while."

"Twenty-eight?" she asked, automatically turning around. He'd managed to put on jeans, but his upper body was still naked. That torso taunted her. She lifted her eyes. "When the hell did you get to be twenty-eight?"

He grinned. A dimple pressed into his left cheek. It had been adorable when he was sixteen. She hadn't seen it when he was twenty. But now? Now it was attractive. Deadly so.

She'd forgotten about her book, but now she clung to it so tightly she was surprised it didn't become part of her body.

"Probably about the same time you got to be thirty," he said easily. "Looking good, by the way. Have you been drinking from the fountain of youth?"

"Oh, because once I turn thirty I'm supposed to look like a prune? Hilarious," she said dryly.

"Thank you." There was a pause. "You do look good." His eyes shone with sincerity. "I wasn't being contrary. Well, not *only*."

She tucked a piece of hair behind her ear. It was loose this evening, annoying her with its thick curls nestling in her neck. But at least it gave her something to do with her hands. And, when she dipped her head forward, covered the blush staining her cheeks.

"Thanks. You, er . . ." The blush got hotter. "You look good, too." When the words lingered awkwardly in the air, she added, "The braces did your teeth good."

The braces did your teeth good?

To think, she wrote romance novels. Her heroines were sassy and cool; her heroes smooth, but she, who created them, said things like *the braces did your teeth good.*

"Thank you. I'm quite proud of that, actually."

He gave her a small smile, then threw a T-shirt over his head. It left his dark, not quite straight hair clinging to his forehead, making him look like a teenager again. Except it didn't, not really. He looked very much like an adult. A deliciously harmless adult, though she knew he wasn't. No man who oozed charm and didn't get disturbed by anything she said could be harmless.

This was why she preferred socially awkward men. Not that she had much experience with men. At least not real-life men. But she imagined socially awkward men to be more hesitant. Less charming. Less dangerous. Or perhaps they would be more charming in their awkwardness.

She'd certainly written them that way in her books. She'd observed some of them being that way, too, when she built up the strength to work outside of her house. Many of the people in cafés during the day were the socially awkward types, working for themselves because they knew the world was a dangerously social place. Or was that just her? In any case, those men would stutter with servers and avoid eye contact, and that was much more on her level.

Men like Jacob though . . . She could already tell he would take anything she said in his stride. He wouldn't be startled if she pointed out something weird—like his teeth—and he'd smile if she told him he needed to put clothes on. There wasn't a taint of blush on his skin at the fact that she'd caught him fresh out of the shower. And her insistence that he was a kid, though he was twenty-eight, had barely fazed him.

No, men who were easy around people couldn't be trusted. She could feel it in her gut.

"Is that a book?"

She blinked. Looked down at her hands. Up again. "Yes."

"You brought a book to a party?"

Now she sighed. "Are you going to give me a hard time about it? You don't have to," she said before he could answer. "Seth's already given me an earful."

"I wouldn't." Again with that sincerity. It was . . . nice. "I was going to ask what you're reading."

"Oh." She took a moment to decide if she wanted to tell him. "It's a romance novel."

"Like the ones you write?"

"You know I write romance novels?"

"Seth's mentioned it a couple"—he lingered—"million times." He smiled. "He's proud of you."

"Yeah, well . . ." She trailed off when she had no good reply. She didn't know how to respond to Seth's pride. He was the only person in her life who felt that way about her. It seemed precious, and overwhelming, and she worried that if she engaged with it, it would disappear. "I dedicated my first book to him," she ended up saying. "He has to be proud."

"Not sure that's it." He sat on the edge of the bed, pulled on his socks and sneakers. "Do you want to tell me about the book?"

"Oh." She swallowed. "It's about a woman. And another woman. And they meet and like one another, but there's a bunch of stuff that happens that makes them think they can't be together."

"But they can."

"Of course." She moved closer. "That's what romance does so magically. You think they can't be together. *They* think they can't be together. And then suddenly something happens. An accident or an incident or a conversation or the sheer fact that they aren't together and they want to be and they realize they deserve to be with one another."

She blushed when she saw him watching her. Smiling at her. Again, she let her hair fall forward.

"I'm sorry. I got . . . carried away."

Was this how it was going to be every time she spoke to an attractive man outside her dreams? Goodness.

"Why are you apologizing?" he asked.

She hadn't expected that.

"I . . . well . . ." She wrinkled her nose. "I'm not sure."

She gave herself a second to consider it. Almost immediately, that first sex scene she'd written with Carlton came to mind. When she'd refused to sleep with him, she'd wanted to apologize for leading him on. She had every right to change her mind, and yet the man she'd written, the man *she* had created, hadn't understood or respected that.

Amongst other things, that situation helped her recognize when in her real life she instinctually wanted to apologize. It showed her how that instinct was isolated to certain groups of people. She tried to change her behavior, but years of conditioning didn't simply go away.

She could change it in her writing, however. She did. She made sure her heroines only said sorry when it was necessary.

"It must have something to do with how the world makes people who identify as women feel as though they need to apologize for taking up space."

He stared, dumbfounded. "Yeah," he said slowly. "It might have something to do with that."

She gave him a half smile. "I try to engage with social issues as often as I can. I mean, I'm not perfect. I fail a lot. But I'm . . . I'm trying."

"Why?"

She studied him. Took in what seemed like genuine curiosity on his face. Since she wanted to redeem herself after the braces comment, she would tell him what she thought. It had nothing to do with proving to herself that she could have a proper conversation with a real man. Nothing whatsoever.

"I want my romances to reflect the world. Or not reflect it . . . I want my romances to *improve* on the world. That means I need to know what needs improvement. Even if that means me. Especially when that means me."

There was a long silence. Slowly, insidiously, tension took hold of her lungs. They were burning before she realized she was holding her breath. She exhaled, trying to make it seem as innocent as possible. After a quick inhale, she decided the silence was enough.

"Look, I should probably get out there." *To find another hiding place.* "It was nice seeing you again. We keep missing one another at Seth's birthdays."

"Work," he said.

"Yeah, I get it. You're a big, fancy businessperson now." She cleared her throat. "I'm going to go—"

"No, wait," he said quickly, moving forward, but stopping when she took a step back in response. "You shouldn't have to go. I should. I came here straight from work and needed a shower. I promised it would be quick." He offered a wry grin. "Seth's probably wondering where I am."

"Okay."

"Okay." He nodded. But he didn't move. Apart from shifting his weight from one foot to the other, he didn't act at all.

"Are you going to go?" she asked some minutes later.

"Yeah, of course."

He still didn't move. The tension inside her was dwindling again, replaced by amusement.

"Jacob?"

"Relax, woman," he said sternly. "I'm leaving."

"Except you're clearly not and if you call me 'woman' again, I might have to kick you somewhere."

He winced. "It's probably safer to leave."

"Yes." When he made no move to, she sighed. "What's keeping you here, Jacob?"

"I want to say something."

She looked at him expectantly.

"I should probably say it."

She dipped her head. She thought it was enough of a sign for him to continue.

"You're impressive," he blurted out. As if he'd been pouring liquid into a glass and stopped too late. Or didn't stop at all, apparently, since he was still speaking. "Everything you said about trying to be better? It was amazing. Not everyone thinks like that. I work with a hell of a lot of people who don't, and it's a challenge." He frowned. The crease between his eyebrows was adorable. Unfortunately. "Maybe some people feel like I'm narrow-minded? Huh."

"That just occurred to you?"

He rested a hand at the back of his neck. "Yeah."

It bothered him. It bothered him that he might not have been as aware, as sensitive to social issues as he hoped. He *hoped*.

"What?" he asked, his hand dropping.

"What, what?"

"You're frowning."

"No, I'm—" She broke off when she realized she was.

"I've upset you."

"No."

"But you're frowning."

"I'm processing."

"What?"

"A lot of things." He didn't ask, but it seemed like he was waiting. Patiently, too, if she went by his expression. And it worked. "I'm thinking that . . . it was silly of me to worry before. When I told you those things. I thought you'd make fun of me."

An embarrassing confession, but the least embarrassing of the options. She couldn't exactly tell him his answer made her brain horny for him.

"Why?"

She struggled to shift gears. When she did, she shrugged. "I don't talk to people much. I always worry I'm going to say something weird or awkward when I do."

"Like commenting on someone's teeth?"

Her lips twitched. "Maybe."

His mouth eased into a smile. "Is that why you're hiding here? You don't want to talk to the people out there?"

"Pretty much." Her arms fell from her chest, and she rested her book at her thighs. "You don't have to stay with me. I have my own entertainment." She lifted the book slightly.

"I'd rather stay here than socialize out there."

She narrowed her eyes. "You're hiding, too."

"No."

"Jacob."

"Okay, fine." He sat on the bed. "I'm only here because Seth thinks I work too much. Which, as your earlier comment about his birthdays highlighted, seems true." Did he realize he was still denying working too much? "I thought attending one of his parties would get him off my back. This is a loophole I hadn't considered. Technically, I'm attending, right?" He frowned. "Why are you smiling?"

"I, too, am here to brush off Seth's concerns about my working habits."

"Is that so?" He angled his head. "Welcome to the club."

"Thank you," she said with a mock bow. "Our first meeting is going swimmingly, isn't it?"

"It is."

He smiled; she smiled. And for a good solid minute, they both smiled. Like fools. Then the air shifted subtly, sparkled almost, as her eyes swept over that dimple and straight teeth.

The kindness in the lines of his face.

The way what he said sounded like something a prototype of the perfect man would say rather than an actual, real-life man.

She took a step back. He was hero material. A Good Man. The kind she'd written after Carlton. She had never met a man like that outside her novels. Yet here Jacob was, in a T-shirt and jeans, smiling right in front of her. No wonder there was a wave of desire crashing over her.

No, wait—desire? Honest-to-goodness *desire*? Feelings of interest and heat in places that hadn't felt interested or hot for anyone in her real life since . . . since . . .

She couldn't remember.

It was time for a pep talk.

Okay, Gaia. You know what's happening. It's called attraction. You happened to see Jacob without his shirt on and he's sexy. He grew into those weird skinny-but-broad shoulders he used to have. Sure, those shoulders are padded with muscle now, but so are your biceps, and you know that means jack shit where they're concerned.

Her self-talk tended to be more vulgar than her usual talk, but since it was working, she didn't pause to judge herself.

Sure, his dimples are cute as hell. Even those dark, unruly eyebrows of his are attractive. Dangerous over those black/brown eyes and paired with that self-deprecating grin? Lethal. But none of that has to mean anything. Of course it doesn't. You're a grown woman who can control her impulses. And Jacob is as safe as—

She froze. Took a few seconds to thaw.

Why would she think he was safe? No one was. Not in this world. The only safe people were the ones she wrote herself. She knew who they were then. Could anticipate their actions. She *wrote* those actions.

None of those people could steal her breath away by unexpectedly hurting her. Letting her down, abandoning her. Even Jacob, with his sexy body and sweet smile, was a human in the real world. She'd learned firsthand she couldn't trust those.

CHAPTER 2

He was having inappropriate thoughts about his older brother's best friend.

To be fair, even if she were a stranger, Jacob would call the thoughts inappropriate. What other explanation was there for imagining what it would be like to act on the electricity pulsing inside his body? He clenched his fists. Relaxed them when he thought that might make him look like a creep prone to violence. Forced himself to take a breath.

"Seth really talks to you about my working habits, huh?" he asked lightly, hoping she didn't hear the faint strain in his voice. "He must have been more upset about me missing birthdays than he told me."

Of course, it wasn't only birthdays. Jacob worked through most special days. Hell, he worked most nights. He needed to keep his business on track. Scott Brand Solutions bore his name—his family's name. But he made up for the days he missed. A birthday dinner after the fact. Regular meetups for drinks. It was weird that Seth seemed bothered by Jacob's absence. Jacob was working at the family company because of Seth, after all.

"Honestly? No. He doesn't talk about you that much. If it

makes you feel better," she said at his frown, "it's probably because he can't stop talking about *my* working habits."

He smiled. "He doesn't understand your dislike of people?"

"It's not that I don't like people." She paused. Wrinkled her nose. "No, it's that."

He laughed. She was funny. Not in a stand-up-comedian-tell-you-jokes way, but quirky. Sharp.

"A party sounds extreme for someone who doesn't like people," he commented. "You couldn't offer to go to brunch or something?"

"Is that another jab at my age?" At his look, she elaborated. "Thirty-year-olds do stuffy things like brunch?"

"Why is brunch stuffy?" he asked. "I love brunch."

"Oh, good," she said with an exhale. "I do, too."

He caught the laugh before it escaped.

"As for your question," she continued. "You don't refuse the kidnapper when they tell you to pose with a picture of the newspaper for the ransom."

He was still sitting on Seth's bed, but he straightened at that analogy. "Are you calling Seth a kidnapper?"

She pursed her lips. "He suggested I come to this party. Brunch wasn't presented as an option."

"And that was him asking you to pose with the newspaper?"

"Yes." Her eyes narrowed by a centimeter. "Maybe that wasn't the best analogy."

"Hang on," he said, stretching out his hand. "Maybe we need to hash it out. Is my brother keeping you here against your will? Literally, I mean," he added when she opened her mouth. "Did he lock you in this room?"

"You know he didn't."

"Do I? I haven't checked the door."

"You're purposefully being vexatious now," she answered, chin up.

"Bless you."

She glowered. It was delightful. And though he had no idea what vexatious meant, he liked that she called him it. Liked how sexy she made it sound. Liked that she was glaring at him now, even though her lips were twitching and her eyes were dancing.

"Your presence here tonight should mean you're free. From the kidnapper," he clarified.

"Not quite," she answered. "I think this is the equivalent of me taking the photo, but shouting 'don't pay' into the camera."

"How exactly would they capture that?"

Her expression went blank, then she snorted. "Why am I still talking to you?"

"To be honest, I'm wondering the same thing."

There was a short pause before the ends of her mouth tilted up and her cheeks lifted. He could have said she was smiling. He didn't, because what she was doing didn't feel like smiling as much as it did the sun shining down on him after a long winter. His skin prickled under its warmth, the temperature seeping into his bloodstream, traveling to his heart. Once there, it thawed ice he hadn't even realized existed. Suddenly he was drinking the water like a man dying of thirst. All because of a smile.

Her smile.

"You're not the worst person to talk to," she allowed as she sat on the edge of the opposite side of the bed. As far away from him as possible, he noted, but he didn't mind.

She'd refused to sit until then, and along with everything she'd told him, he knew she wouldn't have done so if she didn't feel comfortable. Besides, she basically complimented him with her last words. She even set aside the book she'd held like armor since she first came into the room.

He couldn't remember her being this reticent when they'd met. Granted, he'd been a kid, and at eighteen, she'd seemed as distant as the supermodels he'd had crushes on. But she had been kind to him. And her eyes had been kind. It meant her kindness wasn't an act to please his brother, but was in the core of her. It was as much a part of her as the haunted look beneath the kindness. As the uncertainty that vibrated from her even now.

But she was sitting opposite him. He wouldn't take that for granted.

"I'm touched you think so."

He meant to tease, but the words came out sincere.

"You should be." Her lips curved into a wry smile. "You're one of two people I think that of."

He blinked as an explosion of pleasure went off in his chest, his brain. He'd barely begun to process before she asked, "Do you still play rugby?"

It took a while for him to answer. Mainly because of the aftershocks of her admission.

"Do I . . ." His brain cleared. He snorted. "With what time?"

"I remember the days when that was *all* you did with your time."

He laughed. "Things were different then."

"I know." She gave him a small smile. "I'm sorry about your mom."

"Thanks." It was still a jolt when people reminded him his mother was no longer around. But not as much as it used to be. "I'm sorry you couldn't make the funeral."

"I was there."

"You were?"

"I wouldn't let Seth deal with that alone."

She sounded offended. Despite what they were talking about, it made him smile.

"I only meant that I didn't see you."

"I sat at the back. Kept out of the way, mostly." Her finger traced an invisible pattern on Seth's duvet. "I spoke with your dad before you got there. I would have spoken to you, too, but you didn't come until later."

"There was a thing I had to deal with," he said. "With the caterer, I think. My memory of that day's a bit fuzzy."

"You looked rough."

"Thanks," he said dryly.

"It's understandable."

"Sure. Still don't think you're supposed to point it out."

"Oh." She nodded. "Of course I shouldn't have."

"It's fine, Gaia. I'm not offended."

"You wouldn't have said anything then," she muttered.

"You're right." He paused. "I shouldn't have said anything if I didn't want you to worry about it. I'm sorry."

For a moment, she looked confused, but she said, "I appreciate that."

Silence lingered. He waited for her to speak.

"Do you remember when you had the concussion?" she asked.

"Since I was concussed, I'm going to say no."

"You know what I mean."

"I do," he said, smiling at her faint annoyance. "Sure, I remember. It was the last game of the season."

"It was my favorite."

"It was . . ."

"Oh!" she said when he trailed off. "Not because you were hurt. I was thinking about that dopey look on your face. You kept pointing out the most obvious things, too. 'Look, there's a car.' 'Oh—we're walking now.'" She said the last two sentences in a slow, deep voice that he supposed was imitating him. Or was that mocking him?

"*This* I don't remember."

"Well, you did have a concussion," she replied slyly, and he knew she was making fun of him saying he didn't remember earlier.

"I'm pretty sure I'd remember being dopey."

"Would you though?" she asked with a doubtful expression.

"Do you remember taking my hand, telling me I was beautiful and asking me to your school dance? If so, I guess I'm wrong."

She was going to write about him. She knew it the moment his face twisted into the dopey expression she'd been talking about. It was endearing on so many levels, not in the least because Prince Charming really couldn't imagine *not* being charming.

"You're lying."

"Oof," she said, clutching her chest to show him how much his accusation hurt her. "Is this how you treat someone you once thought was the most beautiful woman you'd ever seen?"

"There's no way I would have said that."

"Because you don't think it?"

She was teasing, but something inside her was genuinely concerned he didn't. It didn't matter, she told herself sternly. She didn't need someone to validate her appearance. Just like she didn't need someone to invalidate it. She pushed aside the memories of her foster homes where both things happened in equal measure.

"No. No, of course not."

Jacob's spluttering offered the perfect distraction.

"No, of course not." She bit her lip. "Of course I'm not beautiful. Who would even think that?"

"That's not what . . . Of course you're beautiful . . . I was just . . . I was talking about . . ." He broke off. Took a deep breath. Ran a hand over his face, through the strands of his hair. The result was adorably messy. "I didn't mean that you're not beautiful."

"I know."

His gaze sharpened. "You were pulling my leg."

She laughed. It was a delighted sound she didn't know she could make. "I was. Not about what you said when you were concussed. That part's true." Her eyes swept over his face. "You really don't remember."

"No."

He folded his arms, shifting back on the bed until he could lean against the headboard. He angled so his shoes wouldn't touch the white bedding. White bedding. She made a mental note to ask Lizzy—if they were ever close enough—how she dealt with the white during her period.

"So you broke my heart?"

"Excuse me?"

"I don't recall you going to the school dance with me," he said. "And it was long after my concussion, too, so you can't blame it on that."

"I wanted to go. It's just . . . I was *so* much taller than you," she teased. "Could you imagine the pictures?"

He smiled. The dimple appeared again. It called to her. Told her to lean in and kiss it for the sake of their mutual happiness.

"I had my growth spurt the next year."

She laughed. It drowned out the voice of the personified dimple. "I was teasing, Jacob. You don't have to defend yourself or your body."

"I kind of feel like I have to," he said, chagrined. "I clearly didn't make a good impression."

"Please. You were a kid. I was your brother's friend. You had no reason *to* make a good impression. But you're wrong." She shrugged at the look he gave her. "I liked you. You were passionate about things. Charming, too, in your dopiness." She laughed when his look darkened. "I like dopey. Dopey is harmless. Dopey won't . . . push you against the wall and kiss you until you lose your breath."

It was the first thing that came to mind, courtesy of the book she still had with her. The female main character had pushed the other female main character against a wall after an argument, and kissed her passionately. Gaia had melted when she read that. She loved it when one partner took control. She wrote it, *lived* it, often enough to know the effect it had on her. Even thinking about it now heated her body.

Or was that because of how Jacob was looking at her? His gaze no longer held an easy tease, but was intense and hot and she felt caught in it. It was as if she was standing in the middle of a ring of fire. The fire didn't come closer, and somehow she knew that if she looked for an escape, she'd find it.

But she didn't look. She was too fascinated. By Jacob, and the fact that dopey and charming were a package deal with him. A combination that echoed her earlier suspicions that he was *not* harmless. He was dangerous.

At this moment, she didn't care.

"I'm not so sure dopey is a compliment after all, Gaia."

His voice was so smooth she could see herself sliding down it.

"Of course it is." It came out primly. "You don't know that I want to be pushed against a wall and kissed until I don't have my breath." She swallowed when his eyes dipped to her lips. "Honestly, I prefer not being kissed at all."

"Do you?"

He stood, walked toward her. Sat down closer to her, but didn't touch her.

She didn't move a muscle.

"I suppose," she said hoarsely. Cleared her throat before she embarrassed herself further. "If the occasion arises, I wouldn't be opposed to being kissed. But I'm not going to look for it."

"No, you wouldn't," he murmured. "Do you think the occasion has arisen?"

She opened her mouth, and surprised herself with the chuckle that came out of it. "Is that an *erection* reference?" She laughed again when his eyes widened. Which, of course, made her want to continue teasing him. "Shouldn't you have the answer to that?"

"What is wrong with you?" he asked, but he was smiling.

"To clarify then: you weren't referring to an erection?"

"Not specifically." Now he laughed. "But it does kind of work."

"Does it?"

"If I answer that, does that make it dirty talk?"

"Why are you asking me?"

"Between the guy running a branding and design company and the romance author, I'd say the romance author is best qualified to answer."

"Oh, please. Like you haven't done your fair share of dirty talk."

"Why do you sound so sure?"

"Because look at you!" She gestured up and down his body with a hand. "You look like this. And you speak like that." She waved a hand in the vicinity of his face. "You must have countless people falling over their feet to hear you imply you have an erection."

He closed his eyes. She pursed her lips to keep from laughing. It wasn't what she'd pictured she'd be doing this night; it was better. Somehow this mixture of teasing and seduction made her feel freer than she ever had. Even with Seth. Granted, Seth wasn't seducing her—thank the heavens—but they laughed together. Except *that* laughter felt as though it came at a price. Like he was checking to make sure she was okay instead of making sure she was happy.

Happiness was such a strange concept. No one else could check for happiness. It was a one-person job. Most days, she wasn't sure she qualified. Most days, she was just thankful there was *one* space for her to feel happy. It wasn't in the world where her parents had died and none of her family members wanted to take her in. It was in books. The ones she read for comfort and joy. The ones she wrote and dreamed about every night.

She was happy there. Happy and safe.

Except now, in this moment, she felt both those things and she was awake.

This charming, dopey, attractive man wanted to seduce her. The fact that he was Seth's younger brother no longer seemed to matter. She was *definitely* not thinking about him as any relation to her anymore. She was only thinking that he was making her feel like her heroes made her heroines feel. Like they made her feel, when she fell asleep and became those heroines.

And that thought—that simple, heartwarming thought—helped her decide.

She would let Jacob Scott seduce her.

CHAPTER 3

"There are a number of things running through my head right now," Jacob said slowly. "One is that I think you've said the word 'erection' more in the last few minutes than I ever have in my adult life."

He was rewarded with a grin for that. He wanted to take it, frame it. Put it up on a wall somewhere and charge people to see it. He settled for making her smile again.

"Two, I guess, is thank you? I'm sure your assumption that people want to see my erection is a compliment?"

She winced. "Oh, when you put it like that, it sounds awful."

"No, it doesn't."

"It doesn't?"

"It's not *great*," he allowed, "but it came from a good place."

"The compliment or the erection?"

He laughed. "Is this you being purposefully vexatious?"

Her eyes brightened. "It is!"

He thought he was messing it up earlier. Despite her assumptions, he didn't seduce. That would require time he didn't have. And energy, precious energy, that he could use at work. His lack of experience made him awkward, especially because he desperately, *desperately* wanted to kiss her. Touch her.

Yet somehow, she smiled at his fumbles, her brown eyes dancing to the tune of his awkwardness. She was still smiling at him now, and he knew it was a gift. It felt like they were a part of another world. A cocoon of some kind, where light and romance and happiness were the norm. If they were, he could understand his brother's concerns about him spending too much time at work. He wouldn't experience this when he was at work.

He'd miss looking into the deepest brown eyes and sinking into their depths. He wouldn't be able to memorize the curve of her lips in that smile. Thin, hard-won; the most enticing shape he'd ever seen.

Life at work didn't involve caressing a cheek dusted with a light blush, or curling a hand around her ear to push her hair back.

"Concussion-me knew what he was talking about," he said softly. "You're breathtaking."

The blush on her cheeks darkened, mixing with the light brown of her skin. Her tongue flicked out and wet her bottom lip. He wanted to know what she tasted like. Sweet? Perhaps like citrus, mint. Neither? Both? Something else entirely?

"Dopey isn't harmless, is it?" she whispered, her eyes dipping to his lips.

He shifted closer. "You still think I'm dopey?" In answer, she gave him a look that made him laugh. "Fine." He sobered. "Maybe I could offer you confirmation that you were wrong?"

Confusion fluttered through her eyes. When it cleared, he could see her hesitation. He waited, though everything inside him was alert, as though poised at the edge of a cliff, ready to bungee jump. In real life, he wouldn't do something as reckless as bungee jump. In the cocoon of light, romance, happiness though? He'd jump without a rope. Which was exactly what he was doing with Gaia.

He didn't know her much beyond the few memories they'd

already shared. He didn't know if she'd judge him for working as hard as he did. For taking care of his father. For taking responsibility for their family. He only knew he was attracted to her, that she was smart and kind and hesitant, and that he wanted to kiss her. Was that enough to actually kiss her? He simply didn't know.

But, as it turned out, he didn't have to know. Not when he got the dip of her head, the acknowledgment that she wanted him to kiss her, too. Then he was moving.

He forced himself to do so slowly. He didn't want to frighten her, to concern her because they were moving fast and were basically strangers. But the hesitation he'd seen earlier in her eyes had faded. Now, curiosity replaced it. The realization sent a strange pulse through him. Something that tingled his pride and teased his ego. She wanted to know if he could really change her mind about who he was.

So did he.

He kneeled in front of her, let his hands skim her thighs. She shivered beneath his touch, the vibration of it traveling from his arms to the hardness already pressed against his jeans. He ignored the urgency of it, let his hands travel over the softness of her until he reached her butt.

"Is this okay?" he asked at her inhale.

"Yes," she answered immediately. "I mean, yeah." He was close enough to see her swallow. If he strained, he knew he'd hear it, too. "Sure. I'm fine. This is fine."

His brows lifted. "Are you sure? You sound—"

"Nervous? Yeah, that's because I am. Not that you needed me to tell you that since I interrupted you and I'm talking so much because when you touched me, it was like someone poured acid over my body. It burned and splattered and *things* happened inside me and you only touched me." She drew a shaky breath. "I'm fine though."

"Acid doesn't sound like a good thing."

"No, this kind is good." Her sincerity curled around his heart. "A new kind of acid. Oh!" She straightened. "Maybe acid isn't a good description. Maybe this is what men feel like when they take those pills."

"Those pills," he repeated slowly.

"The ones that make your—"

"You don't have to say it," he said with a chuckle. "I got it."

"Do you need them?"

"*What?*"

She let out a delighted laugh, shifting forward on the bed and setting her hands on his shoulders. "I'm sorry, I'm sorry, I couldn't resist. Not that there would be anything wrong with you taking a pill to help yourself enjoy sex. Not that we're doing that. I just . . . You're so cool, you know." Her voice turned serious again. "Adept, at this seduction stuff, with your kneeling and your charm."

His mouth turned up. "I thought I was dopey."

"You are, which is charming, and you're not, which is confusing."

He smiled and shifted forward. It brought them so close together that her arms wound around his neck instead of staying at his shoulders. If he dipped his eyes, he would see the cleavage he'd resisted looking at the moment he realized her top dipped to reveal it. He would keep resisting, for now, because he wanted her to look in his eyes. He wanted her to see she could trust him.

"I think it's because of this thing called humanity," he said in a low voice. "Have you heard of it?"

Her lips twitched. "Not at all. Please, tell me more."

"Well"—his hands traveled from her hips to her waist—"it's a theory that posits this species, humans, are complex beings capable of containing contradictions."

She gasped. "In *one* being?"

"Yeah."

"Wow. You said they're called humans, right?"

"Yep."

Her hand lifted to slide through his hair. He closed his eyes, letting himself enjoy it.

"Are you one of them?"

He opened his eyes. "I am."

"Hmm."

The hand moved over the back of his neck, down his chest, stopping somewhere in the vicinity of his heart. He should have been worried it would mean she'd feel the rapid beating, the unsteadiness there. Instead, he could only think that she was as adept at seduction as she claimed he was.

He could have blamed it on her romance experience, but he didn't think that was it. He hadn't read her books, but he expected the seduction in them was smoother. Hers came from the fact that she wasn't smooth. She was merely curious, nervous, amusing, and the combination was as enticing as the dip of her waist.

"I've never kissed a human before," she whispered. Her legs parted, and she shifted forward until he was between them, their faces a breath away. "As a student of the behavior of all living forms, I feel this is an essential piece of research."

He folded his arms around her now, grinning. "You're such a nerd, Gaia."

"And you still want to kiss me."

"Damn right."

So he did.

He was kissing her. No, *she* was kissing him. *They were kissing.* It was basically all she thought before her thoughts were silenced by an explosion of feeling.

It started at the contact of their lips, the gentle way he moved his against hers, the way he seemed to be asking even as he was doing it. She hadn't kissed many men before, at least not in real life, and all those experiences had been underwhelming. She had to get creative when she wrote her kissing scenes. She did so by clinging to the belief that the kisses in the romances she read, she wrote, could exist.

This broad-shouldered man with his soft, full lips convinced her they did.

His tongue slipped into her mouth and she felt a bolt of lightning shoot right to between her legs. He didn't move his tongue in what she'd begun to call the "washing machine," since it happened to her with almost every kiss. If what Jacob was doing had to be compared to an appliance, it wouldn't be one designed to clean. The very opposite in fact; something that made her so dirty she'd need to take a shower after.

She knew exactly where those kinds of appliances belonged. Luckily, they were already in a bedroom.

She pushed against his chest and he moved back. Watched her as she lay down so she could reach for the rope that hung next to the side of the bed. She switched off the light. It didn't take long for her eyes to adjust. The curtains were open, the windows casting the room with light from the moon, and the air shifted. Just a little, but enough to make her wonder if she'd done the right thing by turning the light off.

On the one hand, things didn't seem so sharp anymore. It was smoother, easier somehow, and she thought they could do with smooth and easy. On the other hand, the darkness, the moonlight . . . It spoke of romance, and romance spoke of emotion.

Unless it didn't, she thought suddenly. How many times had she written about people using their sexual agency exactly how they pleased? If she wanted to do this, whatever this was, with Jacob, she could do it without involving her emotions. They could enjoy the most romantic date in the world without involving emotion if she didn't want to. She only had to make the decision.

Making it, she sat up and put her hands on either side of his face. He was still kneeling in front of her, and she didn't know if the sign of submission was for her sake or his. She didn't care. It was a powerfully sensual thing, having a man kneel in front of her. She hadn't thought to write it, and she hadn't liked anyone enough to experience it. But it wasn't anyone who was doing it. It was Jacob, and power and sensuality shrouded him naturally. His eyes, even in the dark, bore into hers. It felt like he could see inside her. Right to those dark, forbidden desires she rarely gave herself the freedom to think of.

As long as they were only physical, she didn't care.

As if proving that they were, he kissed her again, slower than before. Her skin went on high alert, demanding to be touched. He obeyed, and she had no chance to mentally praise his intuition when his hands were under her skirt, stroking her thighs. Only the outside of them, only back and forth, and yet it felt like he'd put his hand between her legs and was teasing her. Heat pulsed at her center. Involuntarily, she parted her legs. When she realized she had, her face flushed, and she tried to close them. But his grip tightened, sinking into the generous layer of cellulite.

"Don't stop yourself," he murmured against her lips. He didn't move, didn't do anything beyond what he was already doing. "If you want to open your legs, do. If you don't want to, don't. But promise me you'll let yourself feel. Without thinking."

"It's nice that you think that's possible," she whispered, moving back slightly. "I . . . I have a problem with thinking. I do it all the time."

"All the time?" he asked, his voice seductively low.

"Not in the last few minutes," she admitted.

"But it came back now."

"It's a lifelong habit."

"And we won't undo that in one night."

Since their faces were still close, she could read his expression clearly. There was an understanding there that coated the tension their conversation had sparked in her. That understanding enveloped the tension, comforted whatever had caused it, and seconds later, it disappeared.

"Think if you have to," he whispered. "But let yourself feel, too. Maybe they can both exist inside you."

It was as if he understood something she'd never said before, something she could never bring herself to say. Or think, even. Because despite all her thinking, she'd never thought about *why* she thought so much. In this moment though, it didn't matter. But she felt the significance of it bouncing inside her, and she stopped it by letting her hands run over his shoulders.

She squeezed when she reached the swell of his biceps. "How do people who run branding and design companies get these?"

"They're vain," he said with a chuckle. "They spend the little free time they have in the gym."

"For vanity purposes? I can't believe that."

"Maybe we do it so that pretty girls can squeeze them." When she snorted, he smiled. "Maybe *I* do it so pretty girls can squeeze them."

"You must be going out of your mind that I'm doing it then." At his questioning look, she shrugged. "I'm the most beautiful woman you've ever seen. It's an upgrade from 'pretty girl,' for sure."

He was laughing when he kissed her again. Then he was standing, picking her up with him. Her legs automatically went around his waist, her arms around his neck. And when he pushed her against the wall, he wasn't laughing anymore.

CHAPTER 4

He couldn't get enough. Of her body, which was full and lush and exactly what he wanted it to be. Of her mind, that worked in strange, interesting ways. Of her mouth, because it gave him evidence of how her mind worked and because it tortured him. Teased, plundered. It made him realize that there *were* more interesting things than work.

More desirable things.

But her mouth wasn't his priority right now. He had her against a wall, and the cleavage he'd been avoiding was right in front of him. He gave in to the impulse, bracing Gaia with one arm beneath her, letting the wall do the rest while his free hand skimmed the brown skin over the soft flesh of her breasts. A good portion of it was visible because of the neckline of her top; a V that created an arrow telling him he could enjoy more if he asked.

"Can I?"

She nodded, her eyes wide, serious. He pulled the material out of her skirt, lifted it so he could see her. Decided right there and then that the simple black bra that framed her breasts would be the new star of his fantasies. He slid a finger into one cup, felt the point of her nipple graze against the back of his finger. When he looked at her, her head was back against the wall, eyes closed. With a small smile, he pulled the cup down completely, his breath catching. He took a few moments to admire it, to commit it to memory. The shape, the darker circle in the middle of it, before he traced his fingers around that circle.

Before he lowered his head to take it into his mouth.

Sensation washed over him as he let his tongue swirl, as he licked. It clawed at him when he felt her hips grind against him. Except it wasn't against the part that she needed to move against, so he turned them around, laid her down on the bed.

That's how his brother found them.

And he wasn't happy.

Or so his swearing indicated.

Jacob stood, placing himself in front of Gaia so she had the chance to cover herself. He crushed the disappointment, the arousal, the wonder, and simply gave Seth a level look.

"Seriously, man?" Seth asked, face tight. Jacob shrugged. "*That's* how you're going to defend yourself? I can see the outline of your dick and you're *shrugging?*"

"Seth," Gaia said from behind him, admonishment and shock coloring her tone.

"Don't even get me started on you," Seth growled. "You're supposed to be out there talking to people. Instead you're here showing my brother your breasts."

"Seth," Jacob said now. "Enough."

"No, you don't get to tell me enough." He took a step forward. "I expected more from you." His eyes flickered over to Gaia. "More from both of you."

"Seth," Jacob said again. "Calm down." When his brother opened his mouth, Jacob narrowed his eyes. "This is the last time I'm going to ask."

Anger and surprise warred on Seth's face, but he didn't speak. Instead, he ran a hand through his hair, ran it over his face, then stuck it at his hip. Jacob waited until he was sure Seth had himself under control, and turned to Gaia.

"Are you okay?" he asked.

"Yeah. Of course. Fine."

His brother had put on the light when he walked in, so Jacob could see her cheeks were flushed, her lips swollen. Part of him expected her to avoid his gaze, but she didn't. She looked at him steadily, if somewhat embarrassed. It told him things about her presence and strength of mind. Things he didn't think she knew. Things he wanted to tell her. He didn't think he'd get the opportunity.

"Can I, er . . . can I go?"

Though he expected it, it surprised him. "Where to?"

"Away from here. From him." Gaia looked at Seth, her expression closing before she met Jacob's gaze again. "He needs a moment to cool down. I don't think that moment should be with me."

"You're right."

It was all Seth offered. They both turned to him, but Jacob kept looking at Gaia, so he saw the hurt closing behind her eyes.

"I'll see you around, Jacob," Gaia said. She moved forward, then stopped. Laid a hand on his chest.

The unexpectedness of it, the tenderness after what they'd just done, etched the contact into his mind as strongly as if she'd carved it into his skin. In no way was he prepared for the kiss then. The way she stood on her toes and lightly brushed her lips against his cheek, stopping right before his lips, then making the briefest contact there before she slipped out of the room.

He was still staring after her when Seth spoke.

"It's like you two were magnets attracted to the most inappropriate person you could make out with."

Jacob focused on his brother. "You're a dick."

"Is this because I called out yours?" Seth asked conversationally, though the edge underneath it told Jacob he was pissed.

Good. He was, too.

"You don't own her."

"That's what you think?" Seth's tone indicated outrage. "I know I don't *own* her. I'm pissed because . . . Damn it, Jacob." A slew of expletives followed. There was no order to it, no sense in it, and it would have made him smile if he didn't know it was a precursor to something he wouldn't like. "Now I have to worry about this, too."

And there it was. His brother's perpetual concern for the people he cared about. Except, apparently, for their father. Or the company the man had built and begged Seth to save.

Not now, Jacob.

"You don't have to worry about either of us. We're adults. We're fine."

"What bullshit."

"You don't have to believe me."

"Oh, why, thank you for the permission," Seth said sarcastically. His voice hardened. "The woman who walked out of here was not fine."

Jacob snorted. "You think that's my fault? It had nothing to do with how her best friend treated her?"

Lizzy walked in as Seth opened his mouth. She stopped, looked between the brothers, then took a step back. "Should I come back another time?"

"To your own bedroom?" Jacob asked, offering her an easy smile he fought for. "Nah. I was leaving anyway."

He kissed her cheek as he left, ignoring his brother and nodding at any guests he recognized on his way out. He needed time to figure out how he felt about what happened before he spoke to Seth again. He would get at least a weekend. Seth was too stubborn to reach out first, unless it was spontaneous. But Seth wouldn't spontaneously come to the house, so it would keep until Monday. Jacob had never been as glad he lived with their father as he was now.

Jacob grunted at the thought as he entered the house. He waited a few moments, heard the snores, deep and steady, coming from his father's room. It meant he wouldn't have to talk about his day—or night. A weight lifted from his body, and he walked to the bathroom, dodging the furniture he'd always been half-annoyed, half-amused at his mother for having. Years after her death, his father still couldn't bring himself to give it away.

His mother's hoarding tendencies lived on.

Once, the reminders of her life, her vibrance, had hurt. An open wound exposed to the world. Now, he barely saw those things.

Because you spend every waking moment working.

He ignored the echo of his brother's voice in his head, headed to the shower and tried to think of happier things. His mind skipped past the fact that they'd recently signed a new client, a big client; that the latest project they had for another big client had gone off without a hitch; and that his assistant had booked him seats to a local comedy show—his once-a-year guilty pleasure—and settled on Gaia.

She was a quirky surprise. A woman with a fascinating mind and a skittish demeanor. He wasn't sure why he was attracted to her. Perhaps it was purely physical. How her dark curls sprang out around her head in different directions. The piercing way her eyes saw everything; the delight when the sharpness there was courted by humor.

There were her lips, warm and inviting, and her taste, sweet and addictive, and her breasts, as sweet, as addictive . . .

He took a shuddering breath and turned the water to cold. It drew out another breath; a hiss this time. But he deserved it. He couldn't get turned on by Gaia. She was a nice distraction from the party he thought he'd have a terrible time at. She was cool to talk to, nerdy and sexy, the ultimate combination, but that was it. He had work to focus on, and he had to keep his brother and father from killing one another. Hell, he had to keep himself from killing his brother. How could he add a girlfriend to that? Especially Gaia.

The crush he'd had on her when he was a teenager didn't compare to what he felt about her now. Which was saying something when then, he could have blamed it on his teenage hormones. But he was no longer a teen, and he had enough self-awareness as an adult to know that when he was attracted to someone—when he did something about that attraction—it *wasn't* only physical.

He was fascinated by the way her mind worked, by her unconventional sense of humor, by the social awkwardness that had brought her to Seth's room. Seth wasn't wrong when he'd described them as magnets, at least for Jacob. Because Jacob didn't only feel attracted to her; he felt compelled by her. He wanted to know more about her. He wanted to hear her laugh. He wanted to know why she didn't like to socialize.

Of course that meant anything with Gaia went beyond physical.

And even if he didn't have other priorities, the faint panic in his chest told him he wasn't ready to indulge his fascination with, or his attraction to, his brother's best friend.

Still, he couldn't stop thinking about her. Even as he fell asleep. Even as he dreamed . . .

It was vivid. Everything was. More than Jacob had ever experienced in a dream before.

Gaia was there, standing across the dingy room at the bar. She was vivid, too. So vivid he was sure she was really there. But she wore leather tights and a leather bodice, and that's how he knew it was a dream.

It didn't matter. Spending time with her, real or imagined,

was an opportunity he wouldn't waste. He was about to walk over and talk to her, but a tall, burly man stopped him.

"No."

"Excuse me?" Jacob asked, lifting his head.

He got a stony look in reply. Ignoring it—this was his dream, after all—he took a step forward. Was stopped with a hand to his chest.

"Dude. What's your problem?"

This time, Jacob didn't even get a look in reply. Annoyed now, he tried to dodge the man. Was blocked. He tried again, and was blocked again.

"Get the hell out of my—"

Now his answer came in the form of a fist to his face.

Nick had just hit Jacob. No, *Chris*. She'd named him Chris when she started writing after the party. Either way, Jacob/Chris was lying on the floor and that wasn't supposed to happen.

Gaia's brain responded in the usual way to the unexpectedness.

Paused.

Observed what had gone wrong.

Paused again.

Tried to make sense of it.

Slowly came to life. Once it did, she could move. Still slowly, because this was her brain she was talking about.

"What did you do that for?" Gaia asked, moving forward to make sure Jacob/Chris was okay.

"He presented a danger, Your Highness."

"Really, Nick? A danger?"

She looked pointedly at the man on the floor, then back up to Nick. Her bodyguard—or the Royal Guard; she was still deciding what she wanted to call him in the book—was both taller and wider than Jacob/Chris. A tank, essentially. There was no way Jacob/Chris would be a match for him.

He's a match for you though, isn't he?
She shook her head.

"He was a threat. I took care of him."

"So I see," she said, frowning.

She *did* see. More than the fact that her bodyguard had tried to protect her. She saw that he'd gone off-script completely. Nick was never supposed to hit Jacob/Chris. He was supposed to keep Jacob/Chris from speaking with Gaia—or Princess Jade, as she'd called her heroine—before Jacob/Chris demanded an audience by using blackmail.

"Unless you want everyone here to know she's the heir to the throne no one has seen in the last ten years, you'll let me speak with her."

Gaia would then have a conversation with the man, where he would ask her to help him save his family's farm.

When she'd started writing the book, she had no ideas apart from the fact that she wanted the traditional hero/heroine roles reversed. She wanted her heroine in power, and royalty was a good way to establish that dynamic immediately. She also wanted her main characters' chemistry to be as hot as hers and Jacob's had been. Her characters needed layers of tension, of context for that. Blackmail and enemies-to-lovers were a great way to ensure it—and far enough away from her real relationship with Jacob that she didn't get confused.

But none of what had taken place the last few minutes had gone according to what she'd written. Jacob/Chris had said words she hadn't written. Nick had punched him when he wasn't meant to. The last time there was this level of unexpectedness, she'd just gotten her abilities. Twelve years and over thirty novels later meant there shouldn't have been *any* unexpectedness.

This was disturbing.

A groan came from the ground.

"Nick," she said to her bodyguard, "I'm going to make sure you haven't hurt him too badly."

"Allow me, Your Highness."

"No, I think you've done enough."

It was something Gaia imagined Jade would say. When she woke up, those words would appear in her manuscript. Any changes in a dream would supersede the words she'd actually written.

She'd long ago stopped trying to find logic in any of it. All she knew was that she dreamed the books she wrote. She liked to think of it as if it were a movie where she was the lead actor. The characters all followed the script, her novel, until she improvised. They'd respond to those improvisations, consistent with who she'd written them to be—she assumed that was her subconscious working—and the next day, her manuscript would reflect all the changes. She'd tweak the new words, but unless they changed the plot entirely, she wouldn't relive it in a dream.

But *she* was in charge of everything. *She* was the source of the improvisations, not her characters. The fact that she was responding to them now made her feel . . . off.

The groaning was still happening from the ground, though at her feet now that she'd walked closer. Honestly, it wasn't the kind of groaning she wanted from an attractive man at her feet.

She suddenly thought of Jacob kneeling in front of her, his hands on her thighs, his fingers caressing her skin . . .

Yes, *that* was what she wanted from attractive men at her feet.

She lowered to her haunches, ignoring the prickly feeling in her body. "Sir?" she asked firmly. "Sir, can you hear me?"

He said something incoherent.

"*Sir*," she said more insistently. "I asked you if you could hear me."

"I can hear you." His eyes were closed, but a hand was tentatively touching his face. "Getting punched doesn't take away your hearing ability."

Her eye twitched. Jacob/Chris wasn't meant to be snarky.

He was hard and grumpy, perhaps, but he would never snap at anyone. Or would he? What did grumpy really mean?

Great. Now she had existential questions about heroes when she'd spent over a decade writing them.

"Hmm."

It was all she said, but she reached out a hand, and instantly Nick was at her side, helping her up. A squeak sounded as she rose. It took her a beat to realize it was the leather.

Leather. What the hell had she been thinking? Oh, right. No one would expect a princess to wear leather, so Jade wouldn't draw any attention at the bar. Well, not *that* kind of attention anyway.

Not that it mattered. No one had seen Princess Jade of Aleah. She was somewhat of a myth to her people. A curse had kept her confined to the castle for the first eighteen years of her life. When she was finally free, Jade realized she could move around anonymously if the townspeople didn't know how she looked. It meant freedom when she hadn't had it before, and the Royal Family agreed because it had been their actions that had led to the curse.

Still—*leather?*

"Are you going to help me up, or just stare at me?"

She looked down. Jacob/Chris was staring at her. Despite the swelling around his eye, he was cute. Because he looked exactly like Jacob. Apparently, she was a sucker for the man's face. Maybe she could blame her actions in Seth's bedroom on that?

No. She didn't want to think about that now. Not Seth or what happened in his bedroom.

"Sure." Her eyes flickered over to the guard. "Nick, can you please help him up?"

"You can't be serious," Jacob/Chris said even as Nick moved to follow orders. "You can't expect me to accept his help. He's the reason I'm here."

"Which is why it makes perfect sense for him to be the reason you're not there anymore. Think of it as balancing the scales."

She leaned against the bar, appreciating how no one seemed to care about the drama unfolding meters away. She'd written the place as a haven for misfits. The haven's rules meant no one got involved in anyone else's spats. She was glad that, at least, hadn't changed.

"Balancing the scales would mean I get to punch him, too."

But he accepted Nick's hand. Hiding her smile, Gaia gestured to the bartender to get them both drinks.

"Man, this is not what I expected to dream about tonight."

Her brain did the *something unexpected is happening, help me* thing again. By the time it was done, Jacob/Chris was sitting next to her and the bartender had slid their drinks in front of them.

"What did you say?" she asked, voice hoarse.

"I didn't say anything."

"No, you did. Earlier," she clarified when she realized time had passed during her brain's hiccup. "You said something about a dream."

"Yeah, of course you heard that." He rolled his eyes. "This is the most messed-up dream I've ever had. You're a princess? You have a bodyguard?" He shot Nick, who was sitting on her other side, a look. "Now you're asking me questions about this dream." He shook his head. "I swear Gaia cast a spell on me. This seems like the kind of thing she'd enjoy."

His lips curled, despite what he said. Gaia didn't have a chance to enjoy it.

"You said . . . Did you just say Gaia?"

He looked over. "Yeah, *Princess.* You look exactly like her. Apart from the leather. I don't think she'd wear that to save her life." His expression turned thoughtful. "You know what? Maybe this dream *is* me. If Gaia had anything to do with it, there'd be no leather at all. This must be some kind of fantasy."

He chuckled, as if it amused him. "Hell, the punch might have been, too. You can nurse me back to health."

He wiggled his eyebrows. It was an absurd thing for a grown person to do, and she would have told him so if she weren't in shock.

"Well." She downed her drink, slamming the glass on the counter when she was done. "What the hell does this mean?"

CHAPTER 5

Jacob stared at the woman at his side with interest. She was a fascinating combination of the Gaia he'd made up and the Gaia who actually existed. This look she was giving him, for example, was exactly one the Gaia who actually existed had given him. Multiple times. In his brother's bedroom.

He winced. He needed to reframe that so it didn't sound so gross.

"Well. What the hell does this mean?"

He blinked. "Excuse me?"

She didn't look at him. Only slid off her seat—a feat, considering the leather—leaving him behind as she stalked out of the room.

"Hey," he said, standing. Belatedly, he thought about his own drink. He looked at it, at the bartender, remembered this was a dream and he didn't have to drink it or pay for it, and followed Gaia—or whoever she was in his dreams—outside.

She was on the ground when he found her. Just . . . on the ground. Sitting cross-legged on the sidewalk, staring ahead of herself as if she'd been informed of some tragedy.

"Hey," he said again, approaching her as he would a wild animal. "You okay?"

She didn't answer. He sighed. Lowered to the sidewalk. He wasn't sure what his mind was playing at. Was he about to counsel a figment of his imagination? Did that imply he needed counseling? Did it symbolize his connection with Gaia? Was he being punished for trying to find meaning in dreams when he'd never believed they had meaning before?

"I don't know," she said, interrupting his brain's ramblings.

Also known as thoughts.

"What do you mean?"

"I don't know." She gave him a look. "That's why I said 'I don't know.'"

"Touché," he said wryly. "Is there anything I can do to help you?"

Now he was offering to *help* her? He sighed.

"What's your name?"

He blinked at the soft question. "It's—"

Jacob. His name was Jacob. He'd known that for a damn long time. Why couldn't he say it? It was like there was something malfunctioning between his brain and his vocal cords. His brain sent the word to his mouth, but nothing came out. He tried again, and again. When he finally stopped, tired and more than a little disturbed, a name popped into his head.

"Chris?"

"Chris?" she repeated. "Your name's Chris?"

"No. It's—"

But the same thing happened. She studied him, but it gave him no clues as to what she was thinking. It couldn't have been good when her next move was to rest her elbows on her knees and her head in her hands.

"I don't understand," she said, but she wasn't talking to him. He didn't care.

"What don't you understand?"

"Any of this. You seem almost . . . real. But that's not possible. There must be some kind of mistake. Some kind of . . ."

She trailed off. "It'll go back to normal." Her voice sounded broken as she said it. Then she repeated it, but in a whisper. "It'll go back to normal."

"Okay," he said after a moment. "Okay, this is getting weird now." He stood. "What do I have to do to get out of this? Pinch myself, right?"

He did it. The pain was sharp and short-lived. And he was still very much standing on the sidewalk next to a cobbled street and a woman who was watching him with big brown eyes.

Those same eyes had stared at him vulnerably during their kiss earlier that night. They'd grown trusting as he'd spoken with her. Then they'd gone hot with lust and desire. He wanted that back. He wanted *reality*.

He pinched himself again, but harder. The pain was longer this time, and he winced because of it. But it would be worth it if—

He was still standing on the damn pavement.

"It won't work." She was standing next to him now. He had no idea when she'd stood. "That? Pinching yourself? It won't work."

"Since you're not a real person, I'm going to take my chances with science from the real world. But thanks."

As he said it though, he wondered whether the pinching thing was an old wives' tale or something that had, indeed, come from science. He'd heard it from his mother, who'd been comforting him after a bad dream. Even the prospect of being able to control his dreams like that—one pinch and he'd be out?—made him less afraid. And that was probably why his mother had told him that. Which likely meant science had nothing to do with it.

"You're realizing it's not science, aren't you?" she asked quietly from his side.

"How did you know?"

"I'm a figment of your imagination, remember?" The words were light, teasing even, but he didn't find them genuine. "I know all your thoughts."

"If you were a figment of my imagination you wouldn't know all my thoughts. *I* don't even know them half the time," he elaborated.

"Well, I'm everything you think possible and more," she said with a smile. It was a half smile, curving her mouth in a way that had his gaze dipping to her lips. They were as tempting as he remembered, though he hadn't stared at them for very long before he'd been kissing them. If he truly wanted to check his memory, he would have to kiss them.

"You're seducing me," he said in surprise, taking a step back.

Her brow furrowed. "What? I didn't say anything remotely seductive."

"'I'm everything you think possible and more,'" he repeated. "That's not seductive to you?"

"It depends on what you think is possible."

"See! You're doing it again."

"What?"

"Playing with me."

"I'm not doing anything of the sort."

"You are. And it won't work, so you can stop . . . doing all this, too."

"Too? I'm doing something, too?"

"Yeah. You're smiling at me."

"You're amusing."

"This is my dream. If I don't want to be amusing, I don't have to be."

"Fine. But I find grumpiness amusing, too. So, really, you'll have to remain neutral so I don't think you're amusing or grumpy."

"There are other emotions."

"By all means," she replied, waving a hand as if offering her permission.

He studied her. "You're annoying."

"I don't have to be."

"Seems to me you only know how to be annoying."

"I can't be annoying if I don't speak."

"How am I supposed to prevent you from—" At her look, he stopped. "Oh."

Her smile widened.

"Seduction," he said again.

"It comes in all forms."

He almost smiled at that. Almost.

"Why do you want to seduce me so badly?"

"It's your dream, Chris. You've dreamt Nick out of the picture." A quick look around told him she was right. The man—her bodyguard?—was nowhere to be found. "Now I'm seducing you? Why do *you* think that is?"

He opened his mouth to reply. In the end, he didn't bother. He merely stepped forward and kissed her.

It was hot. Not as much as with the real Gaia, but good. There was no hesitance with this version of her. She opened her mouth to him, moaning with delight when he did the same and their tongues met.

For a moment, he forgot none of this was real and sank into it. Her clothing stuck to her body, literally, leaving nothing to the imagination, as Gaia's clothes had the night before.

But he'd felt that Gaia's body. He'd run his hands over the softness of her thighs, caressed the dips of her waist, her hips. He'd had her breast in his palm, her nipple in his mouth, and perhaps that knowledge now was why this dream version had Gaia's real body. Except now, he'd have the pleasure of peeling off her clothes leisurely, unlike—

"Your Highness," came a voice from behind them.

They stopped. Nick was back, and he sounded concerned. When Jacob turned, he saw why.

There were horses heading in their direction, their hooves harmonizing with the sound of the metal of the accompanying soldiers' uniforms. He was about to say something, and then he was opening his eyes.

In his own bed.

With empty arms and an erection.

CHAPTER 6

Gaia woke up panting. She wished she could say it was because she was aroused from that kiss she'd orchestrated to get out of her dream. But her arousal had quickly faded and now it was . . . She wasn't sure. A mess of emotion she wanted to scoop in her arms and clutch to her chest. She didn't know if that was so she could protect them or process them. It was all confusing. The most significant of it being she had no idea what had just happened.

Slowly, she got out of bed, her movements jerky, her hands shaking. The sky was light behind her curtains, one of the benefits of summer. It was hard for her to get up in the darkness during the winter. But when she woke up from a dream, she was usually inspired to write the next scene of her book.

Not today.

Thankfully, by the time she got to the kitchen after her morning routine, she was feeling sturdier. Not enough to examine what had happened in her dream, but enough to make breakfast. After she made pancakes and added a banana and berries, she settled at the table in front of the windows in her lounge to soak up the early morning sun.

Her phone beeped.

She reached for it, then paused. It was probably Seth. He

hadn't replied to her message that she was safe at home the night before. He'd read it though, which almost made her regret sending him the message in the first place. But she couldn't punish him by holding that information ransom. They always made sure the other got home safely.

Except . . . What if he was messaging to break up with her? Friends broke things off with other friends all the time. She assumed. She hadn't had friends other than Seth; she wasn't sure of the *we're no longer friends* protocol. Steeling herself, she picked up her phone.

It wasn't Seth.

> **Hey, it's Jacob. I was wondering if I could see you tonight?**

She dropped her phone and picked up her utensils. Deliberately, she cut through her pancakes, added both a slice of banana and a berry to it, and put it in her mouth. It was delicious, the sweetness exploding on her tongue. Still, she chewed mechanically, as if she were eating something much less appetizing.

She waited to swallow before she messaged him back.

> **Where did you get my number?**

> **Does it matter?**

No. She supposed it didn't.

> **Why do you want to see me?**

Seconds later she got a reply.

We should talk about last night.

That was frustratingly ambiguous.

I think last night is best left untalked about.

That's not a word.

No, it's a feeling.

I'm not asking you out. I just want to know if you're okay.

Good to know?

She wasn't sure what that question mark was meant to imply. Her indignation? Why the hell didn't he want to ask her out? But that was beside the point.

I'm okay.

She sent the message, then felt bad and sent another.

Thank you for checking.

With that, she switched off her phone. She did it regularly, when she wanted to get words down and didn't want to be interrupted as she did. No one looked for her so urgently that they'd worry if her phone was off. She usually sent the only person who would worry, Seth, a message to warn him she was about to do it.

Seth. He was clearly still mad at her. The night before, he'd been crude and nasty, and it wasn't like him. It bothered her, but she'd deal with that once they made up.

If.

She stopped chewing. Swore at her brain.

Okay. Clearly she needed to stop thinking about Seth.

So, about Jacob . . .

If she hadn't already known her brain didn't like her, the last five minutes would prove it. And apparently future minutes, too, since now she was wondering if Jacob had really been in her dream.

Only that wasn't possible. Of course it wasn't. She was probably projecting. *Definitely* projecting. She had shared an honest-to-goodness kiss with a man she'd felt honest-to-goodness chemistry with. It was rare. No—unheard of. So she'd based her hero on Jacob, and had gotten confused as a result. It was as simple as that.

Because though she didn't know all the mechanics of her abilities—it wasn't exactly something she could do an internet search on—she had twelve years of experience. There had never been a human being besides her in her dreams. It was unlikely to happen now.

Unless there was something about *Jacob* that had changed things. Maybe Jacob was like . . . her.

She shook her head. Frowned. Then went about her day pretending that thought hadn't stuck with her.

When she went to bed that night, she tried to take comfort in the fact that she hadn't written. It was bittersweet. She'd ignored her desire to write, but at least there'd be no dreams. But how long could she keep that up for? She was an author by trade. By passion. By *contract.*

How could she not write?

Jacob didn't usually mind Mondays. This one was hell, and made up for all the others that hadn't tackled him to the ground.

Turned out the big client he thought they'd signed hadn't actually sent the papers through. The man was threatening not to, unless they could match a competing company that was offering them lower rates. He'd just figured that out when there was a power outage. The generator went on immediately, but the system they'd migrated to the month before had to reboot, and they lost an hour of work time. Of course, that meant panic about deadlines and the hum of anticipation and nerves until it went back on. Then came the scrambling. The end of the day was pushed back by an hour, by three for him, and when he was finally ready to go home, he found his brother waiting in the foyer for that spontaneous visit.

"I don't have energy for this," he said. "You can lecture me tomorrow. Right now, I need sleep."

He didn't even know if he'd be able to sleep. He'd struggled since he'd had that dream about Gaia. He thought he manifested it because his brother had planted that seed about her not being fine Friday night. So he thought he'd check in with her on Saturday, see if she was okay. She was. According to her message. Which, of course, he believed. That's why he slept like crap Saturday and Sunday nights.

His brother studied him. "How about we go out for dinner?"

"I said—"

"I won't talk about Gaia."

But his lips tightened in a way that told Jacob he was conceding and he wasn't happy about it. It made Jacob believe him.

"I need to get Dad dinner."

"I had pizza delivered about an hour ago. Said it was from you."

Jacob narrowed his eyes. "Have a solution for everything?"

"Yeah. It's called common sense. You should try it."

He snorted. "If what you have is common sense, I'm not sure I want it."

"Hmm." Seth stuffed his hands in his pockets. "So. Dinner?"

He exhaled. "I could do with a drink."

"Dinner."

"I'll have a drink with my dinner," he said mildly.

"Smartass," Seth replied, smirking. "Do you have your car?"

"Of course."

"Cool. I'll meet you."

"Where are we going?" Seth gave him a look. Jacob laughed. "Fine. I'll see you in fifteen."

Jacob was smiling when he got into his car and drove the steep and narrow road to the hidden Indian restaurant he and Seth had discovered years ago.

It wasn't strange to be annoyed and amused by his brother in equal measure. Their relationship wasn't easy, but they stumbled through it because their mother would have wanted them to. Shortly after she died, they'd found a dimly lit family restaurant that had become their go-to place. They went often enough that they'd endeared themselves to the owners. Neither of them talked about why: that the place reminded them of their mother.

Jacob found a parking spot on the street a short distance away from the restaurant. A miracle. Parking in central Cape Town was a nightmare. Most of the restaurants and clubs relied on street parking, which made every parking spot lucrative. As evidenced by the fact that his brother was still crawling down the road, hoping for someone to pull out. Jacob sighed, and leaned against a wall nearby to wait. It took ten minutes, but eventually Seth came walking down the pavement.

"Nice of you to join me."

Seth swore at him. "Every time I have to park I wonder why we come here."

They both looked up. The restaurant looked more like a house than anything else. It was a two-story building with a bunch of windows, the front of it rounded in some kind of European structure he'd never cared enough about to investigate. The building had once been white, but now the paint was fading and chipped, giving it both an old and haunted look. At first sight, it was the perfect setting for a horror movie.

But another look showed how warm the light shining through those windows was. There weren't many people inside, but those who were, were laughing. Their mother would have noticed it.

"Don't be a snob," she'd tell their father if he hesitated. He almost always had when she articulated unconventional ideas like eating at a haunted restaurant. "This is where they make food with love."

It wasn't a line he'd heard anywhere else, or from anyone else, but she'd been right more often than not. The memory made him smile.

"You know why we come here," he said softly. Seth made a noncommittal noise. They went inside without discussing it further.

The tension faded when Nicki, the daughter of the restaurant's owners, saw them.

"Seth, Jacob, you're back."

"Why do you always act surprised, Nicki?" Jacob asked, brushing a kiss on her cheek.

She was a tiny woman, with straight black hair that went down to her waist. Her skin was a shade or two darker than his own, her eyes lined with dark liner that made the brown of them look light. Or was that the teasing glint in them?

"If I don't act surprised when I see you, you'll think I've grown accustomed to you."

"That's a bad thing?"

"It would be," she said, accepting a kiss from Seth now, "if you stopped coming."

"We wouldn't do that," Seth replied with a half smile.

"Rest assured, we'll never find out." She winked. "The usual to drink?"

"No," Jacob said. "I'll have a whiskey. Neat."

"Er, you can give me my usual," Seth said with a frown. When she left, he asked, "Rough day, huh?"

"What gave it away? Me telling you I didn't want to go out? The coercion it took to get me here? The fact that you promised not to—"

"I get it." He paused. "Do you want to talk about it?"

"Not particularly."

Seth didn't press, but his frown deepened.

Jacob sighed. "Do you ever stop worrying, Seth?"

Seth didn't take the bait. Instead, he said, "Jake, you need to talk to someone. The pressure you're under—"

"Nah," Jacob interrupted. "Let's not do this."

"Jake."

"Fine, you want to talk? How about how messed up your behavior was on Friday night?"

"Oh?" Seth's eyebrows rose. "You want to talk about messed-up behavior on Friday night?"

"Have you even spoken to Gaia since then?" Jacob asked, ignoring the jab. "You hurt her, so I hope you have. I hope you apologized."

Seth didn't say a word. But he was avoiding Jacob's gaze. Looking everywhere *but* his gaze, in fact. Like a guilty baby.

"Ha. Guess your whole 'you need to talk to someone' thing has very limited applications."

Seth swore at him. Jacob retaliated with a smug smile. Nicki returned with their drinks. There were samosas on her tray. There were always samosas on her tray these days. A benefit of having the owners like them.

She gave them a sly look. "Ma told me I should give this to you."

"But?" Jacob asked, playing along.

"It doesn't mean we like you."

He chuckled, breaking some of the tension his conversation with Seth had built. "Nicki, let's not play around. You know you and your ma enjoy us being here as much as we like coming here."

She angled her head. "You keep us in business." As if proving it, she pulled out her notepad. "So, what can I get you?"

They ordered their meals—the usual for both of them this time. When she left, silence descended on them.

"You should ask her out," Seth said eventually.

Jacob merely watched him as he took a sip of the whiskey.

"I'm being serious," Seth added.

"I know you are."

"She's hot and smart."

"Yeah? If you think so, why didn't you ask her out before you started dating Lizzy?"

"She doesn't like me."

"And she likes *me*?"

"She's flirting with you."

"I'm not interested."

Seth's voice hardened. "Why?"

It took a second. Slowly, he sat back. "This is about Gaia."

"No."

"I thought we weren't going to talk about her tonight?"

"*I* didn't," Seth said pointedly.

"Hmm." Jacob stared at his brother for a while longer, then downed the rest of his drink. "Why don't you tell me about your day, bro?"

"Jacob—"

"Your day, or I leave."

Seth exhaled harshly, annoyance and frustration mingled in

that breath. But he began to talk. Of course he did; his brother loved talking. Usually, it was the crap Seth had pulled earlier, with the concern. It didn't confuse Jacob any less today than any other day. Seth was always concerned, yet he seemed content to let Jacob take responsibility for Seth's messes.

Jacob didn't dwell on it. It had been too long a day for him to. Instead, he listened. Seth told Jake about his day, about his opinion on the latest superhero movie, about the series he watched in the last week. Seth kept his promise; there wasn't a single word about Gaia. Even though her name usually slipped out of his mouth as easily as Lizzy's did.

Jacob knew Seth was trying to keep the peace. Except it had the same effect on him as when his brother told him something about Lizzy while she was in the room.

"Don't look at her," he'd say, which of course made Jacob want to look at her.

Now, he couldn't stop thinking about Gaia.

And that's how he found himself driving to Gaia's house instead of his own after his dinner with Seth.

CHAPTER 7

Her doorbell rang at eleven that night.

She hadn't been sleeping, but that didn't mean she was happy about it. Who would be? The pounding of her heart was excessive though, so she went to the door. When she reached it, the doorbell rang again. Three quick rings, followed by one long one. It was a code, but for who, she didn't know. Everyone she allowed into her house were regular people, not spies.

She looked through the peephole, but it was blocked.

"Hey," she said, knocking against the door. "I don't intend on opening. Unless you're someone I know, or someone who intrigues me enough that I want to know you." She almost snorted at the lie. When had she ever wanted to know anyone? "Both options require me to see you. So, you know. Stop blocking the peephole."

She got no reply, then realized she might be a victim of pranking.

"Stupid kids," she muttered, even as she wondered why they were mucking about on a Monday night. Didn't they have school? Or was it school holidays?

Huh. Apparently thirty did turn her into an old coot.

She shook her head. Who was she kidding? She'd always been an old coot.

"It's Jacob."

The voice came almost at the same time she decided to go back to bed. Her heart pounded again, the feeling of it tightening her stomach. Her brain froze for a few seconds, too. She wasn't sure if that was because she hadn't been expecting an answer, or because *Jacob* had given it.

She walked back to the door. "Really?"

"Really."

"Move back so I can see you."

There was a small pause, a shuffling sound, then he said, "I'm back."

She looked through the peephole and saw that it was, indeed, Jacob.

Shit.

He looked *so* good. His shirt was crinkled, as if he'd spent the entire day in it. One side was tucked into his pants, the other not, which made her think he'd . . . Well, she wasn't sure. He wore jeans with the shirt, and sneakers, and his hair was mussed.

What an adorable nerd.

"I don't open my door to strange men who rock up unannounced at eleven at night," she said.

"You'd do it for men you know though, right?"

"Depends. Have they let me know in advance?"

"They would have, if you answered your phone."

Oh. She'd deliberately forgotten it was off for the weekend. That way, she didn't know if Jacob had replied to her message.

Or if Seth hadn't.

"The battery's dead," she lied, closing her eyes with a wince.

"And you don't have a charger at home," he added to her lie. "Yeah, it makes sense."

"Don't get cocky with me, Jacob," she replied primly. "I'm the one with the power here."

"You're always the one with the power."

She didn't know what to say to that. Especially since he said it in a tone heavy with implication. Heavy with . . . something else. She couldn't put her finger on it, but it felt seductive, and now she was considering other reasons to let him into her place.

No—*not* to let him in her place. *Not* to let him. That was an important distinction.

"Why are you here?"

"Can I come in and tell you?" he countered. "Not because I want to be inside your house—though yeah, I do, or I wouldn't have come—but because it's late and your neighbors might show concern and call the police."

She took a second before she unlocked the door.

"You're wrong," she told him. "They wouldn't care. They stole the tires from my car earlier this year and no one saw or said a thing."

He didn't reply. She quickly realized it was because he hadn't been listening. Then she realized she hadn't given a second thought to what she was wearing, which, based on Jacob's reaction, was a problem.

"I'm sorry." She folded her arms at her chest, covering her breasts, which had been roaming free, as was their right whenever she was home. "I didn't expect you and I climbed right out of bed."

"No. No," he said again, lifting his eyes to her face. "You don't have to apologize. I'm imposing."

"I'm going to get something to put over this," she said slowly, taking a step back when she saw him clench his teeth. She didn't know how she knew it, but she could tell he was controlling himself. She didn't think about why that was. "You can, um, help yourself to whatever's in the fridge. Or put the kettle on and make tea or coffee. Whatever. Help yourself."

She was rambling, so she simply turned and hurried to her bedroom. When she was there, she closed the door with shaky hands, and leaned her back against it. It was almost exactly what she'd done when she'd been at Seth's party the other night. The thought had her scrambling forward, to her closet. She couldn't think about what she'd done at Seth's party. Certainly not in the context of repeating those actions. Certainly not when logic had since made its presence known and she realized anything with Jacob would make her life infinitely more complicated.

None of this had even touched on the fact that he may or may not have been infiltrating her dreams. She took a deep breath, then grabbed her tights and pulled her legs through them. She threw off her nightgown—it was silk, for heaven's sake, because she liked feeling luxurious when she went to bed. Except now she felt like a hussy because there was no way Jacob hadn't noticed her nipples responding to the sexual tension between them. She put on a bra, pulled on a long, loose top, and went back to the door.

She stopped before she could go through it and turned toward the mirror.

She looked . . . not as cute as she had at Seth's party. Not a surprise, considering she'd spent an entire week planning what she would wear to the party. But she was struggling to figure out whether it mattered. She had, after all, opened the door to him in her nightgown, boobs free, her hair bound in a silk scarf. She'd forgotten about that little fact. She untied it quickly and retied it so it looked fashionable instead of like she planned on cleaning for the day.

She shouldn't have opened the damn door.

It was too late for regrets now; the man was waiting for her in her kitchen. She pressed a hand to her stomach, to the ball of nerves bouncing there, but she straightened her shoulders and pointed to herself in the mirror.

"You've got this. You're a grown woman who can handle her business."

Her reflection looked back at her skeptically. She stuck out her tongue and went to join him in the kitchen. He was making two mugs of tea when she got there.

"I assumed you wanted something to drink," he said.

"Um, yeah, sure."

"Milk?"

"What kind of tea did you make?"

He blinked. "Er, this one?" He opened the cupboard and gestured to the pot that said "Tea."

"Yes, please, to the milk. And one sugar, too."

He obeyed without comment. She had no idea why she found that attractive. Or maybe she did. He'd done the same thing during their make-out session. Done exactly what she asked. It was an attractive quality in a romantic partner. Specifically, in a sexual partner. She knew that after noticing a pattern in the books she read and then applying that pattern in the books she wrote.

When partners asked the right questions or followed the right orders, they generally resulted in orgasms. This was the first time she'd felt certain of that fact in real life. She was sure Jacob would—

Oh, no. She was thinking about *orgasms* and Jacob at the same time.

"Here you go."

Her eyes flew up to meet his. He was watching her with amusement, one eyebrow raised. Not enough for her to think anything of it. At least not if she'd been in her normal human state. But she wasn't. She was in her horny human state.

Good heavens. She needed to calm down.

"Thank you."

Keep calm and drink tea, was it? She took a sip of the tea.

"Can you drink that when it's so hot?"

"I only drink it hot." Why did that sound dirty? "I had a lot of cold cups of tea when I was growing up," she continued quickly, giving him more information than she intended to give. She couldn't stop though. Talking was distracting her from her hormones. "When I got out of the foster system, I told myself I wouldn't drink it cold ever again."

She stopped when she saw his expression. Rolled her eyes. "Don't feel sorry for me, Jacob. I'm fine."

"I don't feel sorry for you."

"Tell that to your face."

His expression blanked, which made her smile. "I'm sorry about that."

"Your expression or my history of drinking cold tea?"

"Can it be both?"

His tone was so sincere she angled her head. "It can."

She brought the cup to her lips and waited for him to tell her why he was there. He didn't. He leaned back in the chair across from her, studying her in a way that would have made her shift if she weren't stubborn.

Stubbornness didn't change the fact that every day after to-night, she'd think of him like this. Interested, confident, study-ing her easily at the table she sometimes wrote at. It was the same table she'd sat at Saturday morning to eat breakfast, when she'd been freaking out about her dream. But seeing him here, in the flesh, made that morning feel as though it hadn't hap-pened. Which was a mistake. She knew it deep in her bones.

"You have a lovely home."

"How do you know?" she said, mirroring his stance. "You haven't been looking at it."

His lips curved. "I had a few minutes while you changed." His gaze flickered down over her outfit, back up to her face. He must have had heat vision, the way he set her body on fire. "I like the color scheme."

"You like my pink walls? Really?"

"It goes really well with the cream couches," he replied with-out taking a beat. "The beige curtains, too. I love how they match the throws over your couches. It also complements your writing desk. The wood on that thing is a beauty."

She smiled. "Fine, you've looked around."

"Just the lounge and the kitchen."

"It's open plan."

"Your kitchen's nice, too. Modern. And the color of the walls here." He imitated a chef's kiss. It made her laugh.

"You're incorrigible." He opened his mouth but she cut him off. "You can't make that joke again."

"What joke?"

"You were going to say 'bless you.'"

He smiled, confirming it. But he said, "No."

"Jacob." Her tone conveyed a teasing displeasure. "After all we've been through, you're going to *lie* to me?"

"You're right. I'm sorry." He ran a finger around the rim of his mug. "I'm sorry about pitching up here at eleven, too."

It took her a moment to adjust to the change in topic. To the change in his tone.

"Thanks," she said. Debated. Continued. "You didn't wake me though. I couldn't sleep."

"That's part of why I'm here."

"Because I couldn't sleep?"

He snorted softly. "No. Because I thought I wouldn't be able to sleep."

Oh, no. Oh no, oh no, oh no.

"Why not?" she forced herself to ask.

"My brain . . . is too busy. I've had a weird day."

She nearly dropped her head against the table in relief. Though she shouldn't have felt it. There was no way he couldn't sleep because he was afraid of dreaming. She was projecting again.

Another wave of relief crashed over her. She'd almost forgotten how wonderful logic could be.

"Do you want to talk about it?"

"What?" He looked confused. "No. Why?"

"You said it was part of why you're here."

"I meant because I couldn't sleep."

"Are you hoping I'd be able to give you something to help you sleep?" she asked lightly, even though the question didn't seem light to her. It seemed dangerous. "Because I don't know what your brother told you, but I'm not into one-night stands."

His mouth opened and closed enough times that she wondered whether she should interrupt.

"You had a one-night stand with Seth?"

"*What?*" But she was already laughing, despite the indignation. "Absolutely not. No way. I have never even thought about it. Goodness." She laughed again.

"I don't think he would appreciate this reaction," Jacob said with a wry smile. Was there a little relief in it, too?

"No, he would. Because if you asked him that, his reaction would likely be the same."

"He's not that impolite."

"He is when he's with me." Her laughter twisted into a cynical smile. "We have an understanding. We can be ourselves with one another." Mostly, anyway. "No politeness if that's not how we're feeling."

Her smile faded as she remembered how tense things currently were between them.

"Sounds nice." There was wistfulness under the nonchalance.

"I know you two have a . . . difficult relationship."

"I'm not here to talk about my relationship with Seth."

"Why *are* you here?" she asked. "You can't sleep, I get that. But apparently, you're not here to talk either, so . . . ?"

He took a long time to respond. She watched him as she waited, noticing the fatigue in his eyes for the first time. He looked like his day had been rough, not only weird. She didn't know what to do to make him feel better, but her instincts told her to do *something*.

Uncertainty kept her frozen in place though, her mind bouncing between ideas that seemed terrible and wonderful at the same time.

"I did come here to talk."

Her eyes met his. "About what?"

"Friday night."

He had no idea what he was doing at Gaia's house.

Part of him blamed his brother. Seth had put the idea that Gaia wasn't okay in his head. Seth had avoided talking about Gaia. Seth had shown him where Gaia lived.

Looking back, he wondered why Seth hadn't taken him inside that day. Allowed him to talk to Gaia when he was no longer a kid with a crush. He'd already been working at the company for two years then, and had taken another one of his breaks to keep his brother from nagging him—for a while, at least. Seth had wanted to drop off something for Gaia on their way to a restaurant out of town.

Had his brother known something would happen between them if they spoke as adults? Had he wanted to prevent it?

None of it mattered now, when he was sitting across from her at her kitchen table, enjoying the mix of emotions on her face. Feeling guilty for it. Sad when her expression closed.

"I told you I didn't want to talk about Friday night."

"You opened your door to me," he reminded her. "You must have known it would come up."

"Maybe I thought something else would come up."

He gave a startled laugh. "Erection jokes? Really? Cheap shot."

"Don't call yourself cheap, Jacob. Owning your sexuality doesn't translate to that."

"You know that's not what I meant." But he was amused. And entertained. Despite himself. "You're deflecting."

"Yes, I am. Because you've given me a reason to deflect, and that's actually quite annoying at eleven p.m."

She stood, the scraping of the chair loud in the silence of her home. Lights illuminated the space, which he really did think was cool. It felt cozy and warm, and he thought she might have purposefully designed it that way. It made sense if he thought about her past. He'd forgotten she'd grown up in foster care. He shouldn't have. Back when he'd had his crush, he'd made a mental note to remember things about her. Now that his crush had reintroduced itself, he hated that he'd forgotten those things.

She was walking into the living room before he realized it, and he hurried to follow her. Then, he nearly bumped into her when she stopped.

She whirled around. "No. This is my home. I set the rules."

The words were firm. Too firm. Like she was forcing herself to adopt the tone.

"Gaia, I didn't come here to make you feel uncomfortable." He stepped away from her, putting space between them so she could have it. So he could have it. "I just . . . Friday night was . . . I don't know how to describe it." He lifted a hand helplessly. "I'm not being prudish when I say I don't do that. I don't. I don't have the time to. Work is more important to me than going to parties and kissing girls."

"I'm not a girl, Jacob," she said softly. "Which means I don't need an explanation for Friday night. We were both there. We consented."

"We didn't get a chance to talk after."

"What is it with you and talking?" she asked with a shake of her head. "Some things you aren't meant to talk about. Some things are meant to be experiences that blow your mind, and then they're over."

"Is that what Friday night was?"

"Yes."

"For you."

She gave him a pleading look. "For both of us."

"No, not for both of us." He took a small step forward. Waited for her to step back if she wanted to. She didn't. "You want to know why I don't want to talk about my day, Gaia? It's because it was crap. A bunch of stuff happened that I had to deal with. Normally, I wouldn't mind. But I did today. Wanna know why?"

She nodded, her eyes wide. He took another step forward.

"I live for drama at work. It's probably something I need to examine, but for now, I'll tell you it's because I'm good at it. I'm good at solutions. I can only come up with solutions when there are problems. But today, I struggled, because I couldn't stop thinking about you."

As he said it, he finally figured out why he was so off today. Why things he'd have breezed through before caught him so off guard. Dinner with Seth, his link to Gaia, hadn't helped. And he knew, he *knew*, that if he'd told Seth about his day he would have come to this conclusion earlier.

It was a hell of a conclusion. One he hadn't wanted to have without her.

"It's not over for me."

He closed the distance between them, waiting for her to move again. When she didn't, he lifted a hand, brushed her face with his fingertips. Her hair was still pulled back by a scarf, though it was tied differently than it had been before. He hadn't realized headscarves did it for him, but then, Gaia could wear a black bag and it would do it for him.

"I dreamt about you Friday night," he whispered, letting his fingers trail along her hairline. "A dream that made no sense. But it was you, and me, and we kissed again, and it was incredible."

Her lips parted, and he thought she would lean forward and kiss him. If she did, he would accept. That was the only way he knew how to deal with what was happening. If he could kiss her and touch her to his fill, he wouldn't have to dream about her. He would be free; he could continue his existence without her. She wouldn't infiltrate his dreams, his job. He would be able to move on.

"Get out."

"What?"

"Get out," she repeated. Suddenly she was walking away from him, to her front door.

He tried to figure out what happened, but he didn't know. He turned.

"What did I say?"

"Everything. Everything you said was a problem." She pursed her lips. "But I'm sorry, that was rude." Cleared her throat. "Would you please get out, Jacob?"

"I don't understand."

"It's almost midnight on a weekday. I have work tomorrow. So do you."

"Gaia—"

"Jacob, I said go."

He had no choice but to obey.

Gaia wasn't proud of how she'd treated Jacob. But the logic she'd claimed earlier? About Jacob not being in her dreams? It didn't work so well when Jacob was telling her he'd dreamt about *her*.

It was possible it was a coincidence. She could have checked that by coaxing more details from him. But coaxing seemed dangerous when they were both under a spell. A desire-fueled spell that made her want to take him to her bedroom though she'd never done anything like that before.

No, this way was simpler. Relatively. She would write. Start something new. If her hero acted unexpectedly, she would know. If she still had doubts, she would go see Jacob tomorrow and ask him about his dreams.

Either way, she was getting an answer.

CHAPTER 8

Jacob was running, feet hitting soft, plush grass. Before he could fully comprehend that he was running, he leapt over a fence. *Leapt.* As if he were some damn gazelle on a nature channel. His landing was less graceful than the animal's though. The position was somewhat of a squat, somewhat not, and pain shot through his ankles. When he looked down to check the damage, he noticed something else.

He was naked.

"What the—"

A shriek cut him off.

"Hey, hey, hey," he said, moving toward the sound. But he quickly realized he was a strange man standing naked in someone's yard. He stopped moving.

How the hell did I get here?

"You can have it," a familiar voice said.

He blinked. Gaia.

Oh. He was dreaming again. About her.

It felt as if a cat had crept into his chest, curled around his heart, and sat down. Warm, comforting, satisfying. Gaia might have kicked him out of her house, but his subconscious wouldn't allow her to let go. Or was it not allowing *him* to let go? It didn't matter. Not now, when he had her here. A version of her, anyway. He would take what he could get. Because being kicked out of her house showed him how little he wanted to be kicked out of her life.

It was a troublesome realization. More so when he was happy—no, *eager*—to have these weird-ass dreams about her.

"I don't know what you think—"

"You can have it," she said again, lifting her hands to show him she didn't have any weapons. Or to surrender. Both options seemed a tad dramatic.

This Gaia looked more like his Gaia. There was no leather, unfortunately, but she wore an old stretched-out T-shirt over black tights that ended mid-shin. Her feet were bare, a warm brown sinking into the bright green grass. Only her hair was different from the real Gaia's. It was longer, running past her shoulders in curls that were wavier than her real curls. He didn't mind it this way, but he preferred the coily pattern of her real hair. Her curls stuck out in all sorts of directions; he constantly wondered if they might poke his eye out, and somehow that had become his preferred state of being.

"Take the laundry if you want it." She nudged the basket in front of her forward with a foot. "You can have the lemonade there, too."

He looked to where she gestured. A jug of lemonade sat on a small table positioned under the shaded area created by her roof. The rest of the yard was open to the sun, which he now felt over all his skin. Which made sense, of course, considering he was naked. He covered his penis with his hands.

She cleared her throat. "It's . . . um . . . It's a bit late for that."

His lips parted. "Excuse me?"

"If you're covering yourself up for modesty, it's a bit late for that." She tilted her chin up, a move he'd seen the real Gaia do, too.

"It's never too late for modesty."

"It's *sometimes* too late for modesty," she insisted. "For example, when a man jumps into your yard, trying to rob you, but he looks like a male model with shoulders and hair and stuff, and he's naked, so, of course, you look, because you have no self-control, even when you're terrified of being robbed."

It was a lot of information. He focused on one fact.

"I'm not here to rob you."

"Are you sure? Because you jumped over my fence looking pretty fierce, and now you're just standing here."

Good point. "I was running. And I jumped." It was all he could offer her because it was all he knew. "If I was robbing you, wouldn't I be taking stuff?"

"I offered you the laundry. And the lemonade."

"If I was robbing you, wouldn't I be taking stuff worth something?" he corrected.

"Hey," she said, affronted. "People love my lemonade. My neighbors are always coming over to have it."

His eyebrows rose. "And the clothes?"

She eyed the laundry basket. Lifted her eyes to him. Her expression brightened. "You're naked, mister. Maybe you live on the street and wanted my things."

"You think that if I lived on the street, I would be robbing you, someone not my size, for her clothing?" The triumph dimmed on her face. "Yeah, that logic needs some work," he added.

"My logic always needs work," she muttered. "Although, it's a bit annoying for you to offer me wisdom when you're in my yard, trying to—" She broke off at his look. "Okay, fine, you're not trying to rob me. But what *are* you doing here, huh? And why are you naked?"

"Those are both excellent questions."

There was a pause.

She narrowed her eyes. "I assume you have answers?"

"Yeah, sure."

He racked his brain for his own logic, which wasn't something he usually had to search for. Unless he was with her. His logic scrambled for a place in his brain then, showing up at inopportune times to point out how foolish he was being.

It shouldn't happen in his dreams though. He should have control here. He *did* have control here, as proved by the fact that up until now, he could converse with her easily, despite the strange nature of his dream.

But in response to her questions, his brain was offering him answers that made no sense. They were detailed answers, painting a scenario he would never put himself in. And sure, this was a dream, where scenarios didn't make sense. Except in every dream he'd ever had, there was a kernel of himself. In the way he responded to the scenario, in the emotions he felt. The guilt when he dreamed of leaving behind his family and work and moving to a country where no one knew him. Or the anger when his mother, dressed as an angel, asked him why his family was still so broken. They were *his* dreams; something of himself *should* be in it.

So why in the hell was his brain telling him he was running away from the irate husband of a lover? Why, when he was dreaming of Gaia?

He opened his mouth, though he wasn't quite sure what he wanted to say. As it turned out, it didn't matter. Not when a clicking sound had every part of him freezing—including his excuses. It was a very loud, very distinctive clicking sound. He'd never heard it in real life, but he would recognize it anywhere.

"You're the man sleeping with my wife," a voice drawled.

If Jacob *were* running from the irate husband of a lover, that was exactly the kind of thing the husband would say.

Shit.

"Don't move."

He hadn't moved since he'd heard that click of the gun, but he sure as hell wouldn't be moving now.

"If I shot you in the nuts, you'd never be able to sleep with her again."

"Hey, now," Jacob heard someone say. It took him a second to figure out it was him. Another to realize he was still talking. "That sounds excessive."

"It sounds like a fair punishment to me."

"Excuse me? Terrence?" Gaia said, interrupting when Jacob opened his mouth. Apparently, having his junk threatened made him more defensive than smart. "It is Terrence, isn't it? I'm not even sure since you're pointing your gun over my fence without the decency of looking me in the eye."

Jacob followed Gaia's gaze, for the first time realizing the man—Terrence—wasn't in Gaia's yard, only the tip of his gun. Jacob had little knowledge of weapons, but he was pretty sure the tip was all that was needed to do some damage.

Ha, a voice in his head said.

Not the time, he mentally chastised his sense of humor.

A face slowly appeared above the fence. A mean-looking face, with a sneer that could give any villain a run for their money. He could hardly blame the man's wife for seeking affection elsewhere. Probably because if she *had* sought it elsewhere, and elsewhere was Jacob, he should be blaming himself.

"You have a stranger in your yard," Terrence said, voice hard.

"I'm being neighborly."

"Pointing a gun at someone is never neighborly," Gaia replied in the same tone. "Besides, this man isn't a stranger. He's . . . a . . . friend."

"Man's naked in your backyard, Jade. Can hardly call him a friend."

Jade? Wasn't that what the princess was called the other night?

"Okay, fine, he isn't a friend. He's a little more." Gaia, or whoever she was, walked closer to him. He held a hand out to stop her. Her eyes, harder than they'd been before, settled on him.

You fool, they seemed to say. But he might not have trans-lated it properly. He probably didn't. She had no reason to call him a fool.

"We haven't settled on labels yet," she continued, sauntering over to Jacob before placing herself in front of him. In front of the gun. He heard the growl coming from the vicinity of his throat, but she aimed a glare at him that was so sharp it stopped him in his tracks. From shock. Gaia would never, ever be capable of such a fierce, unkind—

"If you want to shoot him, Terrence, you're going to have to go through me. And wouldn't it be heartbreaking for your mother to find out you're going to jail for killing her favorite seamstress?"

The pause that came this time was longer, less sinister, though no less tense. Slowly, after what seemed like a lifetime, the gun was lowered.

"You didn't have to bring my momma into this," Terrence said.

"I clearly did. You wanted to shoot him."

Terrence ran a hand over hair that was graying at the temples. His first show of vulnerability.

"I found Nora in bed, with a man's clothing on the floor. No wallet or ID or anything, otherwise I would have known who to look for. I thought a naked man would be a pretty clear sign of who was messing around with my wife."

His eyes narrowed suspiciously at Jacob. It took that for Jacob to realize he hadn't replaced the hand he'd used to try and stop Gaia from moving. He put the hand back over his penis.

"May I ask why there's a naked man in your yard?"

"You may, but it would be very intrusive." She paused, appar-ently giving him a moment to change his mind. When he didn't, she sighed, and answered the man. Jacob was pretty sure it was only because there was a gun involved. "I like getting him to do household chores naked. It gets me hot and bothered to see a man doing things around the house"—her voice was so dry, he wanted to throw the lemonade at it in case it ground to a halt— "so to see him doing it naked . . . It's foreplay. I jump his bones as soon as he's done, and we have sex for the rest of the day. Does that answer your questions, Terrence?"

"Yes, ma'am," Terrence replied, eyes big and maybe even embarrassed. "I shouldn't have . . . I'm sorry . . ." He exhaled. "Please don't tell my momma."

"Get out of my yard and I won't."

The man's face disappeared in seconds. They waited a while longer before either of them moved. When they did, Gaia sagged. His hands shot out, grabbing her waist and hauling her up before she could hit the ground.

"You're touching me," she pointed out weakly.

"You would be on the ground if I didn't."

"Yeah, but now it's almost like your penis is touching me because your hands used to be there." Her eyes lowered. "Speaking of, I can see it again. I told you it was too late to bother."

He ignored the babbling. Ignored the—reluctant—amusement, too. "Are you okay?"

"A neighbor pointed his gun at me. I'm going to need a minute." She gave him a nod, and because she looked steadier than she had a moment before, he let her go. She walked over to the lemonade, poured herself a glass, downed it. She offered him the next one. He wanted to accept, but he'd covered himself as soon as he had his hands back.

"Towel," she said on a sigh. "There's one in the laundry basket."

"Won't it be wet? Never mind," he added quickly at her expression. "It'll be perfect."

Minutes later, he had a cool towel around his waist. He'd had a rapt audience as he'd done it, too. Gaia hadn't taken her eyes off him since she offered the towel. It sent awareness through his body, which wasn't wise. Awareness was one short trip away from arousal, and in his current state of undress, that would be awkward for the both of them.

"Thanks."

"You're a cheater."

It was a matter-of-fact statement that echoed the lack of emotion on her face. She wasn't watching him in some seductive way—she was watching him out of disgust.

"No," he said, even though all the evidence suggested otherwise.

"Well, you're sleeping with Nora. You wouldn't be the first man to help her try to kill her husband through infidelity, but you're the first one in my yard, so you get to hear me call you names."

"I'm not a cheater."

"You didn't sleep with Nora?"

The scenario his brain had given him earlier told him he'd slept with someone. She might have been Nora. She probably was Nora. And though he wanted to deny it, he couldn't. He *physically* couldn't. It was the same thing that had happened when he'd tried to say his name in that other dream.

"I didn't know she was married, so it's not cheating," he said instead. A line that slipped from his tongue as if he were really this man. This cheater.

"Oh, please. That's a load of crap and you know it."

He did. But his dream wasn't allowing him to acknowledge it.

"You shouldn't have done that earlier. Stood in front of me," he clarified. "You could have got hurt."

"I couldn't stand there and let you get shot. Even if you deserved it."

She stomped over to the laundry basket, picked it up and stomped to the washing line. With movements stilted by anger, she began hanging up her things. After the third item, she turned back to glare at him.

"Are you going to help me?"

"I . . . Yeah."

He went over to help her.

"Not so close," she snapped.

"How am I supposed to help without standing near you?"

"Figure it out."

"You're being unreasonable."

"I'm annoyed. There's a difference."

"I almost wish he'd shot me," he muttered, picking up some clothing items and throwing them over his shoulder.

"I can always call him back and tell him the truth if you like," she offered sweetly.

He glowered. It felt strangely right; again, as if he were this person. But he would never sleep with someone who was married, even in his dream. And he would never snark at Gaia this way either. Although he had to admit he had the potential to.

They worked silently side by side. Gaia didn't complain when he got close this time, and he did her the favor of not mentioning it. When they were almost done, he pointed to the towel at his waist.

"Do you want me to . . . ?"

She shook her head vehemently. "Oh, no. That belongs to you now."

"You don't want it back?"

"It's summertime. I won't need kindling for my fire for at least another three months."

"It's just a penis," he said with a roll of his eyes.

"It's more than *just* a penis," she said under her breath.

"Excuse me?"

"Oh." For the first time since the Gun Incident, Gaia showed something other than irritation.

"Are you blushing?"

"What? No, of course not." She picked up the empty laundry basket and lifted her chin. "It's the heat from being in the sun."

"I don't think it is." He followed her with a grin when she

started walking to the door of her house. "I think you complimented my penis. Thank you, by the way. I'm quite proud of it."

Another dickish thing to say, but it felt right. He was teasing her now though, and perhaps *that's* what felt right.

"It's an appendage. How can you be proud of it?"

"Clearly you haven't seen what it can do."

"Oh, I know what it can do." They walked into a kitchen painted a soft yellow. "Ruin marriages, almost get shot, give the person using it delusions."

"I don't think your reaction to it was a delusion."

"Of course you don't. You're an egomaniac—"

"—if we're calling one another names, can I suggest—"

"—who thinks that someone's offhand comment means you have an impressive penis, which we both know isn't true because if it were, we'd be doing something with it instead of arguing about it."

The tirade ended with a puff of air, as if even the thought of them doing something involving his penis was out of the question. But based on the way her eyes widened, giving the interest she couldn't hide space to dance, it wasn't. In fact, it wasn't a question at all; merely an answer. Since he was only mortal, humble in the face of what Gaia might offer him, even here, he was unable to resist the pull from that answer.

And for once, he felt like *himself* in this dream.

"We could," he said slowly. "Do something with it. We could."

She snorted, but her hands gripped the counter at her back. She thought it a casual stance when she put the laundry basket down, he was sure. But even then, it had given away her tension. Now, that tension was curled around something else. Something dangerous.

"You want to."

"I don't even know you."

"We can change that."

"Except I lied," she said, voice hard. "I *do* know you. I know that you sleep with married women. I know that you think nothing of propositioning another woman minutes after you've been inside someone else." Her face pulled in disgust. "You're not a man I want to get involved with."

"None of that changes the fact that you want me."

He inched closer. Not enough to make her worried. Just enough to make her realize he was telling the truth. As if proving it, her eyes dipped over his naked chest, his torso, lingering at what the towel now covered, before wrenching back to his face. He gave her a knowing look.

She rolled her eyes. "My body might want you, but my mind and my heart don't. Since each of them has an equal say in who I get involved with, my body's outvoted."

"You're a weirdo," he said affectionately, taking another step closer.

"I'm smart. Smart enough not to do this."

He studied her expression—the resolve, the stubbornness, and yes, the smarts. All he could see was Gaia. His Gaia. She had all the traits this version of her had and more. He wanted her more than he wanted anything else in his life. But she *was* smart. Smart enough not to get involved with a man who had family issues and a job that took up all his time.

Perhaps this was the point of the dream. To help him see Gaia had been right to kick him out. He had lied to himself, thinking he could get her out of his system. He wouldn't. This dream—these *dreams*—proved it. She was lodged so firmly in his brain that even his subconscious surrendered to her.

At least it allowed him to say goodbye.

"You're right." He closed the space between them now, waiting before he touched her. When she didn't move, or stiffen, he lifted a hand to cup her chin. "You deserve more than me. You deserve someone who won't pitch up at your door at eleven at night because they can't deal with their emotions. You deserve—"

He broke off when she let out a harsh breath. When her eyes fluttered closed and he had the oddest suspicion that she was trying to keep him from seeing her emotions.

"Hey," he said softly. "Look at me."

"I can't." Her hoarse voice sent a ripple of concern through his body.

"Why not?"

"If I look at you, I'll see you."

"Yes," he said dryly. "That is the point."

"I'll see *you*. Not the character I created."

He was frowning when she opened her eyes. When she let him see the same turmoil that had been on her face when she'd kicked him out. Now, the turmoil was lined with resignation and . . . *fear*.

"It's okay," he said, even though he had no idea what had caused the emotions. "You're going to be fine."

"See, there you are." Her whisper was ragged. "If you weren't so . . . so . . . *you* at that party, I would have never kissed you. And none of this would have happened."

"Party?"

"Party," she confirmed.

"Wait a minute, this is . . . No," he said after a short pause. "Or yes? This makes sense, right? I'm seeing you, and this is us talking about something that actually happened. It's the other stuff—the sleeping with some random woman stuff—that doesn't make sense."

"Except it does," she said softly. "It won't for you, right now, because you have no idea what's going on. But—you will. You should." He was standing close enough to her to see her throat bob as she swallowed. "Just give me a week to figure it out, okay? Then come find me."

"Come find . . . What?"

"I'll explain in a week."

Then she rested her head on his chest, and the words he had coming—the answers he wanted to demand—fell away. He pulled her closer, comforting himself with the feeling of her in his arms. When he woke up in his own room, in his own bed, Jacob wasn't surprised at how cold he felt without her warmth pressed against his body.

CHAPTER 9

Gaia had asked for a week; Jacob gave her two days.

Some time Wednesday evening, her doorbell rang. It was the same pattern he'd rung the doorbell with on Monday. It would have been a cute little code between them—like actual spies—if he hadn't been there to demand what the hell was going on.

She didn't answer the door.

She couldn't answer that question yet. Besides, she'd spent the last two days in a pit of confusion, concern, and hyperventilation. She could handle the confusion, the concern. Or perhaps she couldn't, considering the hyperventilation. Either way, her unreliable breathing patterns were just plain annoying. She was a *human being*. She *needed* to breathe. Those sharp, uneven puffs of air her lungs took in, then expelled, didn't count. The fact that it took her at least twenty minutes of struggling to get it under control again exasperated her.

Human beings breathed properly. How the hell did her body expect her to exist as one when it wasn't supporting the functions she needed to live?

She gripped the pillow she clung to, forcing herself to breathe in and out steadily, though she could feel her body fighting against that illusion of control. Things eased when the doorbell stopped ringing. When the banging stopped. When Jacob stopped calling her name. She had no idea how long it had taken.

Fighting it off cost her all her energy, so she fell asleep again. She woke up feeling tired, so beyond eating small portions of food, she stayed in bed. Thursday night, the doorbell rang again. Again, she ignored it. This time he stayed for longer, and her control nearly slipped. It did the next afternoon, when she realized one day of indulgence had somehow turned into four and she still didn't have energy for anything.

Pure determination capped the hyperventilating at ten minutes. When it was done, she got out of bed on shaky legs, and went to her bathroom. She brushed her teeth, stripped and stepped under the water of the shower. The heat was good for her stiff muscles. She would have loved to have it soothe the stiffness she felt encasing her heart.

She would have been more alarmed if she weren't used to the feeling. It wasn't as acute as it had been when she was in foster care, but when she left the system, that feeling hadn't left her. It felt like a bruise she didn't want to touch. A scab she couldn't bear scratching. It was a strange description for a heart, especially from a romance author, but it served a purpose. It reminded her of where she came from. Of what she'd been: a child no one wanted.

Usually, it was relatively unobtrusive. She had grown used to it, after all. Or she thought she had. Except here she was again, unwanted. How could Jacob want her when her . . . her *magic* had cast a net over him? If she had discovered someone had done that to her—not the universe or some all-powerful being, but a person—she would have been pissed.

It might have been a bad idea for her and Jacob to get involved romantically, but the idea that he didn't *want* to get involved with her romantically was worse.

Heartbreaking, actually.

She soaped her body, tilting her head so she wouldn't wet her hair. She had no energy for that mission. When the water turned cold, she got out of the shower and wrapped a towel around her body. With a deep breath she didn't take for granted, she walked to the kitchen.

And found the Scott brothers standing there.

"This doesn't look concerning," Seth said, eyeing her. "She's fine. If a little pruney."

"I've been here every day since Wednesday," Jacob replied, voice hard, though his gaze was gentle as it scanned her face.

Her heart softened at the concern. But seconds later, her brain reminded her of why he was there. Why he had been there every day since Wednesday. That softness skipped over to her lungs, trying to convince them to let her down.

No, she instructed them. *There are people here. You can't stop working. And if you do, so help me, I'll take one of you out and sell you on the black market. If you don't work for me, I might as well, anyway.*

"She's not fine," Jacob said at the end of his perusal.

"No," Seth agreed, eyes sharpening. "She's not."

"'She' is standing right here."

But she was too tired to say more than that. She went to the cupboard for a glass and poured water into it. Then she turned back to the kitchen and watched them watch her.

"Gaia," Seth said slowly, "you okay, babe?"

She only blinked in return, her emotions swirling. He hadn't spoken to her in a week and *now* he was concerned? She was pretty sure the only reason he was there at all was because of Jacob. And she knew why Jacob was here. He wanted answers. It had nothing to do with concern.

It felt as though a blade sliced through her heart. She folded her arms against her chest in response.

"Okay, this is worrying me now," Jacob said. "We should take her to the doctor."

"I don't need a doctor," Gaia replied before Seth could. "I need space. I believe I said a week."

Jacob's eyes widened. Disbelief skipped through them. Confusion scurried after the disbelief. Then he shut them both down, biting down so hard his jawline bulged.

"I feel like I've stepped into a lovers' tiff," Seth commented slowly, his voice suspiciously devoid of emotion. "I think I'm going to go and let you two sort this out."

"I'll walk you to the door," Gaia said.

"You're not denying there's something between you and Jake now?"

She snorted. "I knew it! I knew this was a test to see if Jacob and I—"

She broke off. She didn't want to dive into that. She didn't want to feel the disappointment and anger and *hurt* toward Seth either. But she clung to it because it was better than feeling nothing. Or not nothing—fear.

It was better than being scared she was losing her best friend.

"Dude—seriously?"

"You're the one who asked me to come here," Seth answered his brother.

"I thought you'd be concerned about your best friend."

"I thought you needed my key," Seth said flatly.

"I should know why the idea of me and Jake freaks you out, but I don't, which I guess means our relationship is as broken as this entire thing seems to indicate," Gaia said softly. "So, Seth, I will walk you out, and you can give me back my key so you never have to be put in the position to care about me again."

"Gaia—"

"On second thought, maybe Jake should walk you out. Give him the key."

She drank the water, set the glass on the table, then walked out of the kitchen to her bedroom. There, she lowered to the bed, gripping the sheet between her fingers. Had she worried about Seth breaking up with her? She shouldn't have. She should have just faced the reality that someday, Seth would realize he didn't want to be a part of her life, like everyone else.

She bit down on her lip to distract herself from the explosion of pain inside her. When voices sounded from the kitchen, she stilled. Because she hadn't closed her bedroom door, she could hear every word.

"You should go," Jacob said.

"No. She obviously needs me. I think I'll stay."

"She obviously *needed* you." Jacob's voice was steady. She closed her eyes. "Now, she needs something else."

"You?"

"You did this, Seth. You pushed her away for a week for some stupid reason. You should have come to see her like you did with me."

"You're family."

She hissed out a breath at that. Because of course she wasn't Seth's family. Just because he was the closest thing to family *she* had, didn't mean it was the same for him.

But Jacob was laughing.

"You know she's as much family as I am. But, hey, if it makes you feel better to believe that instead of knowing you treated your family like shit, sure." There was a quick pause. "Then again, that's not a new thing, is it?"

Seth didn't reply for a long time.

"Take her to Between the Covers."

"Excuse me?"

"It's a bookstore in Stellenbosch. You'll find it with GPS."

"You're telling me to take her to a bookstore?"

"It'll make her feel better." He paused. "And if it doesn't, she's always said she'd prefer a death by books." Another pause, shorter this time. "Don't bother walking me out. I can do it myself."

There was a metal clink that told her Seth had thrown down

his key on the table. Seconds later, her front door slammed. She held her breath, then let it out shakily when Jacob didn't immediately come to find her. But she didn't move, so when he eventually did appear in her doorway, she was still sitting on her bed in a towel, gripping the sheets.

"You heard that," he said. She nodded. "Is he right? Should I take you to a bookstore?"

She didn't reply. Couldn't summon the emotional energy to engage with knowing her best friend—or whatever he was now—knew the exact right thing that would make her feel better.

"Personally," Jacob continued, tone conversational, "I'd want to die in a more dramatic way."

"You don't think dying under an avalanche of books is dramatic?"

Something pulsed in his eyes, but he only smiled. "Not dramatic enough."

"How can that not be dramatic enough?" she asked, indignance creeping over the emptiness of the last few minutes. "It's something the world has never seen."

"Are you sure?"

"Of course." At his raised eyebrows, she reconsidered. "Well, I mean, if someone had died because a pile of books fell on them, surely we would have heard about it."

"You're proving my point."

"I am, aren't I?" Her gaze rested on him, amusement fizzling into a stronger emotion. "I'm doing exactly what you want me to do."

He stepped into the room. "What's that?"

"Getting out of my head."

There was a pause. "Is it working?"

Amusement slithered back in, and she brought her hands to her lap, curving one under the other. "Somewhat."

He studied her. Unashamedly, without any pretense that he

was doing something else. She tried not to stiffen, tried not to show how much it bothered her that he was looking at her as if he wanted to *see*. She didn't know what he'd see.

No—she did. And that was the problem. She didn't want the shards of her brokenness to poke him in the eye.

"You. Me. Between the Covers."

"Excuse me?"

Jacob opened his mouth again, but paused before he could speak. Color, red and telling, crept over the gorgeous brown of his skin.

Gaia sucked her bottom lip in, pressed her front teeth down on it. She didn't want to smile. She wasn't in the mood for smiling.

Except now, both those things seemed like lies. She wanted to grin at Jacob's phrasing and tease him about it. She wanted to laugh and let the light that seemed to surround him seep into her soul and banish the darkness there, force away the weight of it. She didn't understand it. It made her heart thrum and the chaos that seemed to live in her chest buzz.

But those light feelings—those feelings she felt when she looked at Jacob—came from the vicinity of her chest, too. And as if she needed more going on there, they seemed to be at war with the darker feelings. *Those* feelings were draining. Like they were there for the sake of being there, not because they needed to be there.

None of it made sense.

"I . . . I didn't mean it like that. I was talking about the bookstore Seth told me to take you to."

She didn't answer his stammering. Mostly because it stomped on her negative feelings, replacing them with good things. Jacob things. It was merely a bonus that the lack of reply seemed to prompt more stammering.

"Between the Covers. That's the name of it. I assume you like it or Seth would have suggested another place."

"Yes," she said primly. "I like Between the Covers." She clutched the front of the towel. "I like it very much."

He stared at her. His lips split into a grin. "You're messing with me."

"No, I'm not. I like Between the Covers. It's my favorite place to be."

"Yeah, but you're talking about the bookstore, not the other . . ." He faded.

"Of course I am," she replied, as if he hadn't. "What else could I be talking about?" She didn't give him a chance to answer. "Can you give me a moment? I need to get dressed."

"Yes. Yeah."

She waited until he'd almost closed the door before she said, "Sucker."

"I heard that!"

She smiled as the door clicked closed and she inhaled. Her lungs, for the first time in a week, seemed to be working fine.

CHAPTER 10

He couldn't believe how relieved he was to hear Gaia teasing him. To see the tension that had been on her face, in her body, fade to something that didn't make him want to pull her into his arms.

When she walked out of her bedroom, when she offered him a tentative smile, the fist clutching his heart loosened. They didn't talk much on the way to the bookstore. Her fingers curled into her skirt. She occasionally exhaled sharply, followed by a quick inhale. But other than that, she seemed okay. Not like someone who didn't answer the door for two days because . . . he didn't know.

He desperately wanted to find out, but he was afraid asking would push her right back into wherever it was she'd come out of. He kept the questions to himself, and let the books comfort her.

Personally, Jacob didn't understand the appeal. The bookstore was, quite frankly, chaos. Books lined almost every wall. Which was more concerning considering the small space those walls enclosed. The store looked like a four-bedroom house if four-bedroom houses only had tiny bedrooms. Somehow, the owners had managed to fit a long table in the middle of each of those tiny rooms, which created an aisle of sorts, with books stacked on and around the table.

There was barely space to stand, let alone walk, yet Gaia slipped through the aisles like a pro. The other patrons did the same. There were about fifteen of them, snaking past one another without so much as an "excuse me." They scanned book stacks, read blurbs, flipped through pages as if in some magical world. No one looked upset if someone bumped into them by accident. They barely acknowledged the hit, caught in what they were doing.

So—this was what it was like to watch book nerds in their natural habitat.

Smirking at himself, at the thought of what Gaia would say if he ever chose to voice that, he moved through the narrow spaces, apologizing to whoever he bumped—because he was an outsider here, and the rules didn't apply to him—and went to stand on the veranda. It was cute, more spacious than inside the store, and had three small tables on one side with huge, handmade SALE signs on top of them. More people stood in front of those, the open air making it seem less stuffy.

He stared out at the car lot in front of the store. It was a large gravel space without any outlines for parking. Gaia told him the only criteria was that they should be able to pull the car out as easily as they got it in. He hoped to heaven she was right.

A car door slammed, drawing him out of his thoughts. He found the sound in time to see a tower of books crash to the ground and a woman drop to her haunches with a curse.

"Hey, can I help?" he called as he walked toward her.

He kept his distance, knowing it was evening and he was a man and that didn't generally make women feel safe.

The woman looked up. The familiarity of her features hit him in the gut, though he had no idea why. He hadn't met this woman before, and he couldn't think of who he did know that looked like her. Her hair was brown and straight, running past her shoulders. She had a wide nose, a wide mouth, and big eyes that were framed by thick lashes. Her expression was warm, confident, and when she smiled, everything on her face made sense.

Which was a compliment, despite how it sounded.

"Yeah, thanks. I don't know why I thought bringing these here without a box was possible. I suppose I didn't think, because if I *had* thought, I'd probably have brought a box. Oh, well," she said with a shake of her head. "On the other hand, if I had brought a box, this wouldn't have happened, and I wouldn't have met you."

She smiled at him as she stacked books on the ground. Again, he thought about how lovely she was. He wouldn't call her beautiful in the same way he would call Gaia beautiful. Her features were too confusing for that. But there was something stark about her face. Striking. And he was so caught by it that he didn't realize what she'd said for a while.

He cleared his throat. "How nice."

"Isn't it?" she replied, beaming. "You seem like a good person, too, and that's honestly a bonus. I like meeting new people. Friends."

"Friends," he repeated. "I don't think that's the best description for—"

She didn't let him finish.

"Not everyone I speak to is like you." She picked up some books and put them into his arms. As she bent down for more, she continued. "I don't want to say that they aren't good people because I'm sure they are. They just have a weird way of showing it."

Intrigued now, Jacob asked, "What's weird?"

"Um." She frowned. "I met a woman in line at the post office and she tried to steal my purse."

"At the post office?"

"Hmm. I think the post office wouldn't give her the grant money she needed, so she tried to take my purse."

"You think that's weird? Not . . . *wrong*?"

"No, it's wrong," she agreed. "But in the end, she let me keep my purse and was very grateful when I gave her some cash."

"You gave her—"

"So, yes, weird and wrong," she interrupted him, nodding her head.

He took a moment. "Ma'am, I think your definition of *weird* needs some work."

She looked at him for a second, then her expression softened and she laughed. "Probably. But that's okay. It's not hurting anyone."

"I'm pretty sure it's hurting you."

Her expression went blank, as if it never occurred to her to think about how things were affecting her. Then she waved a hand. "I'm still here, aren't I? Alive and well and making friends."

"I think you need to redefine the word 'friend,' too."

"Now *that* I don't agree with. Friendship is like an onion. You start off with the really crispy layer that's relatively safe and then, as you become closer, you get to the people who have the power to make you cry." She shrugged. "You and I are on the crispy layer."

It would be easier to accept her way of thinking than to question it. To point out the disturbing premise of her metaphor or try to figure out her logic.

"So am I the same level of crispy as the woman who tried to steal your purse?"

She chuckled. "At this point, yes. But you make me want to get a knife and peel you so we can move to the next layer."

"You might want to start with something other than his head," Gaia's voice interrupted. His head snapped to where she stood. In her arms she had a brown bag stuffed with books, and she was looking at him strangely. She turned to the woman. "It's pretty hard, so you'll blunt your knife there."

"It's nice to know the first thing you do when someone threatens to cut me is give them advice on how to do it efficiently," he said dryly.

"Someone has to," she replied in the same tone. "Besides, I'm sure you could handle her if you had to."

He looked over at the woman, and for the first time noticed her silence. She didn't seem like the type to be silent. They'd known one another for a few minutes, and she'd called him a friend. Shouldn't she be doing the same for Gaia?

No, apparently. She only stared.

"Are you okay?" he asked.

The woman kept staring. Gaia shifted, angling toward him in a way he didn't think she realized. It was almost as if she was using him as a shield.

Before, he wouldn't have thought she needed one. In fact, Gaia was the person he would have thought least needed a shield. But today, after seeing how vulnerable she'd been—with Seth; on her bed before they'd come here—he understood. And he remembered that she hid the night of the party. That she told him she didn't like socializing with people.

If she felt half as exposed as she looked when she had to socialize, no wonder she didn't like it.

"I'm sorry . . . Excuse me," he said again, when he still hadn't gotten the woman's attention. Finally, her gaze settled on him. "Is something wrong?"

"No, no." She dipped her head in a show of nerves that, again, seemed uncharacteristic for someone who claimed to be friends with strangers. "It's just . . . it's her."

He frowned. Shifted in front of Gaia a little more. "What do you mean?"

"I mean, it's *her*."

The answer gave him no clarity, and he was about to tell Gaia to get in the car when she murmured from behind him.

"The books. They're mine."

He looked at the pile of books in the woman's hands and noticed the name. Gaia Anders. There must have been twenty of them. All new; all in different colors.

"You're a fan."

The woman blinked slowly, lifting her head to meet his eyes. Vulnerability flashed there. For a second, it made him think of Gaia. Then it was gone, replaced by a bright smile that was so far from Gaia, he dismissed ever making the comparison.

"A fan. Yes. Yes, I am. A reader. Of your books," she clarified, looking at Gaia. "They're superb. So well-written. Such great characters. So much romance."

"I . . . er . . . thank you," Gaia said, moving out from behind Jacob slowly. "Thanks for reading them."

"Yeah, definitely. I love these books. Really love them. They're great."

Jacob's senses tingled. He looked over at Gaia. She wrinkled her nose at him. Something didn't feel right.

"You're really a fan, huh?" he said slowly. "What's your favorite book?"

"Oh. It's, um . . ." Her eyes went up and down the pile of books he held. Down to the books she held. But it was pointless. She wouldn't be able to see any titles. "It's the one with the man. And the . . . um . . . the woman. And they meet at a . . . um . . . at a bar. And they're lawyers?"

Her voice went up at the end, as if she were asking a question. She was also looking at them as if she were selling a product she knew wasn't very good.

"*Love at the Bar*," Gaia offered. "I thought the title was catchy because they meet at the bar and they're lawyers . . ." She shrugged. "It's not very original, but what are you going to do?"

"Yes, *Love at the Bar*," the woman replied, clearly relieved. "Anyway, it was great."

"I was hesitant about the way the hero encouraged the heroine to leave her job to pursue her dream of singing telegrams— ridiculous, I know, but I wanted it to highlight her agency—but readers seemed to love it."

"Yep. Yeah." Her hair flipped with her aggressive nods. "It

worked wonderfully. I realized the singing telegrams was a metaphor for something else. You're a genius. Anyway," she said for the second time in as many minutes, "I should probably get these inside so they can get into the hands of readers. It was really—*honestly*—a pleasure meeting you, Gaia."

That last sentence was the only sincere thing she'd said since Gaia had joined them.

"It was nice meeting you, too."

The woman walked past them, and Jacob gestured to the books in his hands before following her. Inside, the woman went straight to the counter and engaged the man behind it in conversation. Jacob dropped off the books, got a smile of acknowledgment from the woman, though she kept talking. That was as good of a goodbye as he was apparently going to get.

When he joined Gaia outside, she was leaning against his car, frowning.

"I didn't realize romance novels were that on-the-nose with their titles."

Her gaze settled on him. "Three things. One, you obviously don't know much about romance novels. Two, they can be, but they can be subtle, too. Which brings me to three: You can't judge the entire genre based on one book you read. Or think you've read. Or think you know."

He angled his head. "Fair enough."

He unlocked the car, they got in, and for a while, they both sat there.

"Just say it," she said into the silence.

"*Love at the Bar* because of a bar and because they're lawyers?" he blurted out. "Singing telegrams as a metaphor? Seriously?"

She shifted, staring at him. "It was one of my first books, okay? I was still learning. But I'm sure you knew all about the business you entered into when you started, since you're so unsupportive of growth."

"No. No, of course not. I'm sorry, I wasn't implying that

you . . ." He trailed off at the amusement on her face. "Oh, you're pulling my leg."

"Only because you were being an ass." She reached for her seat belt. "It's possible a romance novel along the lines of what I described to that woman exists out there. I just didn't write it."

"You were testing her," he said.

"Not testing. Trying to figure out whether she really had read something of mine."

"Sounds like a little bit of an ass move, if you ask me," he muttered, starting the car.

She smiled slyly. "Probably. Except . . . why did she lie?"

Jacob was wondering the same thing. He doubted they would ever find out.

Gemma left the bookstore immediately, though she couldn't resist looking around in the car lot in case they were still there. They weren't. So she drove home, went straight to her freezer, and took out the emergency ice cream.

There wasn't much left—she had a lot of emergencies, like when she'd forgotten the milk she'd gone all the way to the store for—*in* the store—but she could drown her sorrows. Or her nerves. Her delicate constitution—whatever. The point was, she'd just met her sister *by accident* and she'd lied to her.

She shoveled a spoonful of mint and chocolate into her mouth, hoping it would freeze the memory out of her head.

It didn't.

She was strangely disappointed.

Ever since she'd started looking into her biological family, she'd tried to prepare herself for this. Not that she'd had the intention of ever meeting someone she was biologically related to. No. It was more trying to fill in the blanks in the picture of her life. She wanted to know where she came from, who her dead parents' families were, what their circumstances were, so she could make up things about who *she* was.

It was for no other reason than context. Context for herself, which sounded strange, but was somehow quite important. It couldn't come from the people who loved and raised her. She already knew all there was to know about them. Or so she thought.

As it turned out, they'd kept a fairly big secret from her: she had a twin sister.

Her parents hadn't adopted her sister from the foster system. Nor had anyone else.

The knowledge had . . . disturbed Gemma. More than anything else in her life had. She couldn't bear to tell her parents she knew the truth—she knew they'd separated her from her only sibling—and she couldn't bear to introduce herself to her sister. So she did what every reasonable person would: She stalked her sister. Found every piece of information Gaia had made public and savored it.

When Gemma discovered she was an author, she ordered all of Gaia's books. She ordered two copies each, in fact, because it was a simple way to support her author sister. She hadn't begun reading any of them, oddly nervous at the prospect. But they'd only arrived that morning, so instead of staring at them, at the author picture, at the bio—all of which she absolutely had *not* done; certainly not for forty minutes—she went to donate the extra set of books to the bookstore.

Where she'd met her sister.

And acted like a fool.

She was lucky that Gaia had written a book about two lawyers or else . . .

Slowly, she set the ice cream aside and grabbed her phone. Typed in *Love at the Bar by Gaia Anders*, and found nothing. Absolutely nothing.

So her sister thought she was a fool, too.

Wonderful.

CHAPTER 11

Jacob didn't complain when she asked for takeaways. She didn't know why she expected him to. It was probably the years where asking for any kind of food seemed like a terrible burden. There were foster parents who made her feel that way. There were also foster parents who couldn't understand why she wouldn't ask if she was hungry.

That was years ago though, and she had trained herself out of feeling that way. The only remnants of even the memories were moments like this. But Jacob only asked her what she wanted, then drove until they found the place. After getting the food, they went to the beach a short distance away and ate in silence. Sat in the aftermath of contentment that only indulgent food choices brought, in silence, too.

"You feeling better?"

He didn't look at her. Kept staring at the ocean. She did, too.

The crashing of the waves was rhythmic, coming so far onto the beach that the people walking by had to dodge them. She supposed they knew it was coming. It was nighttime after all, the tide high, as to be expected. They were probably there for the calm. She felt it now, just looking at the waves.

Realizing it, she angled her head to Jacob. "Did you bring me here because you thought it would be therapeutic?"

"Tell me if you're feeling better and I'll answer that."

She snorted, rolled her eyes. But she couldn't lie. "I do." There was a long pause before she said, "Thank you."

"You don't have to thank me. This is what . . . friends do."

They weren't friends. They both knew it. But "friends" was an easier description than what they were.

"I'd like to say thank you," she said softly. "Not only for this, but . . . for . . . not asking. About . . . You know."

She couldn't say it out loud. He would think she was unstable if she'd made up the fact that he was in her dreams. A desperate part of her was still clinging to the possibility.

Besides, she hadn't spoken about it out loud . . . ever.

"You're not ready for me to ask." His words were quiet.

Any hope she had that she was making it up was dashed. The faint tension in his voice told her he wasn't as calm about it as he seemed to be. Perhaps he wasn't ready to ask either.

"No, I'm not."

"So we wait."

She wanted to thank him again, but her throat felt too thick to push the words out. Silence stretched.

"If it's going to happen again soon, please warn me," he said.

Her gaze flickered over to him. He was clenching his jaw. She wanted to press her fingers to the slight swell of it. She clenched them into a fist instead.

"It won't happen again soon."

"You sound sure of that."

"I am. I haven't . . . written, since . . ."

He looked at her. "It works with your writing?"

"Yes."

"Okay." He nodded. "Cool." There was a pause. "Cool, cool, cool," he muttered under his breath.

It almost made her smile. If they weren't talking about something outside of the realm of logic, she would have. But his reaction was expected. Consistent with his personality, too. He didn't want to upset her, but he was confused. He was keeping the confusion to himself. Beyond the clenched jaw and nervous murmuring.

She leaned back against her seat, looking at him. He was as handsome at side profile as he was front. Even when there was barely any light illuminating him and all she could see were the angles of his face. It was the same thing that had happened at the party. She'd put the light off and the moonlight had illuminated him, and the only things she'd felt were lust and trust. A combination she hadn't even considered a possibility, and yet somehow, it coated what she felt for him.

Trust.

Something uncomfortable turned in her chest. Thoughts, memories beat against her skull. She chose to ignore them. Chose, instead, to focus on how her lungs seemed to be on her side again. Each breath seemed almost normal, though the act of breathing still felt a little strained. Like she'd been running for a long time and was finally still.

But she was breathing. For someone who hadn't been able to for a while, that was enough.

"I can feel you staring at me," he murmured.

"Good. I wanted you to."

His cheek lifted. "Isn't it polite to pretend like you weren't looking at me?"

"I don't see the point in that."

She waited as he turned to her. And though it was dark, though she couldn't handle the idea of trusting him when she couldn't see him—and that felt like a metaphor of some kind—she felt a warmth she'd only felt with Seth settle in her body. It wasn't the same kind of warmth as with Seth, and not only because they weren't on the same page at the moment. No, this warmth was more solid, more prickly, more intense.

"We both know that I was looking at you," she continued, her voice a little hoarse.

He rested his head back against the headrest now, too. "I'm surprised."

"About what?"

"That you admitted it. That it had nothing to do with politeness," he clarified. "You just . . ."

She waited for him to finish. He didn't.

"Say it."

"It might offend you."

"You don't know that."

"It might . . ." He hesitated. "It might hurt you."

He was considering how she felt. The warmth coiled up like a snake, poised above her heart, ready to strike.

"I appreciate you considering that," she said carefully, as if somehow she could avoid that snake's attack. "But don't tiptoe around me because of what you think I might feel. I've survived a lot worse than an honest conversation."

He exhaled. "Fair enough." Still, it took him a few minutes before he continued. "You run away a lot."

The warmth completely dissolved, but the snake remained. Except now, it felt as though it was curling around her heart, actually threatening *her* rather than threatening her feelings.

She swallowed. "I'm not sure . . ."

"At the party," he said gently. "Which I get isn't exactly a fair comparison to make since I was running away that night, too."

"You weren't," she disagreed after a moment. "You were avoiding a situation. It's not the same as running away."

"Isn't it?"

"As someone who does both in equal measure, no, it's not." She inhaled deliberately, her lungs feeling tight again. Exhaled as deliberately. "Avoiding something is not putting yourself in that situation at all. Running away from it is being in that situation and refusing to deal with it. With any of it."

"Neither seems healthy."

"No."

Even in the silence, Gaia could hear Jacob list the occasions she had run away since she'd met him. The situation with Seth. That very first dream. When he'd contacted her after. The night he'd come to her house. The aftermath of the second dream.

If she was being honest with herself, she wanted to run from him now. But there was that warmth. It made her want to stay, to face it.

"What are you doing?" Jacob said, straightening as soon as Gaia moved.

"I'm taking off my shirt," she answered, because she was, and she didn't want to think about it. "It's probably another form of running away, which is ironic, considering I'm trying *not* to run away from you telling me I'm running away." But she pulled the top layer of clothing over her head, leaving her in only a tank top. "I'm also fairly certain you're not going to push, since my breasts are semi-visible now and they'll probably stun you into silence."

He made a face, as if to protest, but then his eyes dipped to her chest. She looked down, too. Smiled.

Her breasts had shown up to work.

She'd worn one of her sturdiest bras, which, while not entirely comfortable, did amazingly supportive things to her boobs. Onwards and upwards, apparently. It helped that the top she wore pressed against her body, making both onwards and upwards look pretty darn good.

Great job, she mentally told them, before reaching out and tapping Jacob under the chin.

"My eyes are up here."

"Hang on a second, I'm not done." When he finally managed to look at her, he was grinning. "You can't blame me. You pointed them out and they really are impressive."

"Thank you," she said as she kicked off her shoes. Removed her socks. "Wait until I take off my pants."

She was out of the car before he replied, though she heard

him scrambling behind her as she ran toward the beach. There were so many thoughts in her head about how this was a bad idea. But there were always thoughts. And they were always telling her the things she did were a bad idea.

She ran away from *them* now. Ran toward the freedom she hadn't had the last week. Apparently, freedom came in the form of literally running.

Into an ocean on a Friday night.

She shimmied out of her pants, leaving them on the beach only because everything of value was in her handbag in the car. Also, if someone took her pants, they probably needed them more than she did.

"Gaia," Jacob called from behind her. "What are you doing?"

"Swimming!" she exclaimed, and ran into the ocean.

And screamed as soon as the water touched her.

"*It's cold!*" Gaia shouted soon after her somewhat cute scream. "*Why is the water so cold?*"

He laughed at the expression, at the words, and lowered to pick up her pants. He was close enough to hear her talk, close enough to reply, but a safe distance away from the waves.

"I told you not to do it."

"No, you didn't."

"No, I didn't." He grinned.

Teeth chattering, she walked toward him. Her eyes narrowed. "You wanted me to do it."

"That sounds oddly accusatory."

"You *tricked* me."

"I didn't trick you. You barely gave me a chance to respond to anything you did in the last five minutes. How was I supposed to come up with a plan to trick you?"

"Damn it," she muttered, looking down at herself. "My panties are wet."

"Um . . ."

"I heard it," Gaia said, shutting her eyes. "Sorry."

"Don't apologize. Especially if you think I'm the reason your panties are wet." He gave her a wicked grin when she looked at him. "Gotta take the recognition where you can."

She snorted. He was sure she meant it as a scoff, though it came out vaguely impressed. He didn't point that out.

"I think I turned you into a monster." She took her pants from him.

"If it makes you feel better, I was a monster long before we met." He paused. "Before you seduced me at that party."

She gave him a look. It said *I'm not falling for that.* "You've never been a monster, Jake. You couldn't be, even if you tried."

He smiled, but his brain turned into a web, catching the words as if they were flies.

What if you did try? What if, for once in your life, you didn't think about your responsibilities, your family, and did exactly what you wanted to do? It would make you a monster, sure, but you'd be free to figure out whatever is happening with Gaia. Doesn't that sound tempting? Doesn't it sound like something you want *to do?*

"Hey," she said, studying him. "That was supposed to be a compliment."

"Yeah, I know. Thank you."

And he was still smiling. So how the hell did she see into his brain?

"Are you okay?"

"Fine."

"Jake." Her eyes were soft. Understanding, though that was impossible. How could she understand something he didn't understand himself? How could she even *know* what he was thinking? "Your face is telling me you're lying."

"I'm not—" He exhaled. "I was thinking."

"About?" When he didn't reply, she nodded. "You're not ready to share." It was a statement. "Well, I think the best solution is to shock your thoughts out of whatever pit they've sunk into."

His relief that she wasn't pushing quickly gave way to suspicion. "What are you thinking?"

"Some ice-cold water."

He was shaking his head before she finished. "No."

"I promise you. It's a shock."

"I have no doubt about that. I don't need it."

"I think you do."

"I guess we'll have to agree to disagree."

"I can't accept that."

He snorted. "What are you going to do?"

"Push you in?" He snorted again. "Yeah, okay, fine. Your strength gives you an advantage there."

"Indeed."

She rolled her eyes. "I could bribe you though."

He stilled. "Go on."

"A . . . story. I'll tell you a story if you go into the water. No farther than I did, which is basically up to your knees."

He took a second. "I'm sure the story would be great, but the stakes are too high to offer something that simple."

She narrowed her eyes, but dipped her head in a *continue* motion.

"A date. Tomorrow afternoon."

"A lunchtime date?" she asked. "Are we skirting curfew, or—"

He smiled. "I was going to suggest breakfast, but that makes it seem like I want to stay overnight. I didn't want to imply that."

"You have an aversion to evening dates?"

"No. But . . ." He trailed off. "Well—slow, right? We do this slow. So we can both get used to it."

He was doing it largely for her, and the look on her face told him she knew it. If she asked, he would say it was for him, too. Things were shifting. He could feel it happening, that it was tied up in her, and slow worked, so he could figure it out.

But she didn't ask. She didn't respond for a long time. Then she said, "It's a deal." Her voice was hoarse. She cleared her throat. "Now, strip."

He laughed at the instruction, at the feeling of triumph that shot through him when she agreed. "Do you have some music?"

There was a beat of silence.

"I know you're joking, but there's a huge part of me that wishes my phone wasn't in the car."

"I'm not joking," he said, untying his shoes and very clumsily removing his socks while trying not to touch the sand.

"Considering how smoothly this is going, it's probably a good thing I don't have my phone."

He chuckled, removing his pants and shirt next and handing them all to her. Then he faced the ocean. Gaia gasped from behind him and he whirled around.

"What?"

Her eyes were wide, and under the light of the moon—brighter now that they were on the beach—he thought he saw her blush. "Nothing."

"You gasped?"

"I . . . am thirsty." She closed her eyes, as if *she* didn't believe the lie.

"Gaia—"

"The bet's off if you don't do this in the next minute."

"That's cheating."

"Only if it works." Her expression shone with the challenge.

She knew she had power over him. It was like the night he had gone to her house, before she had opened the door. He'd told her she would always have that power, and it was the truth. He wanted to spend time with her, to find out if she was okay. Plus, she had the answers to his questions about his dreams.

Yes, she had power. She had *all* the power.

Fear flew into his chest, hitting his heart as hard as a bird flying into a glass wall.

"Gaia, I think—"

"Jake, your clothes are off. You do realize that, right?"

He only looked at her.

"So whatever you were about to tell me—whatever put that serious expression on your face—can wait. Clothes are there for a reason, and they shouldn't be off unless there's another reason."

"I don't know if that logic is—"

"*Ten seconds!*" she shouted. "Nine, eight, seven . . ."

Fool that he was, he turned and ran into the cold-as-ice water.

His swearing mixed with Gaia's laughter. He knew even then it would be the soundtrack to all his memories of that night.

CHAPTER 12

Gaia slept better than she had all week. She woke up once, her heart pounding, stomach tight, which wasn't abnormal. She was nervous about the next day. A date. With Jacob. The man who told her they could go slow because he knew she needed time to adjust.

Also the man seemingly appearing in her dreams. The precious, private place that had been hers alone for as long as she'd had her abilities.

But she had fallen back asleep eventually. And it wasn't the restless, drug-like sleep she'd had the week before. When she woke up, she didn't feel as tired as she usually did.

The idea of what she had to do that day still concerned her. Thinking about it was like continual snowfall on the top of a slope: too much, and it would turn into an avalanche and suffocate her.

There was a lot she could do to distract herself. The house was a mess after the week she'd had. She should drag herself to the store for food, too. Her laundry needed to be done. She needed to wash her hair. All of those were perfectly adequate distractions.

They wouldn't make her feel like she was escaping the avalanche though. She would still be aware of it, knowing it would happen if she gave it any power. But if she wrote, she would escape. Into the thing that made her feel good and capable. Into another world where she had control and was safe from avalanches.

Writing always did that for her. The actual writing. The business of writing, not so much. But that didn't matter in the drafting stage. Only the writing mattered. And she didn't want to avoid it anymore.

So when she was done with her morning ritual, she took a cup of tea to the table and opened her laptop. It took a long time, with many pep talks, but eventually, she turned it on. With a deep, steadying breath, she opened two documents. Read through the first.

It documented exactly what had happened in her first dream about Jacob. After days where she had avoided thinking about it, she had to face the possibility—or the inevitability—that the dream had been *with* Jacob. She didn't know how to deal with it; she'd never gone through this before.

When she started experiencing her dreams, she was sure she had misremembered what she'd written that day. Shortly after, she convinced herself that her dreams were really her sleep-writing. There had been other such explanations, but they'd quickly been refuted by fact.

Misremembering everything she had written was impossible.

If she had been sleep-writing, her flatmate at university would surely have said something.

So it had continued until she finally accepted that the dreams were part of her reality.

She was *in* them. Now, so was Jacob.

The second document, detailing what had happened in the second dream, including when she'd told him to give her a week, proved it.

She took a deep, deep breath, before catching her head in her hands when it dropped.

Jacob had infiltrated her dreams.

Jacob was playing the hero in her books.

Jacob had . . . had *magic*.

Just like her.

The week she spent processing—struggling with—the suspicion fortified her in this moment of confirmation. It had happened, it was real, and she couldn't run anymore. She needed to accept it. She . . . she did.

Relief and confusion filled the breath she released. Thoughts tumbled into her mind. Did Jacob have magic? He seemed confused by it all, needed answers from *her*, so he definitely hadn't been magical before her. Had she inadvertently shared her power with him? Perhaps she had shared more than saliva through their kiss. Maybe her magic had somehow seeped into him.

Which made it sound like an STD of some kind.

She wrinkled her nose, but continued with the metaphor since it made sense.

If her magic were an STD, one of the men she had shared bodily fluids with before Jacob—all two of them—would have had it. She would have known, too, since they would have appeared in her dreams. But this hadn't happened before. So obviously this had something to do with Jacob.

She didn't particularly want to delve into why, so she wrote instead.

She erased and polished the ending of the chapter where she and Jacob had gone off script. She leaned into the banter. Sharpened the characters and their motivations. It felt good to write again. It felt good to not fear it. To feel capable of handling it and what would come that night.

She sat back after a thousand words, assessed, and dove in again. This time, there were only a few hundred for her to think about. Her eyes shifted to the clock, and she knew she could get in another hundred words or so before she had to get ready.

She hunkered down, knocked out another two hundred, and left the table feeling better than she had in a while.

Until she walked into a chair.

"What the—" Pain shot up her toe. "Shit. *Shit.* What are you doing there?" she asked the chair. "You're supposed to be . . ."

She trailed off when she realized the chair was exactly where it was supposed to be. Under the table. She'd walked into it anyway. Which happened to her more often than she cared to admit. With a limp, she went to her bedroom and tried to figure out what she should wear.

When the simple task began to take more time than necessary, she threw on a T-shirt and a skirt, which were cute together. *Too* cute. She eyed her reflection suspiciously. Yes, this thing with Jacob had gone from sexy make-out session to some real stuff quickly, but he didn't know that. Well, okay, he probably did know that. Still, it didn't mean she should show him how much she appreciated him. She needed to find the sweet spot between trying and trying too hard, and she wasn't sure this level of cute hit it.

In the end, she put on sneakers so she could look more casual, slid some hoops into her ears, and pulled her hair up. Her eyes caught on her mother's pendant. It hung over the side of her mirror. She kept it there to remind her that once upon a time, she had been loved. She didn't know that for sure, of course. Her parents had passed away when she was too young to be able to make that assessment. But she had to believe it. The alternative was too heartbreaking.

Although some part of her must have believed that alternative because she never actually wore the necklace. Even when she wanted to, like today, she resisted. It felt too . . . personal. She had no idea what that meant, so she left it alone and moved on to makeup.

She settled on mascara and some lip gloss. Enough to make

her look better than she did before, but not enough to make Jacob notice.

She was satisfied with the result, and more than a little pleased she could fuss over something as straightforward as an outfit. After the last week, she needed the lightness, the unimportance of it.

When he rang her doorbell in the pattern she now came to recognize as his, she was ready.

Jacob watched Gaia suspiciously. She was in a good mood. That haunted look in her eyes had disappeared, leaving only shadows of it behind. Her smile didn't seem like it came at a price she couldn't pay. Her laugh came often.

He kept expecting her to pivot. To become the woman he saw the day before. Or, hell—even the woman from the day they met. The reserved, hesitant one. And while she still had some of those traits—she had quietly asked for a seat in the corner of the restaurant, away from most people—she was mostly . . . open.

He was finding it a bit unsettling.

True, that could have been from the lack of sleep he'd had since that last dream about Gaia. He suspected he was trying to avoid dreaming at all. He'd stuck it out for two days before going to find Gaia for some answers. Then she hadn't answered her door, and worrying about her had kept him up for the remainder of the week.

Until the night before.

The night before, he couldn't sleep because he was plagued by the memory of the look on her face when he and Seth had found her. The strain, the worry lining her expression. That jumped to memories of her full breasts peeking out at him from behind her top; the way she looked wearing only that top and panties; the idea of those panties being wet. Those memories were punctuated by her laughter, the flashes of vulnerability and emotion, and his own feelings about how she was already distracting him from his life.

He had worked very hard not to be distracted from that life. Now that he was, he was questioning his motives. Was it because the family business was failing and needed him and his attention? He had still been studying when the decline began, his father so distraught after his wife's death that he needed help. Seth had helped, for the first year, but when Keenan Scott had offered him the reins, he'd refused. He'd pretty much stepped back entirely, and since Jacob had graduated and intended on working for the business anyway, Jacob had stepped in.

Seth had told him not to, but he had no answer when Jacob had asked who else would do it. And to Seth's credit, he'd helped Jacob transition into running the company. But the credit didn't count for much when he still left a twenty-one-year-old inexperienced graduate to fix a failing company. Jacob had interned at Scott Brand Solutions, but in the design department, where he had once believed he and his degree in graphic design would go.

It had taken everything he had to learn the ropes, to manage the shit-show his father had left behind, only slightly improved with Seth's help. He had to be humble, acknowledge to the senior management of the company—most of whom had left when his father had, anyway—that he didn't know much, but he was trying. Trial and error had been his way for the first two years, but pure determination and stubbornness had pulled them out of the red. Eventually, they started moving forward again. His hard work had done that.

But it had also given him an excuse not to examine whether he was living the life he really wanted.

He was so lost in his thoughts, it took him a moment to realize Gaia had stopped speaking. She was watching him now, a frown between her brows. Even with that frown, she was beautiful. Cute in an effortless sort of way, what with her skirt and sneakers and that hairstyle.

But her brown eyes had gone guarded again. He cursed himself for questioning when they weren't. The guardedness was more unsettling.

"I zoned out."

"Yeah, I saw that." She bit the inside of her lip. "I . . . was talking a lot."

"No, it wasn't that."

"It's fine if it was," she said with a small smile. "This is the longest I've spoken to anyone besides Seth. Maybe even him." She paused. "I was kind of curious about what would happen if I was allowed to speak uninterrupted. Someone zoning out seems like an appropriate reaction."

"Don't do that." It came out too sharp. He softened his tone. "Don't make it seem like it's some kind of internal flaw that made me respond this way. It's not. Not in you, anyway."

Her eyes narrowed by a fraction, before widening back to normal. She brought her cup to her lips, but spoke before she drank.

"Will you tell me?" she asked.

"What?"

"What you were thinking about."

He ran through his options. If he didn't, she would probably take it personally. Blame herself when it had little to do with her. If he did, she would know more about his life than he wanted to say out loud.

"I want to tell you that you should forget I asked," she said before he could speak, "to be polite, and unobtrusive or whatever, but honestly, I think we're past that."

Of its own volition, his gaze dipped to her lips, and memories of how they tasted flashed through his mind. That, along with the frank emotion on her face, made him agree with her. "You sound fine with it."

"I sound like someone who spent a week trying to come to terms with it." The words were honest, unassuming; her expression the same. "Maybe you need a week, too. Or maybe," she emphasized, "you need to talk about what's going on so you don't end up in bed for days."

He gave himself a moment to figure out what to do with that information. In the end, he asked, "It was really that bad?"

"Yes."

"But . . . you're okay now?"

"I'm better." She took a sugar sachet and began to shake it lightly. "It . . . happens. I get in my head about something, freak out, but I come back." She set the sachet down and went about leveling the sugar granules inside. "It's how I process, I guess."

"It's happened before?"

She answered with a nod.

"And you always bounce back this easily?"

She gave him a look. "You mean, how could I be in bed for a week, then flirt with you?"

"Well—yeah. How *are* you better? You're laughing."

"Didn't you tell me human beings are complex? Capable of containing multitudes?"

He winced, though she spoke gently. "To be fair, I was trying to get you to kiss me at the time."

"Hmm."

He couldn't fault her for that response.

"I'm glad you're better," he said quietly.

"Me, too." She paused. "And to answer your question, I'm really good at pretending to be okay when I'm not."

He didn't let his surprise show. "You're pretending now?"

She took a moment to answer. "You know how they say fake it until you make it?"

"Yeah."

"For me, it just feels like faking." She stopped fiddling with the sugar. "Maybe I haven't made it yet, though you'd think three decades would get you there."

He exhaled. "I'm sorry you—"

"I'm not done yet," she interrupted with a coy curve of her

mouth. "Sometimes the faking feels like faking, and it exhausts me. Other times, faking it barely takes any energy. But—" There was a long pause before she continued. "But it helps me know what's real, too." She blinked up at him. "Me? Now? It's real."

She didn't look away from him, though her eyes shone with a vulnerability that left him breathless. He wanted to thank her for letting him see that vulnerability. It didn't seem like an adequate response. It didn't seem appropriate either. He wouldn't say the wrong thing, or something that wasn't enough, when she had offered him this.

He told her the truth instead.

"I'm not sleeping. Since the . . . You know."

The guardedness snapped back into place. "I do know." She cleared her throat. "Are you scared of it happening again?"

"Trying to figure out what's happening, to be honest."

She nodded. Took a deep breath in and let it out slowly. "Okay. This is going to sound . . ." She shook her head. "I don't know. Illogical. Impossible."

She paused. He waited.

"I need you to promise you won't tell anyone."

"I . . . I don't know if—"

"You can't tell anyone," she cut in, tone clipped. "If you do, you'll make us both sound . . . It wouldn't be good for either of us."

"Fine. I promise." She gave him a hard look. "I promise," he said again. "You're like a detective in some undercover sting, sheesh."

"I'm too clumsy to be a detective." She sniffed.

"Wait—am I the first person you're telling this to?"

"The *only* person."

"Seth doesn't know?"

"No."

Since talking about Seth wouldn't make this conversation any easier, he didn't ask the questions going through his mind.

"I won't tell anyone."

"Thank you." She paused. "I'd like to ask one more thing." Her voice had gone small. "Don't leave."

"Why would I—" He broke off, taking in the trembling lip. "I won't leave. Of course I won't leave."

"You'll have to process," she said a little mechanically. "And you might be tempted to . . ." She let out a shaky breath. "I can't ask you to stay. It's unfair."

"I will though," he swore. He would swear anything if it made her look less . . . small.

She nodded. Exhaled. Let silence give birth to anticipation, nerves, a thousand more questions.

"Okay," she said eventually. "Okay." She cleared her throat. "I have . . . abilities. Magical abilities. And I think now, you do, too."

CHAPTER 13

She probably shouldn't have started it like that. She blamed it on her writing background. In her books, every revelation had to be dramatic. But seeing Jacob's face made her think it didn't work in real life.

It didn't matter. She had said the words. She was in it. She needed to tell him the rest.

"On my eighteenth birthday, the abilities . . . appeared. I'd bought myself a notebook for my birthday to celebrate the new life I was going to have once I got out of foster care. It seemed like a . . . I don't know, a symbol of some kind. Silly, I know."

"It's not silly."

She softened at the fierce words. "Thank you." She exhaled. "Anyway. I started writing a new story in it that day, and when I went to bed, I . . . I dreamed about the story. Exactly as I had written it that day. Everything was so vivid and detailed. It felt . . . real. And I saw all of it through the eyes of my main character."

It had been her first romantic suspense attempt. It had also been her last.

"I thought it was a fluke. It was *too* real to be a dream. And I wasn't seeing it through the eyes of the main character—

I *was* the main character. I had her hair, her clothes. My nose was pierced like hers was." She shook her head. "I mean, it was me, but the outer layers . . . That was all her. But—fluke. So I kept writing. The next night, I dreamt about what I had written that day." She took a breath, remembering the confusion. The denial. Eventually, the panic. "It went on for about a week. I stopped writing. And the dreams stopped."

Jacob didn't speak for a long time. "Are you saying you wrote those dreams?"

"I'm saying I dreamt what I wrote." Realizing he needed more, she continued. "I *dream* what I write. Sometimes, it's a man trying to approach me in a dingy bar when I'm wearing leather. Sometimes the man is naked, being held at gunpoint, and I pretend I'm in a relationship with him." She paused. "It's not me, not really. It's the characters I create in the scenes I wrote that day."

Jacob's lips parted, but he didn't say anything. She let him have the time. Her hand lifted to her chest, over where her heart was thudding against her skin. It went hard and fast, as if it were trying to escape. She rubbed lightly, trying to provide the thumping organ some comfort. All the while, three words repeated in her head.

Please don't leave. Please don't leave.

"Gaia," he said eventually. "Are you telling me you have . . . you have magic?"

"Yes."

"What else can you do?"

"What do you mean?"

"Can you make rabbits appear out of a hat?"

"Oh." He was making fun of her. "No. Only this."

He closed his eyes. "I'm sorry. I'm sorry. I didn't mean to make that sound . . . Just . . . magic? Like rabbits-out-of-a-hat magic?"

His question was sincere. *Had* he been making fun of her then? She took another look at him. No. He hadn't been.

"This is my only ability."

"Okay." He took a deep breath. Took a couple more before he spoke. "This has been happening to you your entire life? Since you were eighteen, I mean?"

She nodded.

"How?"

"I'm not entirely sure."

"Is it everything you write?"

"Only fiction."

"And do you— Are you— Is it always the same?"

"What do you mean?"

"Are you always . . . *in* them?"

"Every novel I've written, I've been in, yes."

It was another long while before he asked, "And me? What does this have to do with me?"

"To be completely honest, I don't know."

"You don't know a lot of things about this ability."

She didn't wince, though she wanted to. This reaction was normal. The doubt, the disbelief. When she'd allowed herself to make the link between her writing and her dreams, it had taken her months to accept it. Had she expected Jacob to have a better reaction than she had?

Yes.

She tried to shake out the tightness from her shoulders. It didn't work. "You're right. One day I didn't have them, and one day I did."

"Did you . . . did you ask for them?"

She frowned. "What? No. From who?"

"I don't know."

But she saw the flicker in his eyes. Her swirling emotions suddenly stilled, laid down, and created a path for her ungracious response.

"Ah, you've seen through to what I really am: a witch." His eyebrows rose, but she was too into it to care. "On the night of my eighteenth birthday, I offered myself, a virgin witch, to the god of writing, under the full moon. I told her to use me as her muse as I danced naked to the rhythm of my chants under the night sky. And here I am. A vessel for her powers."

His jaw had dropped. "I—"

"Please don't say whatever you were going to say. I am *not* a witch, you dork. None of that happened. I just went to sleep on my birthday and dreamed. I don't know why. I don't know how. Maybe if I had—" She broke off when even the thought had a truck ramming into her heart. "I don't have anyone to ask," she said instead. And left it at that.

But Jacob saw through her in that unnerving way he had. His hand covered hers. As if his touch would cast away the rest of her sentence.

Maybe if I had parents, I could ask them. Is it inherited? Or am I a fluke? Or am I . . . am I delusional?

A part of her was wondering if his doubt, his disbelief meant that she *was* deluding herself. Maybe it wasn't magical abilities, but some kind of psychiatric breakdown. It wasn't the first time she'd considered it.

But she couldn't be delusional. Not if Jacob, the steadiest person she knew, was experiencing it, too.

The relief of it, of that question she'd had for the last twelve years of her life, stole her breath.

"This is my reality," she said when she could breathe again. "It's a part of my life. Now, it's a part of yours."

"Is it?" he asked. "Or is it happening to me because of you?" He took his hand away. It was as if he'd slapped her. "I'm sorry," Jacob said curtly. "I . . . I shouldn't have said that. This is . . . it wasn't what I was expecting."

"What were you expecting?" she asked, keeping the emotion from her voice. "A logical explanation for why we've been sharing dreams? A neatly wrapped rationale for why that man punched you in the face because you wanted to speak to me?"

"I don't know," he said, his body deflating. "I certainly wasn't expecting magic."

"Neither was I."

He didn't reply. Stared out the window instead of looking at her. She knew he wanted to leave. Could tell by the way his foot was tapping, by the restlessness of his hands. But he wasn't leaving because she'd asked him not to. Even when she had told him it was selfish of her to ask. Even after she'd taken it back. He was staying because of her.

It should have meant something, but knowing that he didn't want to, that he felt forced . . . It somehow made it worse. She was used to people leaving. She could handle that. She didn't think she could handle people staying when they wanted to leave.

She grabbed her handbag and took out some cash.

"Drinks are on me."

His head whipped to her. "What? No. No, don't go."

"You need space."

"I don't . . . It's not . . . I have more questions."

"Write them down. Email them to me. Call me and ask. Come . . . come see me once you've worked through this."

"How do you 'work through' magic?"

"You just . . . do," she said. "It's not going away."

His expression tightened. "It can. If you don't write."

She gathered all her emotions inside her, good and bad, and set a cover over them. She would deal with them later. Right now, she had to get through this.

"You're asking me not to write?"

He gave a tight nod.

She angled her head. "You said Seth called you a workaholic."

"What does that have to do with this?"

"You work a lot," she said as if he hadn't interrupted, "but you don't enjoy what you do." She ignored his surprise. "If you did, you would understand what happens when you enjoy what you do. You *want* to do it. With me, there's more—I *have* to do it. If I don't write, my brain . . . It doesn't like me not writing." It was the simplest explanation for the compulsion she felt when she wasn't writing. "And if I don't write, I'm thinking about writing. Even in this past week, when I couldn't get out of bed, I was thinking about writing. When you feel that way about something, Jake, you don't not do it."

He had gone unnaturally still. There was none of the earlier fidgeting. No leg tapping, no twitching muscles in his face. He was watching her, but his gaze had gone dead.

It was so out of place in the bustling café. They had chosen to sit in a corner, away from most of the busyness, but the energy touched them nevertheless. Jacob sat with his back to the open room, its counter a few meters away, the brick walls that enclosed the space stopping opposite to where they sat to allow for the glass wall. It was a bright summer's day, completely wrong for their current mood, and light shone on them. It should have been hot, but the café had air-conditioning right above them, sending a blast so strong that the plants in the corner behind them rustled.

And still, despite the people walking and talking behind him; despite the music playing softly through hidden speakers; despite the waiters weaving between tables, Jacob was still.

She pursed her lips. "I can give you a few days."

He leaned forward, rested his forearms on the table, and dropped his head. The posture was so defeated that she wanted to reach out to him, but she was afraid touching him would sear her hands and she'd never be able to eradicate the memory.

"I . . . I don't know how to deal with this."

She didn't either. But she knew they had to accept it. It wouldn't change. Unless . . .

She slammed her hands on the table.

He looked up, alarmed. "What? What is it?"

"Let's try to reverse it." There was more confidence in that statement than she felt.

His alarm turned to bewilderment. "How?"

"The night at the party. It started that night, right? And what did we do? We kissed," she answered for him. "So that's it. We have to kiss and all of this will stop happening."

He sat back and rubbed a hand over his jaw. "I don't think—"

"Do you have a better idea?" she demanded.

He sighed. "No."

"So we'll pay the bill and then go outside and kiss, damn it."

To say the logic of Gaia's plan was flawed was an understatement. But he didn't have a better idea. He didn't know how magic—*magic?*—worked. Plus, what she'd said about his work had struck a chord. Sure, he'd already written the music with his recent thoughts, but someone he had only known for a week pointing it out?

Maybe *this* was a dream.

Could be, he thought as he paid the bill. The details here were as vivid as they were in the dreams Gaia claimed they shared. And there she was, waiting for him outside. Sitting on a bench under the trees as if she had nothing to do but wait for men to kiss her.

The branches were high above her, casting her face in a shadow and making the suffocating heat seem more manageable. The bench she sat on was on the pavement, but behind her, the ground was covered in green. Plants of various kinds spread between the trunks of the trees, giving him only a glimpse of brown soil.

All of it looked magnificent, though he would expect no less from the small town of Stellenbosch. Technically, it still formed part of Cape Town, though it felt like a different place. Perhaps what Cape Town would have been like if urbanization hadn't necessitated that nature be replaced by buildings.

He didn't spend much time here, since he lived closer to the city center, although he had been here more often since he and Gaia had . . . reconnected. The beauty of the place could easily be something Gaia had created. No—it would be something *he* created if this was a dream. *His* dream. Not anyone else's.

Yes, this was *his* dream, damn it. It was about time he acted like it.

Gaia's eyebrows rose when he stopped in front of her. "Did you *saunter* over here?"

His mouth curved. "Did it look like it?"

Her brows lifted higher. He full-out grinned.

"I take it you're feeling better about things," she commented, setting her bag down on the bench beside her before she stood.

"Indeed I am."

"Indeed?" Her eyes narrowed. "Are you okay, Jake?"

"I'm fine. Never been better."

She frowned and bit the inside of her lip. "I know this hasn't been an easy day. I'm sorry."

"Don't apologize. Kiss me."

Her lips parted. His gaze automatically dipped to them. A prickling feeling spread in his body. A tightening that came with anticipation. The kick of his heart that told him he was going to kiss her.

It didn't matter if he was dreaming this. He was going to kiss her. That's all that mattered.

"You want to do this right here, right now?"

"I mean, not all of it," he said, smiling. "Unless you want to, in which case, I'd be into it."

She tilted her head. "You know that isn't what I meant."

He moved toward her, snaking an arm around her waist. "You're no fun."

Her breath caught, and though she still looked at him suspiciously, he didn't miss how her eyes darkened.

"I'm a lot of fun," she contradicted, voice soft, caressing his skin as she brought her hands to his chest.

"Yeah?" He brought their bodies closer together. Again, he heard that little snag of breath from her. "Prove it."

Her hands moved from his chest to the back of his neck. Then, she slid them up, into his hair, putting a light amount of pressure on his head. Obeying, he lowered. Before their lips touched, she whispered, "I hope for both our sakes this works."

She kissed him.

CHAPTER 14

Gaia heard herself moan when their lips touched. It was a soft, light moan. Approved by her brain as appropriate for the public, before coherent thought became a challenge. But she couldn't help it. His lips were so soft. And it had something turning low in her belly. A ballerina of desire, pirouetting around and around, faster and faster, until there was only the turning, the spinning, the want.

She felt the moment the dancer collapsed. Jacob had slid his tongue into her mouth. There was no more dancing, only a spreading heat. Lava, flowing down between her legs. It would destroy her. Turn her into ash.

Ah, well. She'd had a good run. And this kiss was a worthy way to die.

Giving up the desire for self-preservation allowed her to sink into the kiss. To let him seduce her lips, her mouth. To let his hands squeeze her flesh.

She deepened the kiss, sweeping her tongue into his mouth, asking him to open for her without saying the words. He did, and for a moment, it felt like they were one. She curled her arms around his neck, pressing into him. Willing him to break the rules of public decency and slip a hand between her thighs. Or pull down her top as he'd done the night of the party. To take her nipple into his mouth. Let her feel the roll of pleasure even as it built to something more intense. Something she'd once been afraid of.

But fear had no hold over her if she didn't care about surviving.

Someone coughed. Then cleared their throat really loudly.

Gaia pulled back, her gaze not leaving Jacob's. She saw many, many things in that moment. Pleasure, satisfaction. A light bouncing in the deep brown of his eyes, so vehemently and completely, her lips twitched with a smile. But it was the emotion there that gave her pause. Or the emotion that *wasn't* there. The doubt. The turmoil. The things she'd seen on his face before they'd left the café.

Denial, she realized. He was in denial.

The stranger cleared their throat again.

"Yeah, we get it," Jacob said, throwing the words over his shoulder.

Gaia pulled away from him completely, feeling the blush in a wave from her head down to her toes. "Sorry," she muttered to whoever had thought they needed to interrupt the kiss. She grabbed her handbag, walked a few meters down, and pulled up a car app.

"Gaia," Jacob said, taking the phone from her before she could confirm. "What are you doing?"

"I'm going home."

A perplexed look settled onto his face. "Why?"

"What do you mean, *why?*" She stood on her toes to try and reach the phone Jacob held above her. "Really?" she asked when he lifted it higher. "This is childish."

"I'm trying to figure out why you would be going home after that kiss. Unless we're both going to your place?"

He gave her a self-assured grin that was so far from the man who had taken her to the bookstore the night before, the man who'd taken her to the beach after, that her heart twisted.

"No, we're not." Even she could hear the defeat in her voice. "Can I get my phone, please?"

"Gaia." The teasing tone of his voice was gone. "This isn't the version of you I want in my dreams."

"In your . . ." She trailed off. "Wait—do you think this is a dream, Jake?"

"It isn't?"

He spoke slowly, watching her as she watched him. As she saw the emotions she'd missed after their kiss return to his face.

It hit her harder than expected. Took her a few seconds to figure out why.

In the last two days, Jacob had made her believe that the real world could be safe. It hadn't even been a consideration before, not with her past. Yet somehow, she hadn't thought feeling safe with Jacob would come back to bite her in the ass.

Now, she felt stupid for not anticipating it. Stupid and raw and vulnerable.

Those feelings weren't fair to him. She'd had twelve years to get used to what she was able to do; Jacob barely had more than an hour. But she couldn't help how she was feeling. In the same way Jacob couldn't help how he was feeling, she knew.

It was for the best if they gave one another space.

"No, it isn't a dream," she said, then asked for her phone again.

He handed it to her, looking numb. "None of it . . . It doesn't make *sense*. Magic can't be real. You're . . . you're lying. You *must* be lying."

His obvious desperation didn't take away the accusation's sting.

"You don't have to believe me," she answered stiffly. "But I'm not lying."

"I *can't* believe you, Gaia." He stood in front of her. "Do you realize what you're asking me to believe? In magic. *Magic doesn't exist.* It just . . . doesn't."

A car slowly drove up the road. One look on her phone told Gaia it was hers. Based solely on the timing, she was going to give the driver a good rating.

"It exists," she told him, holding out her hand so the driver knew it was her. "I'll prove it to you."

"How?" he asked.

She didn't bother answering. He'd find out soon enough.

Jacob replayed the last time he'd seen Gaia many, many times over in the following days.

I'll prove it to you.

And though she hadn't answered him then, the answer became pretty clear the Monday after their date. When, for three consecutive nights, he dreamed something new.

Something torturous.

He was fairly certain she was doing it for her amusement, too.

The first night, he was locked in a tower. An actual tower. Like Rapunzel. Which, he discovered after answering a call from his window, was exactly who he was meant to be.

"Rake, oh, Rake, let down your hair. It's long and it's strong and it's oh so fair."

Oh, shit. Long blond hair was growing out of his head as the woman he was yet to see called up to him.

"Let it down for a moment, as it is so meant, that I may kiss you, oh, Rake, and prove you are my mate."

The hair was filling up the room he was in, had done so pretty damn quickly, and unless he wanted to be suffocated by his own hair, he had no choice but to throw it out the window. And feel her climbing up on it.

It *hurt.* Who the hell thought it was a good idea to let someone climb up something that was *attached* to a *body*?

But he wouldn't give her the satisfaction of hearing him complain. So he endured until the woman climbed into the room. It was Gaia, of course, which a part—a large part—of him had suspected. In this dream, she was dressed for battle. All in black, in clothing that was tight-fitting; not for aesthetics, but for flexibility. For movement. Her hair was in an intricate arrangement of plaits. Again, not for aesthetics, but to keep the strands out of her way.

All in all, it was a package that would have struck fear in him had he not been so damn annoyed.

"What a pleasure it is to see you, Rake."

She dipped into a bow of sorts, somehow managing to make it mocking and reverent at the same time.

"Is this the game you're playing now?"

"Excuse me?" she asked innocently. "I have no idea what you mean. I am merely here to free you from the tower you have been locked in." She paused, twitching her nose as if she couldn't help it. "If the tower is meant to represent your rigid thinking—the same kind that has you believing I would lie to you—then so be it."

"I take it you're the knight in shining armor then?" He kept his voice bland, though anger and confusion tried to convince him to give a more passionate response. "Freeing me from my tower."

"No," she denied. "The heroines of those stories never really needed knights in shining armor. They needed allies. People who believed them and tried to help them. Not save them."

"So you're doing this to make some kind of social justice point?"

"To who?" She dipped her head. "You?" Then she was shaking it. "No. I'm only *proving* that this is real." She stepped closer, bringing her lips a breath away from his. "This is what you wanted, isn't it? Proof?"

She kissed him lightly and he woke up.

Annoyed and aroused. Unable to go back to sleep.

* * *

The following night he found himself in a club. A *strip* club. Based on his outfit—black, spandex underpants, cowboy chaps, boots and hat; nothing else—and the pole a few meters away from him.

"You look good," Gaia said from where she sat in the middle of the stage. She was tied to the chair, as though she were a sacrifice of some kind, and the room around them cheered at what he assumed was her sass.

It took him all of a minute to figure out it was happening again.

"I get your point," he said, startled when the sound amplified over the room. For the first time he noticed the mike curved in front of his face.

"Actually, I think I'm supposed to get yours," she replied, challenge in her eyes.

Damn if he didn't find it sexy.

Damn if he didn't find her annoying.

He ripped off the microphone pouch he discovered at his left hip, pulled off the headset and threw it to the side. It landed with a thud and a shrill sound, causing the crowd to boo, then cheer when they thought it was part of the show.

He leaned forward, bracing against the arms of the chair.

"I get the point," he said again.

"It's only been two days." She tilted her head in a way he was beginning to recognize as defiance. "Are you sure you don't need more?"

He narrowed his eyes, then took in the ropes around her.

"You talk a big game for someone who's tied up." He played with the ropes at her arms. "Not entirely smart for you to give me the power here."

Something akin to appreciation lit in her eyes, but her smirk showed none of that. No, that smirk was something he'd never seen on Gaia—had never thought he would see on Gaia—and, to be frank, it scared him a little.

"It's cute that you think you have the power here." Her eyes flashed. "Now—strip before your manager fires you."

She nodded her head toward a big, bulky man behind the curtains at the side of the stage. He looked an awful lot like that man who'd punched him during the first dream. He was wearing a suit now, and his hair was longer, but that menacing expression . . . Yeah, it was him.

Still, he wasn't stripping.

"I'm not stripping."

"Dream doesn't end until you do."

He blinked. "Seriously?"

She smiled, though honestly he thought it more a baring of her teeth. "Seriously."

Definitely scary.

"You control that?"

"Dream plays until the end of what I write that day, yes."

He thought about it. "The day I was naked in your kitchen?"

She sighed. "It was supposed to end in an embrace. Which I was planning on clarifying the next day, considering I already suspected you were . . . you."

"The night at the bar?"

"A kiss."

"And you wrote all that? Everything I said?"

She shoved her shoulders back. A feat, since she was still tied up. "No. Some of it seems to be coming from you."

"What do you mean?"

"I write the scene, dream it, and play the heroine. The ability is really only useful for writing books—"

"—and torturing me—"

"—and usually, I use it to figure out whether the scene I wrote needs work," she continued, ignoring him. "I follow the script until something doesn't work. If it doesn't, I pivot, and my characters respond."

"How?"

"I'm not sure." She shrugged. "I stopped asking those kinds of questions a long time ago."

"So they just . . . respond? If you change something, they change, too?"

"Within the personalities I've given them. It's like improv. You're still playing a specific character, but you're responding to what the other person says. Except they only respond to me." She lifted her head. "And now you."

"What does that even *mean*—"

Three things happened then. One, someone shouted *Strip!* loudly and alarmingly aggressively. Two, his supposed manager turned, his movement too big for Jacob not to notice, and pulled a rope. Three—he was suddenly completely drenched with water.

His only consolation was that Gaia was wet, too.

She grinned up at him. "Worth it."

He was still spluttering, his body adjusting to the realization that the water had been ice-cold.

"You *planned* this?"

He woke up with the image of her smiling still in his mind.

Night three was perhaps the worst of all.

This time, he was tied up. To a bed, with no audience, which made things marginally better. The room itself was large. A gray-brown wood ran in lines across the floor, the walls painted white, two small armchairs opposite the door.

Gaia was currently sitting in one of those chairs, wearing a long brown coat that swept from her collarbone down to her ankles. Her hair was loose, spiraling around her head in a hairstyle that made her look the most like herself. Daylight streamed through the glass wall on her right, his left. If he could inspect it, he was sure he'd find a built-in door of some kind.

"I really do get your point," he said softly.

Her gaze was steady. "You believe me now?"

"Yes. Though I could have done without the trapping-me metaphors."

"Where's the fun in that?" She leaned forward. "Besides, you weren't trapped yesterday."

"Not physically, no. But that stage was a trap. The manager behind the curtains was a trap. The water was a trap."

Her mouth curved. "You're sharp. Smart."

"And logical," he added. "It's why I found it hard to believe in your . . . abilities."

"I get it. Honestly, I do."

She stood, the coat falling over her like a nightgown. It was strange seeing buttons down the middle of the fabric. It was like she wanted him to see one thing, but believe another.

He looked up, searching for any signs of water. Just in case.

"And I'm sorry."

He brought his attention back to her. "For what?"

"For this."

"Tying me up?"

"No." She smiled. "I don't feel bad about that." The smile faded. "No, I'm sorry for drawing you into this. If you've never had magic before"—she paused, giving him an opportunity to refute it. He shook his head—"then this is because of my magic." After a beat, she continued. "I'm sorry the kiss didn't work, and you're still here. I'm sorry for not giving you the chance to properly process."

His fingers itched to touch her, but she was too far away. Not that it mattered. He wouldn't be able to reach out to her even if she hadn't tied him up.

"I should be apologizing, too. I reacted poorly."

She simply stared at him, waiting for him to continue.

He sighed. "I can't tell you that I regret it. That's . . . It's how I worked through it."

"Have you?"

"I . . . have."

She studied him. "You're lying."

"No, I'm not." He closed his eyes. "There's a part of me that understands. That believes. But the other part . . . It's resentful. Of you, of this. Of the fact that I can't focus at work because I'm thinking about you and this. If I can't focus, I can't push the company forward."

She sat down at the edge of the bed. "And that's it? That's what you need?"

"It doesn't matter what I need. It's what the business needs. And that isn't a managing director who's distracted by a woman or by dating or by dreams and magic."

His chest was heaving by the end of it. He waited for it to settle, then braced for the questions. They didn't come. Instead, Gaia stood, walked to the side table on his left, and picked up a book before she returned to the armchair. Her back was toward him so he had no warning she was removing her coat until she turned.

She slid the material off her shoulders, revealing a lace out-fit that was surely, *surely* illegal. It was as though a spider had woven a nest over her body. The intricate design started at her breasts, clinging to the two, full curves, skimming the narrower line of her waist, before settling on her hips. From there, the pattern grew more chaotic, spindling over parts of her body he'd only seen that night at the beach, where he hadn't allowed himself to look, to see. It ended mid-thigh, allowing him to see the thickness of her legs; the light strength and the deepest seduction.

"Shit."

She sat down, crossing those glorious thighs, and opened the book. Without acknowledging that he spoke. Without even looking at him.

He tried to say her name, but the word wouldn't leave his mouth. His memory told him it was the same thing that had happened with his name in earlier dreams. There must have been some rule about names in this world of hers. There were other rules, too, he was sure, and he would ponder them later, when he was awake. For now, he hated that he didn't have anything to call her. Not the name he desperately wanted to use, nor the name of whoever she was here.

"What the hell are you doing?" he asked, or rasped, his voice hoarse.

"Reading."

As if emphasizing the point, she turned a page.

"You can't seriously be reading in that . . . In *that*," he ended up saying, because he genuinely couldn't figure out how to describe what she was wearing.

"A true reader can read in anything, and anywhere." Her head shifted, telling him she was now reading the next page. "May I remind you of the party we were at?"

"Believe me, I'm unlikely to forget it. Even if I tried."

Her eyes flickered up at that, before she lowered them to her book again.

"I have about twenty more pages before this ends."

"Seriously? Twenty? What am I supposed to do until then?"

She snorted. Lightly. In a polite manner that didn't fool him. "We both know I've provided you with ample entertainment by wearing this outfit."

And because he could hardly argue, he didn't. Instead, he entertained himself and watched her.

CHAPTER 15

For the rest of the week, Jacob didn't dream. It didn't take him long to realize she was giving him the time she promised. She had given him the day of their date—she must have erased what she'd written or something, for them not to have had a dream that night—and now.

He didn't dwell too much on the reprieve. Instead, he focused on work. His attention had been slipping and he couldn't afford that. They had to meet with their new big client, the one they'd had issues with on signing, about how they intended on balancing the ideas they'd pitched, with the client's notes. The team working on the project seemed relieved when he called them for a check-in, concerns and creativity spilling out in equal measure.

He addressed the concerns, directed the creativity. By the end of it, the overall morale of the team had improved dramatically. And he was exhausted. Had he always felt that way after a meeting? Did he just not allow himself to feel it? Or had things changed that radically in the last two weeks?

Maybe a little of all of it.

He could remember times he had enjoyed the challenge of the work. But that enjoyment had never mattered. He wasn't there to enjoy it; he was there to fix. That had overshadowed everything else.

Now he wondered if he'd fooled himself into thinking that he'd enjoyed it, even then.

"Er, Jake?"

He looked up to see Charity, the team leader, lingering in the doorway. "What can I do for you?"

"I, um . . ." She closed the door and sat down across from him, hesitation the only sign of nerves. "I noticed that you haven't been . . . yourself lately. Are you okay?"

He studied her face. Recognized her concern. Could forgive the intrusion on his life because the concern was genuine.

Charity was one of the few employees who had stayed after the decline under his father. She'd stuck around when clients began to leave because of a lack of leadership. When employees began to leave, too, one after the other, until there were only thirty left.

Jacob had had thirty employees when he'd taken over. Half of them were so grateful someone was committing to the company again that they didn't question his age or his authority. The other half were resentful. Of his father, for putting them in the position where their jobs were at stake. Most of them hated their work already, but they couldn't leave because they had bills to pay or had no options for other work with their qualifications.

He made sure they were compensated through bonuses when the scales tipped back into black. Then, he nudged them out. Found jobs for them or offered retirement packages to those who applied.

He couldn't move a company forward with people who resented him or the work. Scott Brand Solutions was a family business, small in the grand scheme of things. They needed people who wanted to be there, who enjoyed the work, and not people who felt they had to be there.

Like you?

He ignored the thought. Focused on Charity instead. She was one of the good ones. She had stayed, offered her knowledge—an asset, he could readily admit. He could live with her asking if he was okay.

"Yeah, I'm fine. I haven't been sleeping all that well lately."

"Oh, well, if it's only that."

His eyebrows rose. "Are you being sarcastic?"

"Not at all," Charity said in the same biting tone, "why would you not sleeping concern me?"

He stuck his tongue into his cheek to keep from smiling. Charity was loyal, and one of his steadiest workers. She didn't do sarcasm. Witnessing it amused him, until he realized how much she must be worrying if she was resorting to sarcasm.

"I know I've been distracted," he told her solemnly. "It has nothing to do with the company, I swear."

"Your dad's distraction had nothing to do with the company either," she noted. "I'm sorry for saying it, truly, I am, but . . ."

She trailed off. And frankly, he understood. The line she was crossing came from fear. She'd already been through one Scott breakdown, after all.

"I'm fine, Charity." It came out sharper than he intended. He swallowed and tried again. "I promise you, I'm fine. I haven't been sleeping because I've been worried about a . . . a friend. And even when I'm distracted, it doesn't mean we're going back to what happened with my father."

"Okay," she said after a moment. "I know you being distracted isn't . . ." She sighed. "I'm sorry. It's been eight years, Jacob. Eight years, and never, not once, have you acted the way you have been recently. It's probably unfair of me to expect you to be the same all the time, but—" She broke off with a shrug. "I'm sorry if any of this was inappropriate."

"I appreciate your concern," he said in lieu of answering. "But again—everything's fine."

She gave him a tentative smile before leaving, which he returned. But the moment she was no longer in sight, the smile dropped and a weight settled on him.

Did enjoying his work even matter? The company—and everyone in it—relied on him. It was also the only thing he had in common with his father these days. They had never been close, but after his mother died, his father had completely closed up. The only time Keenan engaged was when it came to Scott Brand Solutions. Jacob suspected Keenan only tolerated the rare forced family get-together because he felt he owed Jacob for saving the company. What would happen if Jacob no longer worked there?

His mother had asked him to make sure the family stayed together. It wasn't pretty, but he was doing his part. Even the semblance of family they had now was better than nothing. Would he be risking that if he tried to find something he *did* enjoy?

He shook his head. This was what he got for allowing himself to be distracted. Gaia was making him indulgent. He had responsibilities. The company, the people working in it, his father, Seth . . . They relied on him. He couldn't be distracted.

Not by magic—he was still processing that—not by dreams, and certainly not by the woman who made him believe both were possible.

Now, he only had to convince himself he was happy to live his life that way.

"Gaia? Gaia Anders?"

Gaia looked up at the name, recognizing it as her own, but not registering the person who said it. She was still thinking about the fake relationship theme in her book. Did she have to continue it now that Terrence was no longer a threat? Maybe . . . But what if she put her characters in a forced proximity situation instead? Or not instead—*also*. They would have to fake when the need arose, increasing the tension that already existed between them. Tension that was already growing because they were forced to work together in some capacity . . .

She had taken to plotting over the last few days to give Jacob space. She wasn't particularly a plotter. But she could be one, if she wanted to.

Now she was mainly trying to prove herself right.

"Gaia?"

She blinked a couple of times. Oh, she was in a coffee shop. She had forced herself to work at a coffee shop. One, because her house felt a little claustrophobic after she'd spent that week in bed. Two, because she was trying to prove to herself that she *could* leave the house. Her heart had protested loudly at the thought, an annoying vibration in her chest, but she was out in the world.

See! Proof! she told her brain. *I'm not scared of leaving the house!*

"You probably don't remember me."

Finally, Gaia focused. There was a woman in front of her. The one from the bookstore. The one who had pretended to read her books.

There was a nervous smile playing around her lips. Gaia got the impression it wasn't normal for her.

"I remember you." She shut her notebook and set both hands on it. "Are you stalking me?"

The woman made a face. "What? No."

A man, seated at the table directly behind them, snickered. Gaia's eyes shifted to him, but she decided she could do without noticing a man who looked that good with a beard. Or rather a man who looked that good with a beard who was also an eavesdropper.

"I'm Gemma, by the way. I don't think I introduced myself last week."

The way she spoke made Gaia think of how in children's cartoons, they had a dot bouncing over words to get the kids to sing along. It was lyrical in a . . . bouncy kind of way.

"And okay, yes, I am stalking you." Gemma sat down opposite her. "I swear it's not for creepy reasons. Or maybe it is? I'm not sure."

Again, that snicker.

Gaia narrowed her eyes. "Do you know him?"

"Who?" Gemma asked brightly.

"The man behind you. The one who keeps making noises through his nose."

Gaia might have heard a curse come from his direction, aimed at her, but she couldn't be sure.

"Oh. Well."

Gemma didn't say anything else.

Her fingers tapped against the table, tips only, an annoying *ba-ba-ba-ba-ba* sound. She wore a ring on each of her fingers, so Gaia supposed she was being saved from a louder sound had Gemma been tapping her hand. Some of her rings were plain bands, some carved in an intricate design. Only one had a stone in it. Topaz. She recognized it because it was her birthstone. And the pendant her mother had left her had that birthstone in it. Something about Gemma's ring reminded her eerily of that necklace.

"Who are you?" she asked.

"I'm your . . . I'm your biggest fan," Gemma said in that bright way she had.

It was vaguely annoying, and yet somehow endearing at the same time.

The snicker now turned into a full-on snort. Both she and Gemma ignored it.

"And you've been stalking me?" Gaia asked, a fluttering in her chest. "I don't know how I should feel about you doing it, or admitting it."

"I'm not dangerous," Gemma assured her, as if that was the only troubling part of her admission. "I promise. I just . . . I really love your, um . . . your books, and I wanted to meet you. Properly. And I know you work in here sometimes. Not a lot, because I've been in here—" She broke off with a smile. "Well, you're here now."

This was . . . weird. It made her feel more exposed than working outside her home usually did. It could have been from the turmoil of the last few weeks. It could have been because she still wasn't feeling completely clear of the darkness that wanted to bring her down. She could feel the temptation of it slithering around her, waiting to strike. But she wouldn't let it. Not this time. Not when she'd worked so hard to get it together again. To get *herself* together again.

"Do you want to talk some more about your favorite book of mine?" Gaia asked blandly as she worked out an exit strategy if things turned from weird to dangerous. "I would love to know your thoughts on the themes or character development."

The brightness dimmed for a moment. "Hmm." Gemma sniffed. "It was unfortunate that we met on the night I got your books before I could read them."

"You were giving my books away."

"The second set of books, yes." She shifted from tapping her fingers to twisting her rings. Left hand to right hand, right hand to left. "I bought two sets. One for me and one to um . . . donate."

Gaia tilted her head. "Why?"

"Don't sales matter to your career?"

"They do," she said slowly. "But it's unusual for someone to buy all of an author's books when they haven't read one yet. It's even more unusual for that person to buy two sets of those books, and donate one set."

"Oh," Gemma replied, as if the unusualness hadn't occurred to her. "Well, I wanted to support you."

"You don't even know me."

The other woman was silent for a moment. A short moment. Gaia thought that might be a part of her character.

"Maybe I feel as if we have a bond of some sort."

Gaia blew out her breath. "So you're going to keep leaning into the weirdness then."

She closed her notebook, took out her purse to check if she

had enough cash to pay the bill. She didn't. She'd have to pay by card. She gestured to the server.

"You seem like a very nice woman," Gaia said, "but we don't have a bond. We're not connected in *any* way. I would really appreciate it if you stopped, um, stalking me, and maybe—"

"We might be." The words were uncharacteristically quiet. Gaia had known Gemma for all of ten minutes but that gave her pause. "Connected, or—"

"Right-o," a man said, touching Gemma in a too familiar way. It wasn't only *a* man—it was *the* man. The one who kept making noises. "We're done here. Very nice to meet you." To Gemma, he said, "We need to leave. Now."

"Hey!" Gaia said, a little too loudly since she heard it over her heart racing. "You can't touch her like that. What the hell?"

They drew the eyes of the nearby table, which made Gaia's heart pump even faster. She tried to ignore the attention. The man did not, however, and let go of Gemma's arm.

"We're in a relationship," he said.

Gaia narrowed her eyes at him. "Are you sure? Because she didn't even admit to knowing you earlier."

For a moment, Gaia could have sworn he shimmered. *Shimmered.* As if he were some ethereal being and air had flown right through him.

But a blink later he was there in front of her, solid as any entitled man, expression just as bland. He looked down at Gemma; Gemma looked up at him. They seemed to be communicating, the man's face shifting almost imperceptibly from bland to concerned. When he touched her shoulder this time, it was vaguely reassuring. As if he were trying to reassure her, but didn't want her—or himself—to know it.

Then he dropped his hand, bland expression back, and Gemma turned to face her.

She offered Gaia a timid smile. "Yes, he is my . . . partner. Levi." She swallowed on the last word.

Gaia studied both of them. "You two have a really weird dynamic."

"I know," Gemma said at the same time Levi said, "Yes."

Her eyebrows rose. "Maybe you are in a relationship then. Who am I to judge?" But for her conscience's sake, she looked at Gemma. She quickly realized what she had to say wouldn't work if the man was still standing there.

She looked at him. "Do you mind giving me a second here? I would like to talk to my biggest fan." The woman who claimed to be stalking her.

If Gaia were murdered, it would be her own fault.

"We have to leave," he replied, giving Gemma a hard look.

"And you will," Gaia said with a polite smile. "In a short while."

The server brought her the bill as she said it, and Gemma's boyfriend sighed and walked out.

Gaia looked at her. "If you're in an abusive relationship, I'll try to help you."

Offering help to a stalker. Something to check off her bucket list before she died.

"Oh! Oh, no. No, no, no, he's not . . . He's just really intense. He's fine." Gemma waved a hand.

"He's managing the time you're allowed to talk to people," Gaia said as gently as she could.

"He's trying to keep me from making a fool of myself. Which I have been doing." Gemma offered her a half smile. "So he has a point."

"It's okay to make a fool of yourself. It's part of life."

Gemma blinked. "That sounds terribly wise."

Gaia's lips twitched. "Is it terrible? Can't it only be wise?"

"Of course, of course." The smile Gemma gave her now was brighter. "I'm sorry that this was so awkward. I wanted to meet you, and sometimes I can trip over myself in excitement. Then, you know, fall flat on my face."

"I wouldn't call what happened falling flat on your face. With the whole *we're connected* thing, I'd say you tripped at the top of a hill and kind of rolled your way down."

Gemma laughed. It was light and musical and exactly what Gaia expected. "That's a lot worse! I'm sorry."

Gaia studied her. "I'm guessing the tripping thing happens to you a lot."

Gemma angled her head in a familiar gesture. "Well, I suppose—" She broke off, rolling her eyes. "Probably, yes."

Gaia allowed herself a small smile. "Maybe don't apologize for who you are then. Unless, you know, you're confessing to criminal activities, in which case, an apology might help."

Gemma blinked a couple of times and smiled the brightest smile Gaia had seen her give. Instinctively, she reached for her sunglasses, but her brain told her she was being dramatic and that somehow, the smile had endeared Gemma to her more. She could hardly judge Gemma's quirkiness when she had her own quirks, could she?

"I should go," Gemma said softly, eyes on the door. Gaia didn't have to look to see who'd caught her attention. "I hope we'll meet again. But . . . um . . . I won't be stalking you. I promise. I promise," she said a little more firmly, and stood.

"Thank you. I think."

Gemma laughed. "You're welcome."

She stood there for a little longer, staring at Gaia, eyes sweeping across Gaia's face as if she wanted to commit it to memory or something equally alarming. In the end, she dipped her head in greeting and left.

Later, when Gaia opened her bill, she found that it had already been paid.

It didn't take a genius to figure out who'd paid it.

CHAPTER 16

"Let's sleep together," Jacob said as soon as Gaia opened her front door.

The only indication of her surprise—at his appearance after a week of silence when he'd battled to stay away from her—was her eyebrows. They lifted a fraction.

"Aren't you supposed to take me out to dinner first?" Lazily, Gaia leaned against the door frame. "Woo me? Tell me you've missed me this past week, and ever since you've met me, you haven't been able to get me out your mind?"

She was disturbingly accurate on that last part, but he would never admit it.

"I meant actual sleeping."

"Does that make it better?" Her voice was still casual. "What you're suggesting is still a form of intimacy. I don't hand out sleep vouchers to every man I meet."

"Good to know," he drawled. "Can I come inside?"

There was a beat where he thought she might refuse, but she inclined her head and opened the door, letting him through. The door clicked quietly behind him as he took in the room.

It looked as if a hurricane had passed through it.

Not the kitchen. That was mainly tidy, with only a few dishes sitting next to the sink. It was a stark contrast to the mess of her living room. Stacks of papers sat on a table he knew had once been in her kitchen. There were several papers strewn over the desk, some with lots of words on them, others with a single line. One such page caught his eye, in no small part because of the big red circle that had been drawn around it, over and over and over.

It said, *What about his father?* Jacob desperately wanted to know the answer.

But that was only the tip of the iceberg. Her walls were full of sticky notes, pink and blue and yellow, stuck in an order he couldn't recognize, but appearing on every open surface. There was a notebook—no, notebooks—on the floor, along with a plate with a half-eaten sandwich on it, three empty cups, and one cup filled with what looked like tea, some loose papers, pens of every color, highlighters, a file, and for some inexplicable reason, an ornamental bird.

"I hate to be impolite—"

"Do you?"

"—but what the hell happened in your house?"

Gaia surveyed the room with a little sigh, then looked at him. "Firstly, that *was* impolite, and you didn't look as if you hated it one bit."

He barely stopped his laugh.

"Secondly . . . I'm writing a book. Well, I'm writing a book without actually writing, because, you know, space"—she lifted a hand to gesture to him—"and it's proven to be a . . . challenge."

He looked at the mess again now that he had context, and it became clear. "You're trying to game the system."

"If by system, you mean my powers, then yes." She bit her lip. "I've never actually tried to before."

"Why not?" he asked, genuinely curious. "Especially at the beginning. There must have been some kind of denial."

The quirk of a brow was the only way he knew she knew he was referring to his own experience. "Denial came in the form of not writing." She got a glazed look in her eyes, remembering. "But not writing felt like I was giving up a part of myself. The part that made the crap I had lived through for years seem tolerable."

She looked at him now. "Not writing isn't an option for me, as you know. It wasn't back then, when I found out, because I wanted to continue pretending I was a normal, well-adjusted human being." Lips curved into a small smile. "So I faced it. Embraced it, or whatever. Gaming the system never occurred to me." She paused. "Not to mention it seems horribly unproductive. I spent over a week on this." She spread her hands. "I could have been writing. Actually writing."

He tried to think of a way to respond, but truthfully, he was caught by what she'd said. What she'd implied. He couldn't imagine life was easy in foster care. But he also hadn't thought about the smaller things. About the coping mechanisms that lingered; the scars that healed but were still there, if they'd even healed at all.

What would have happened if he hadn't come to find her that week when she'd been struggling? Would she have stayed in the darkness that had seemingly claimed her? What had happened before him? Before Seth?

He reached out to take her hand. More for himself than her. Of course, more for himself than her. She had no idea what was happening in his head. More importantly, she was there. Talking to him, teasing him. She was *there* even though she hadn't had anyone in the past to help her out of the darkness he knew had come for her.

She didn't need him to come find her. Or help her. She had herself.

What was it she'd said about knights in shining armor?

The heroines of those stories never really needed knights in shining armor. They needed allies. People who believed them and tried to help them. Not save them.

She didn't need him to save her either. It left him feeling oddly unsettled.

"Not to make this any stranger than it is," Gaia said slowly, "but is there a reason you're holding my hand?"

"Thank you," he replied, ignoring the lightly mocking edge to her voice. "You need to write, but you gave me space."

Her free hand pushed back a strand of hair. Nervously, he thought.

Hmm.

"I tortured you first though," she said, her voice higher than usual. "Don't forget that."

"Oh, I won't."

He pulled at her hand. Not with enough pressure to move her, but to ask her to move. She did. She faced him, her fingers threading through his.

"In fact," he continued, "I believe that torture means payback."

She smirked. It reminded him of the expression she'd had in one of the dreams where she'd teased him. Instead of finding it scary now though, he found it sexy. He inched forward, leaving barely a breath of space between them. They didn't touch, but the tips of her breasts were so close to his chest that if either he or Gaia moved, they'd graze his skin.

Would it turn her on to feel it? To have her nipples scrape against his skin? Would it turn them into tight peaks he could take into his mouth? To test whether she tasted as good as he remembered. To see if she'd arch her back, pressing further into his mouth.

He swallowed.

"You're thinking dirty thoughts," she said softly, staring at him.

"No," he lied.

Laughter danced in her eyes.

"So revenge for me keeping you in a tower, making you a stripper, and tying you to a bed is—what? Dissing the mess of my home?"

"You forgot that outfit," he said, gaze dipping to her lips. They glistened up at him, as if she'd slipped her tongue between them when he wasn't noticing.

His already aroused body complained, telling him to focus.

"What outfit?"

He met her eyes. "The thing you created from your imagination for the exact purpose of torturing me."

"Honestly, Jake, not everything I do is to torture you."

"Isn't it?" he asked, seriously now. "I spent years not dating, working, barely seeing my family while still keeping them together without even considering that it might not be what I wanted to do. Then I meet you, and . . ."

He trailed off, the heat in his body cooling as he realized what he'd said.

"I . . . shouldn't have said that."

He stepped back, then farther when he wanted to push her against a wall and do dirty things to her until he forgot about the discontent echoing in his brain.

She was biting her lip when he looked at her again, still standing where he'd left her. She tilted her head from side to side, as if debating what to say next. Not for the first time, he braced himself for her to ask.

And not for the first time, she didn't.

"So," she said, dragging out the O, "you want to rethink this sleeping together thing?"

He laughed, something spiking in his chest. Relief, he thought. Relief that she hadn't asked.

Not disappointment.

Did Jacob know how much emotion was on his face every time he spoke about his work? His family? She didn't think it was a coincidence that he kept mentioning it. Dancing around it, really.

Maybe he'd forgotten that she had context. That her best friend, despite evidence to the contrary, was his brother, and she knew that Jacob had done what Seth couldn't.

Seth was about as forthcoming about his feelings on this issue as Jacob was. He tiptoed around it, the hurt and guilt too much for him, she knew. Occasionally, he'd show up on her doorstep drunk, ready to vent about his father and brother, and would then refuse to talk about it when he was sober.

She got it. In theory, more than practically. Family was complicated, and Seth's situation was no different. Gaia chose to respect that instead of push—not that she wouldn't have had the right to, considering how often Seth pushed her. And if she thought Seth's avoidance was for toxic reasons, or that he *needed* to talk, she would have pushed.

But Seth was aware of the trappings of their society. The idea that men couldn't feel what they needed to feel, so they channeled their feelings into sports or video games or whatever the hell made them feel better. But that didn't change that they had those feelings. It didn't help them process it. Only allowed them to set it aside for a short period of time.

Seth didn't blurt out his feelings on most things, but he didn't shun them either. His family was the only issue he didn't readily open up about, and before it became a problem, he'd appear on her doorstep. He knew it wasn't healthy, but somehow, he figured the purging of his emotions balanced the toxicity of getting drunk to do so. Despite his relative awareness, no one could use Seth as a perfect example.

In any case, Seth's drunken therapy sessions were the reason she knew he felt guilty about what had happened after their mother's death. They'd all fallen apart. Seth and his father were too similar to get along smoothly, but their adoration of Seth's mother had kept them from not getting along at all. Their grief had ravaged them both, in equal measure. So when his father had asked Seth to take over the business completely, he couldn't say yes. He had already suffered through a year of running things. The company was still struggling, and Seth was afraid of what failing would do to their relationship.

In the end, saying no had destroyed that relationship anyway. The only thing that had kept them from lingering in the destruction was Jacob.

Seth had never told Jake any of that. Just as Jake hadn't told Seth how much the responsibility of keeping things together was hurting him.

Thankfully, she had a plan to help Jacob deal with the situation in a much healthier way than Seth did.

"I thought sleeping together here would be a good way of dealing with this. If I have questions—like why can't I say my name? Yours? And sometimes, when I want to say something, I can, but other times, I can't?—you'd be here for me to ask."

She took a second. "We can't say our names because we're not ourselves in the book. Not really. As for your second question . . . I'm not sure. That's never happened to me. I can do what I like. Maybe your abilities . . . are more limited."

He exhaled. "This is hard to figure out. Not in a *how is this happening* way—I don't think I could figure that out. Just . . ." He trailed off. "Just in a *how do we deal with this* way."

She liked the way he said *we* a little too much.

"It's not a bad idea," she said. "But I haven't written anything, so it won't happen today."

He checked the time. "You can't do anything in a couple of hours?"

She let out a light laugh, enjoying the slightly mocking way it echoed after her as she walked to the kitchen.

"Writing doesn't work like that. Not mine. I need to prepare myself mentally to write. It's not a spur-of-the-moment thing."

"Really?" he asked, following her. "What do you do to prepare?"

"No, it's not like that." She checked the refrigerator for the groceries she had finally managed to get to the shop to buy. "I don't have a ritual, but I have to know that I'm going to write today, so my brain can gather all the words and put them in an easily accessible place."

She put water in a pot and threw some pasta in it, added oil to a pan. When she turned to Jacob, he was watching her with a bemused expression.

"What?"

"You said your brain gathers all your words to make them easily accessible."

She gave a curt nod of confirmation. Grabbed her chopping board and a knife and began chopping an onion.

"You realize that's not how brains work?"

"That's how my brain works," she said, giving him a sly smile. "It's like turning a packet of chips on the side so you can reach the chips easily."

"No one does that."

"I do that."

"I think this officially makes you weird."

She snorted. "Not the magical powers then?"

His mouth lifted, but he didn't reply. He leaned back in the counter seat she hadn't heard him sit in and watched her like some sexy chef judge on a reality show.

"You know what is weird though?" she asked, mainly to distract herself from that disturbing thought. She didn't need any more of those. She had plenty left over from that moment in her living room. "That woman we saw at the bookstore? Apparently, she's my stalker."

She told him about the café as she cooked, answering his questions and soothing his concerns. It was almost normal. Except this wasn't normal for her. She didn't cook for people. Didn't particularly want them watching her.

It was either because she had grown used to no one watching her in one of her foster homes, or someone paying too much attention to her in another. She didn't know which was better, frankly. She only knew that it made her wary of people. They either didn't care about her, or they stopped caring about her even when they did.

She had waited for the same thing to happen with Seth. But in the twelve years of their friendship, it hadn't. She should have known the man who had been determined to be her friend that first year at university, even when he stopped dating her room-mate and in spite of the fact that she allowed no one else close to her, would defy the odds.

Until now.

She would be a fool to deny it was Jacob's involvement that led to her and Seth's current situation, but part of her did. The part of her that curled into itself when she'd learned she had family, her mother's cousins, but none of them wanted to take her in. She grew up feeling alone and unwanted for most of her life. She couldn't trust that that wouldn't change as an adult.

She *hadn't* trusted it. Perhaps that's why she was so torn about Seth's reaction.

Yes, it hurt that he was acting this way. But then again, she always knew he would, and she could hardly blame him for it.

"Why does it sound like you're not concerned about a woman claiming to be your stalker?" Jake demanded, though he'd just laughed at one of Gemma's responses.

"I don't know. She doesn't seem like a stalker."

"I'm sure plenty of stalked people have felt that way."

She rolled her eyes. "My instincts on who to trust over the years have become pretty sharp. She's okay."

"You trust her?"

The question seemed perfectly innocent on the surface. But one look at Jacob's face told her there was more to it. He was trying too hard to feign disinterest. Leaning back in his chair, watching her almost lazily. There was a jump at his mouth though. And his voice was too soft, too unassuming for her to believe it.

She answered carefully. "In a general, she-won't-kill-me way, yes."

"It's significant, isn't it?" he asked, again in that casual tone of voice. "You don't give that kind of trust away easily."

"I have to, on a very basic level, believe that people don't want to kill me," she said, unsure of what he expected. "I wouldn't leave the house if I didn't."

"You don't leave the house though, do you? Or you didn't, at least. Not for a week." He shifted, placing his forearms on the counter. Her counter. He was leaning on her counter and he was trying to trap her. The nerve. "Because, on some level, you don't trust the world."

The nerve.

He had it, and he'd struck one in her, too.

She didn't particularly like it. Didn't like how he saw something inside her that she hid from people. From herself, most days. She didn't like the casual way he pointed out her deepest insecurity; the building block of some of her most intense emotions. She most definitely didn't like that the man who did all of that had been given access to the world she did trust. He could see how she struggled with the real world, with the people in it, and they'd only known one another, really known one another, for three weeks.

What would spending more time with him do? What would sharing her safe space, making her more vulnerable than she'd ever been, *do*?

And how long would it take before he picked up that she preferred her dream world to the real world?

"I've crossed a line," he commented, eyes on her.

A blush crept over her face, the color a confirmation that he had, and a shameful admission that she didn't want him to see that he had. Not so easily.

The only sound was the sizzle of the pan as she sautéed the onions. When they were ready, she got the beef and put it in with the onions. Her hands were shaking as she did, but she shook her head. She wouldn't let him see it.

It wasn't for him. Her emotions, her fears weren't for him.

"Does this mean I don't get dinner anymore?" Jacob asked.

It was out of the blue, said in a teasing voice meant for reconciliation. She took a second to adjust, then turned around with a smirk. A mask. "Who said you were getting dinner in the first place?"

CHAPTER 17

A few nights later, Jacob was standing in that soft yellow kitchen again.

He was prepared for the dream this time though. That morning, Gaia had sent him the outline of the scene she planned to write that day.

Instead of asking if she was okay, he replied with his thanks. Because he couldn't bear to push her again. He had crossed a line with his remark about her not trusting the world. He'd done it for selfish reasons, too; he couldn't understand why she trusted a complete stranger when she didn't trust him.

That wasn't even true. She trusted him to some extent. Enough to let her guard down the night they'd met. To allow him to be there for her. To accept that he would share this deeply personal experience of her dreams with her.

His real issue was that she didn't trust him in the way he wanted her to. In the way that would allow her to admit she didn't trust the world and not recoil from him.

It seemed like a hell of an expectation when he didn't trust her in that way himself.

"We could," he heard himself say, the words spilling from his lips easily. "Make use of it, I mean."

He was going along with the script already written, hence the ease. He assumed. He didn't know the mechanics of it, but if he was going to believe in magic—and he did, apparently—then he needed to understand it. For himself. So he didn't try to control anything. He let whatever needed to play out, play out. And found that ease again, as if he were a vessel for some god. For Gaia.

Gaia snorted, or the character did, and gripped the counter at her back, as she'd done the first time they'd been in this scene together. But Gaia had warned him she needed to rewrite the ending, so the repeat didn't surprise him. In fact, he was interested in seeing how things would play out now.

"You're offering to have sex with me minutes after someone tried to kill you for having sex with their wife?"

He opened his mouth, then winced. "When you put it that way . . ."

Her grip on the counter slackened. "Good heavens, you're a douchebag."

"I prefer cad."

"Is there a difference?"

"Not to you, I suppose."

She frowned. "Is that . . . is that *judgment* in your voice? You're judging *me* for not wanting to have sex with you after you've had sex with someone else? Like, minutes ago?"

He stood up straighter. "I'm judging you for judging me."

"I have a right to judge you. You just offered to have sex with me—"

"Yeah, yeah, I got it. We all got it," he snapped, opening his arms. "It was a mistake, okay? I didn't set out to sleep with her. I was there to quote her on retiling her place, but then she came on to me and one thing led to another."

She was studying him impassively. Or it would have been impassive if not for that swelling at her jaw that told him she was clenching her teeth.

"So let me get this straight. You're saying that you were there to provide a service, but you ended up servicing her instead because you have zero self-control?"

"No, of course not," he snapped again. Then realized he had absolutely no ground to stand on. "Well, actually, yes. That's exactly what happened."

She snorted again, but this one was less mocking. In fact, he thought she might have been amused.

"Heaven save me from men who think sex with the wrong people won't add to their problems."

Those words sent a staggering amount of information into his head. About his mother, who needed his help to pay for her blood pressure medication. About the fact that he actually needed the tiling job so he could do that. He'd messed up his life with sex yet again. This time it was worse because he was putting his mother at risk.

"Ah, you're realizing it, aren't you?" Gaia said, watching him. "You've added to your problems by sleeping with Terrence's wife. Now, someone wants to kill you."

"I was more thinking that now, I can't pay for my mom's meds. But yeah, sure, let's make it about the killing."

He moved toward the door, and thanked the universe he'd parked away from Terrence's house, farther down the road. There'd been no street parking near the house and he was happy to take what he could get. His keys were still in that house though. He supposed he could break into the car, but that would mean paying for repairs. He had to save all the money he could get.

With a sigh, he turned back. "I need a favor."

Her eyes narrowed suspiciously. "What?"

"I need you to get my keys. They're in my jeans pocket. In Terrence's house."

Which made him realize he still didn't have any clothes on.

As he said it, the towel at his hips unraveled and fell to the floor.

"For heaven's sake!" Gaia exclaimed.

* * *

When Jacob woke up, there was a smile on his face. A smile. As if he'd enjoyed the dream. But that couldn't have been it. If he'd enjoyed the dream, it would mean he didn't mind being in it. If he didn't mind, he was accepting that magic was a part of their world and he was somehow a part of that magic.

It made him realize that he hadn't asked Gaia if there were more out there like her. There must be. It didn't seem plausible that only one person in the world had been granted abilities. But there was no way he would know. If those people were anything like Gaia, they would keep their abilities to themselves. Hell, he was like Gaia now, wasn't he? And he had no intention of telling anyone he was playing the part of Gaia's heroes in her dreams.

Maybe *everyone* had magic and they were all just keeping it a secret from each other.

He went down to breakfast with that suspicion in his mind. His father was already there, chomping down dry cereal.

Jacob sighed. "If you'd waited ten minutes, you could have had eggs and toast with me."

"Was hungry," Keenan said between chomps.

It was all his father offered. Jacob refrained from commenting further. He didn't have to guess which magical power his father might have had. Jacob already knew it was the supernatural ability of ruffling his feathers even when he spent days smoothing them down, telling himself no one had the power to disturb them but him.

His father almost always had the power.

"What happened with the Jefferson account?"

Ah, a full sentence. No food splutters, either. His father was remarkably eloquent when it came to work.

"Nothing yet. We only pitch next week."

"Talk me through the pitch."

He felt tension seep into his body, but he talked it through with his father. Listened to Keenan's advice and made mental notes about what he wanted to add to the presentation. By the end of it, when his father walked away without asking about anything else—about why Jacob had been distracted lately; about where Jacob went when he left; about his late nights—Jacob had a headache. Tension and disappointment had merged and crashed into his skull. It was barely eight a.m.

He left for work, calling goodbye to his father. As he drove, he opened the windows all the way down, let the air fill the car. And the farther away he got from the house, the more the tension in his body dissipated. By the time he got to the office, the headache was a dull throb he could live with.

And, through pure determination, he went back to wondering whether his staff had superpowers.

Gaia was putting the finishing touches on a chapter when the doorbell rang.

It wasn't Jacob. He always rang the doorbell in that vaguely annoying but recognizable pattern, and this was simple. Straightforward. And with that, she thought she knew who it was.

She was wrong.

"Lizzy?" Gaia didn't let the question linger. Of course it was Lizzy. She was standing right there. "Hey. Is everything okay?"

"Hi. Yes, everything's fine. I know it's odd that I'm here, but . . ." She trailed off. "Can I come in?"

"Yes. Yeah, of course."

Gaia shifted away, feeling oddly out of place now. It was a strange feeling to have in her own home. It was a familiar feeling though. She'd felt it every time she had to move to a new foster home. That must have been six or seven times in the sixteen years she was in the system, and she knew that made her lucky.

It was that knowledge that helped her move on from it. She'd escaped the system relatively unscathed. Sure, she struggled to make meaningful human connections, but she could hardly blame the system for that. Humans were unpredictable. There was a solid portion of them who were terrible. She didn't want to connect with people who were terrible. She'd rather be alone.

Really? an inner voice mocked her. Reminded her of how terrible it had been to be alone for sixteen years. Becoming friends with Seth, being included in his life . . . That had shifted things inside her in ways she still hadn't taken stock of.

And had apparently taken for granted as a result.

"Can I get you something to drink?" Gaia asked, distracting herself from her thoughts. They'd been a lot more annoying than helpful lately. So she would continue ignoring them, she supposed.

"Er, no. I'm not here to chat."

Gaia barely resisted the wince.

You'd rather be alone, yet you're hurt she didn't come over to be social.

Ignore, ignore, ignore.

"That sounded terrible. I'm sorry. I . . . I don't know how to make small talk. With you."

Gaia's lips parted, but she stopped herself from speaking until she knew what she wanted to say. "You don't know how to make small talk in general, or with me specifically?"

"With you." Lizzy grimaced. "You're Seth's best friend. I've constantly had to negotiate my space in his life around you. Doing that makes it hard to have small talk with you."

Well, that explained why she never did anything but smile and make a few snarky comments when she and Gaia were alone. It had suited Gaia. She didn't have to think about what to say, how to start a conversation. She could simply smile back. But now, it had been two years and they were nowhere near to being friends. They tolerated one another, in the least contentious way people could. As if they were different animals in the wild who encountered one another often, but didn't care that they did.

"If it makes you feel better, I don't know how to make small talk in general. So, it worked for me." She waited a beat. "I'm sorry you felt as if you had to negotiate a space in Seth's life. He adores you. You don't deserve to feel that way."

"Oh, no. I don't mean it in a bad way. Just being frank." Lizzy stuffed her hands into the coat she still wore despite the summer heat weighing down the house. "It was the same way I had to negotiate with Jake's relationship with Seth. And Seth's other relationships." She shrugged. "I didn't expect to become the most important person in his life. Except it's been harder with you because you're so . . ."

Gaia was curious more than anything else, though her heart did feel like a record that had skipped a beat.

"Reticent. You're not exactly willing to make new friends. The only thing that made me feel better about it was that it wasn't because of *me*. You're like that with everyone."

"Well," Gaia said on an exhale, "that's a lot better than what I thought you were going to say."

Lizzy gave her a small smile. "I can try something else."

"I think that's fine," Gaia said dryly. "Thank you." Again, that curiosity flared. "Why are you here, Lizzy?"

She didn't care that the question was straightforward. That had been Lizzy's energy from the moment she opened the door. And Lizzy didn't seem to mind it.

The woman took a breath. "Seth. He's been . . . difficult since you two fought. I can barely get a word out of him about what happened, but he's been the worst version of himself since the fight. I'm here to try to save my relationship by saving yours."

There was a long silence. Lizzy was expecting Gaia to answer, obviously, but she was struggling. She didn't know which of the things in her head she should say first. Or if she should say them at all; they would likely get her into trouble.

But Lizzy seemed to be going the honest route. Gaia had watched her interactions with Seth enough to know that was how Lizzy preferred to handle things. Coming here then, speaking with Gaia, was totally within character. It was still odd to interact with that character though.

"Seth can get stuck in his emotions," Gaia said slowly. "You know that."

"Usually, he gets unstuck by himself, too. Now he seems to need a little push." She offered something Gaia thought might be a smile. "I'm pushing."

"And he'll need that, too, so great. Except you can't push me." She felt as if she were holding her breath, even though she was breathing fine. "You need to push *him* about this. He was the one who . . ." Her stomach clenched. "He doesn't like that Jacob and I are friends," she said flatly.

"But you're not only friends. I think that's what he's really upset about."

"I . . . I don't know what we are."

"Yeah, you do." Lizzy's voice was surprisingly gentle despite the assertion. "You're afraid of calling it what it is."

Gaia clenched her jaw to keep from saying what she wanted to. And what she wanted to say was that Lizzy was being very annoying.

"I can't do anything about Seth's feelings regarding the situation with me and Jacob," she said instead. "I can't do anything about Seth not trying to save our friendship of twelve years because he has feelings about me and Jake. And your relationship shouldn't be dependent on a reconciliation between us."

Lizzy was nodding before Gaia finished that last sentence. "Yeah, I probably phrased that poorly. I don't think saving your friendship will save our relationship. But I did think your friendship would mean enough to you that you'd want him to be happy. I thought you'd want to save your friendship, too. Though you seem content to let it end because of a stupid situation."

Gaia exhaled, hating the tension in the room that had slowly crept up her body, her spine, her neck, and landed in her throat. It tightened there, making each word she said next feel costly.

"I know you don't mean for it to come out that way, but you're manipulating me." She spoke quietly, carefully, wanting each word to matter. "You're making it seem as though Seth's emotions are my responsibility."

Lizzy didn't reply, though emotion rippled across her face. Gaia was too busy containing her own to try and figure out what Lizzy's were.

"You're right about one thing, though," Gaia continued. "I've let things between me and Seth get to this point." And she would think about that later. "In the same way you've let things between the two of you get to where they are now. To where you're at my house, trying to get me to snap him out of himself."

Gaia understood, and she wouldn't blame Lizzy for wanting to avoid it. To avoid her part in a relationship, which, by definition, was two parts. "He needs to take responsibility for how he's been acting. He won't if we don't force him to."

"We," Lizzy repeated faintly. "You're going to, too?"

Gaia sighed. "Seems like I have to. I can't exactly tell you to do something I can't do myself."

"And I can't be annoyed at you when you're right and you plan on doing good on your word."

Gaia studied her. "But you are."

Lizzy's mouth split into a grin. "I am. It'll fade, I'm sure."

"I wouldn't count on it. I annoy people a lot."

"People who aren't afraid to face their mistakes tend to." Lizzy folded her arms. "It's a reminder to everyone that we can all face mistakes and the world doesn't end. In fact, it makes us better. But that would entail admitting we're wrong and that's . . . It's hard." There was a beat. "I was wrong to come here and expect you to save my relationship."

"But I'm glad you did," Gaia said, though a different kind of emotion replaced the tension in her throat. A good kind of emotion. "I wouldn't be able to face my part in the Seth saga otherwise."

They stood in silence for a few moments.

"I like you, Gaia," Lizzy blurted out. It was the first time she'd sounded nervous, despite their conversation. "I really hope we can be friends."

"I hope so, too," Gaia replied. This time the good emotion prickled her eyes.

Again, silence. But it didn't feel weird. It felt oddly right. The kind of silence that came after a long hike to the top of a mountain, as she stood there and took in the view.

She assumed. She would never actually hike to the top of a mountain.

"I suppose I need to deal with this now," Lizzy said.

"Me, too." Gaia exhaled. "But maybe not *right* now."

"Easy for you to say," Lizzy muttered. "I have a date with him tonight."

"Whose fault is that?"

Lizzy snorted in reply.

"I will go see him," Gaia said. "I need time after this conversation, but I will."

"That's fair."

"Doesn't change that he's a complete idiot."

"Doesn't change it at all," Lizzy agreed.

A beat of silence. Then they laughed.

CHAPTER 18

"I'm taking you out," Jacob said when she opened her door that Friday evening.

She lifted her eyebrows. "You really need to stop making grand proclamations when I open the door. My instinct is always to shut it on you, and one of these days, I'm not going to be able to resist."

He smiled. An easy, charming smile that had desire exploding in her body and, more concerningly, her brain. Objectively, she recognized his smile was amazing. The dimple, those teeth, the way, when she stood close enough, she could see his eyes sparkle. Those were all facts, and had nothing to do with her body's reaction to him.

No, her body's reaction to him was pure lust.

Those reviews of her books were right: she was a hussy.

The names had bothered her at first. They made her heart beat uncomfortably, her mind spin with questions. Was she a thoughtless author who had no talent? Why *did* people read her books? Was she a shameless human being because sex was a part of the romances she wrote?

To be fair, those questions had roamed her mind long before the reviews. She had been convinced, for the longest time, that she had no right to be an author. She wasn't sure who was handing out those rights, but she didn't have them. When she got an agent, a publisher, she was sure it was a fluke. There were stretches of time where she expected them to call and say they'd made a mistake. The call never came, but the readers did. More readers than she could imagine over the years.

She learned her lesson fairly quickly. The negative things people would say damaged her in a way she hadn't developed defenses for. She avoided reviews, good and bad, as far as she could manage. Occasionally, something would sneak past her efforts and she would learn that she was a hussy or harlot.

If only they could see her now.

"If you stop fighting your instincts where I'm concerned, our relationship is going to get a lot more interesting," he said, undeterred.

"I think you're overestimating my instincts."

"You keep writing me naked." His words were easy as he walked into the house. "Something is definitely happening in your subconscious where I'm concerned."

In the novel, Gaia's heroine Jade felt sorry that Chris needed to pay for his mother's meds and didn't have a job because of his straying penis. Partly because she was a bleeding heart; partly because her father had needed medication for a chronic condition, too, and she knew how pivotal it was to quality of life. There was the added complication of Jade's mother's visit from New Zealand at the end of the year. They had a strained relationship, her mother was overly critical, and Jade knew her cozy little home needed a face-lift of some kind if she wanted to avoid the critique.

So, against her better judgment, Jade hired Chris to tile and paint her home. As Gaia expected, the forced proximity was wreaking havoc on her characters and their reluctant attraction. Jade had no intention of dipping her toe into the bad-boy pond, despite the sizzle of that attraction. And Chris had no intention of dipping his toe into the judge-y pond, despite the heat that simmered in his veins whenever he got near Jade.

It made situations like Chris watering himself down on Jade's lawn after a hot and hard day's work uncomfortable. It didn't help that it happened on the first day of the job, heightening the sexual tension right from the get-go.

"Technically, you weren't naked," Gaia told Jacob, going to the fridge and getting him a drink.

"My shirt was off."

"Not naked."

"If your shirt was off, would you claim you're not naked?"

"*My* nipples serve a purpose."

He had no response to that, as she expected. She set the soft drink down in front of him triumphantly.

"Another technicality is that it's not you." She poured herself a glass of water. "It might seem like you, but it's not."

"I get that. I think," he added with a frown. "It's almost like being on autopilot, now that I understand what's happening. I say and do the things you've written, and it comes easily. But it doesn't feel authentic."

"It shouldn't feel authentic. I didn't base Chris on you."

He dismissed that with a snort.

"No, really," she insisted, though heaven only knew why, when it was shaky ground to take a stand on.

"Gaia."

"Okay, yes, maybe that first night, with the princess stuff . . . Maybe *then* I based Chris on you. But this Chris is . . . He's not . . . No," she ended. It made no sense, but she shook her head to emphasize it.

"Do you think that's why it's happening?" he asked after a pause. "Why I'm in your dreams, I mean. Is it because you based him on me?"

"I did not. And honestly, it's rude that you don't believe me."

"It's rude that I don't believe your lies?"

"A-a-a-nd," she continued with a sniff, dragging the word out, "I considered it. It didn't stick. I've based heroes on men I've seen before. Hell, even men I've kissed. They've never appeared in the dreams after that."

Jacob's eyes darkened. It had the faint waft of danger. Or was that what he was wearing? She took it in. Plain white T-shirt, well-worn jeans, sneakers. But it was the leather jacket that got her. It would have eventually, even without that darkened expression. With it? She had a vague desire to call the police. Except that would imply she wanted to be saved.

Yes. Yes, that *was* what she wanted. Definitely. *Definitely.*

She needed an escape plan. Things with Jacob were . . . Well, there was *more* with him. More than the fact that he'd been drawn into her dreams. More than that she found him attractive. She was sure the one thing had to do with the other, and that both those things had to do with the emotional things she was ignoring when it came to him.

How she liked that he rang the doorbell in a unique way, like he knew she would want to prepare to see him. How his words were always ridiculous when she opened the door. How he made her laugh and smile and feel.

She liked it, and she didn't like it, and that told her that noticing his dimples and sparkles and desire . . . It was a bad idea. She knew better than to entertain bad ideas.

"Are you saying I'm not your first?" he asked in a voice that was another bad idea.

She opened her mouth to say something when he rounded the counter.

"What are you doing?" she asked instead.

"Nothing," he said easily. Suspiciously. "I wanted to hear you better."

She clucked her tongue. "Grandma, why are your ears so big?" she said, repeating the famous words. "All the better to hear you with, said the wolf."

"You're calling me a wolf?"

"Are you one?"

His eyes swept across her face and he lifted a hand to pull at a stray piece of hair. The curl popped out entirely, bouncing in front of her face. He tugged it again, and it bounced again. It would have been a ridiculous thing to experience if it weren't for that faint smile on his face. It burrowed itself into her heart, bypassing desire in both her brain and her body. She inhaled, and she got a whiff of . . . She wasn't quite sure. He smelled like him, like Jacob, and that scent in itself seemed like an adequate description. But there was something more, too. Something familiar.

She couldn't let it go, even when his fingers left her hair and trailed lightly over her face, passed her temple, the curve of her cheekbone, the edge of her lip. She felt as if he were trailing a path, as if her skin was sand and she would see the indents of his fingers. He was marking her, she thought. Marking her skin for where to come back to later, just as Hansel and Gretel had done on their way to the witch's house.

On their way to being devoured.

"Books!" she said, the realization unexpected. "You smell like books! Or"—she sniffed again—"or a bookstore. You smell like . . . like Between the Covers."

He snatched his hand back. "No I don't."

But he'd reacted too strongly for her to believe him.

"Did you go to Between the Covers? Or have you been reading?"

"You can't seriously smell that," Jacob said incredulously.

"There's a simple way to answer that. Have. You. Been. Reading?"

Jacob didn't respond for a long time. Eventually, he said, "Get dressed. We're going to my side of the world for dinner."

She bit her lip, but it did nothing to hide her smile.

"Don't you dare," he warned.

She lifted her hands. "I did nothing."

"Just get dressed, Gaia, or I swear I'll strip right now and we can figure out whether you have an obsession with me being naked or not. And I mean me," he said, "not Chris."

"Pretty sure you're threatening sexual harassment."

"Gaia!" he barked.

Laughing, she went to her bedroom, and tried not to linger too long on choosing her clothing. She grabbed jeans and a top she really liked—a loose, flowing thing that clung to nothing and would entice no one—and paired it with a cute pair of wedges. She fixed her hair, tying it on top of her head so it could be wild and out of her face before adding a patterned headband that matched the loose, flowing top. After a minute of deliberation, she put on some makeup and looked at herself in the mirror.

"This is . . . good," she said with a nod. "This is . . . You look nice."

Her reflection blinked back at her, as if it couldn't believe she was complimenting herself. Her eyes shifted to the pendant again. She resisted taking it, putting it on, not understanding the desire to. Shaking her head, she got her jersey and handbag and went to find Jake.

He was staring at the sticky notes she hadn't bothered taking down from the wall.

"You should add a spoiler warning to these notes," he said as he turned around. Then he blinked at her. And blinked again. "Wow. You look . . . You look really nice."

"Thanks." She brushed a hand over her jeans. "I took your outfit as a sign of how formal I should go. It's okay, right? I'm okay?"

It sounded so terribly insecure that she regretted asking it. But his eyes softened, warmed, and she braced for his touch when he brushed his fingers over her cheek.

"You've always been more than okay, Gaia."

The words sank deep inside her, filling a hole she tried not to think about. No—not filling it; coating it. He couldn't possibly fill it. They weren't in a relationship. They were barely friends. Besides, she'd spent her entire adult life writing about people who weren't filled by their relationships. They were supported by their partners, and that allowed them to realize they needed to fill themselves. A fact that seemed rather pointed now that her hole had forced its way back into her consciousness.

"You're a flirt."

Something tightened in his eyes, but he smiled and took a step back. "Only with you."

The frown that took the place of his smile worried her, but he asked if she was ready to go and she nodded. She was still thinking about it in the car, staring out the window at the greenery of Stellenbosch.

They had to take the main road to get to the freeway, which would eventually take them to Jacob's side of town. Trees leaned over the tar, shading most of it, while people wove between cars at red lights and ran when the lights turned green. The roads grew quieter as they drew closer to the freeway, and by the time they got on it, Gaia realized how long it must take Jacob to visit.

She knew it, of course, on a fairly basic level. He lived near central Cape Town, which was about forty minutes away. With the stops, the turns, the traffic, it was pushed closer to fifty minutes, which was essentially an hour, and he was driving *an hour* to get to her every time he visited. Those visits had become at least a weekly fixture since the party, and she looked forward to them.

Except she made little to no effort to make it worth it for *him*. She fed him, but that didn't seem special when he was always going to feed himself. He only came because she'd caught him in her abilities. It seemed selfish and she would have hated it if the roles were reversed.

So why did he keep coming?

"Does anyone else have magical abilities?" Jacob blurted out before she could ask him.

"Oh," she said, as her brain shifted gears. "I'm not sure. I assume not, or we would have heard about it by now."

"Unless everyone is hiding their magic like you do. Afraid people are going to riot if they find out." His hand gripped the wheel.

"Has this . . . has this been bothering you for a while?"

She stared pointedly at his hands when he glanced over. He slackened them. So much so that the car veered slightly. He tightened them again.

"No," he denied with a strained smile. "Why would you ask that?"

She didn't want to laugh at him—the issue was clearly bothering him—but he was making it hard. She focused on answering him.

"I used to wonder about that, too," she said. "At the beginning. I wondered if I was the only one or if there were more. I thought about my parents and imagined they had abilities. They'd have told me to expect it if they'd been alive. They would have taught me how to handle it."

The admission was more personal than she expected it to be, but the rolling tension in her chest didn't compare to the weight she felt lessen on her shoulders. Not even when that tension grew because it was sharing something personal with Jacob that had lessened the weight.

"I'm sorry. That they died *and* that you had to go through all you did."

One of his hands left the steering wheel and settled on her thigh. When she tensed beneath the contact, he lifted it again, but her own hand snapped out, taking his before he could put it back on the wheel. The car remained steady.

"Thank you," she said.

There was a long stretch of silence.

Then Jacob spoke.

"When my mom died, I felt empty. For a long time, there was just . . . nothing. But after . . . when my dad asked Seth to take over the company and he refused . . . I could see that it would break them. Us. And my mom"—he sucked in a breath—"she asked me to make sure we stayed a family. Before she died, I mean."

"I know what you mean," Gaia said softly, the information breaking her heart. "Is that why you did it? Why you stepped in? To keep the family together?"

"Yeah." He paused. "Don't tell Seth. I don't want him to know."

He needed to know though. Seth needed to know that Jacob had done it for Seth and their father and not for himself. But she wouldn't be the one to tell him. Not when Jacob had asked her not to. And not when really, *Jacob* needed to tell his brother.

"I am not currently talking to Seth, so that's not a problem," she replied lightly. "And even if I were, I wouldn't say anything. This is between you and him."

He squeezed her thigh. "Thanks."

They drove until they hit traffic a little closer to the beach, which wasn't unusual for a Friday night. Sand dunes rose on either side of the road, interspersed by tall green bushes. In the distance, Gaia could see buildings that must have cost a fortune to live in since they were so close to the beach. She opened her mouth to make some inane remark about it, but then she saw Jacob's face. His jaw was tight, his mouth in a thin line. He'd long since moved his hand from her lap to drive, but he hadn't put it back after changing the gears. She didn't need to touch him to know he was tense though. And now the inane comment didn't seem like enough.

She pulled her gaze back to the window, contemplating what to say.

"You know," she started before she lost courage, "I don't think about my parents that much. It sounds awful, because they're dead, and it seems like I *should* think about them. I did—a long time ago. For pretty much the entire time I spent in foster care. I wondered what type of parents they'd be. I thought about how different my life would have been if they hadn't been in that car crash." She let it linger for a moment. "But that changed when I got out of the system. I worked hard to get into university. To get some form of financial aid so I could pay for it and for accommodation. And then I was out, and my life . . . It was my own. Not dictated by a system or by people I didn't trust."

The road lights flickered on around them. It didn't do much to illuminate the area since the sky was still dusted pink and purple, edging into night slowly, as if realizing it was a weekend and wanting to stretch it out for as long as possible. Jacob made a left turn, and slowly the beach came into view. Dark blue waves crashed against the sand. It made her remember the last time they'd been together at a beach. Her lips curved at the memory.

"But I didn't know them," she continued softly. "I didn't know my parents. I didn't know what I had lost beyond an idea. Perhaps beyond the concepts of parents and stability that I had made up for myself." She paused. "You knew your mother though. It must have hurt."

He didn't speak for a long time. Not until he pulled into an empty parking space in the car lot next to the shopping complex he'd brought them to.

"Losing someone always hurts," he said curtly. "More so when you're expected to replace them."

With that, he got out of the car.

It wasn't how he wanted the night to start. He wanted to woo her with beachside dining and romantic sunsets. He'd left work early for that very reason, ignoring the strange looks he'd gotten. He was the boss; he could leave early if he wanted to, damn it.

But it had made him feel uneasy, despite the assurances.

He didn't leave work early. It wasn't an official rule, but it was one he'd lived by for years. There was always more to do. He always did it. And with the big presentation coming up the following week, he *should* have been working.

Except when three o'clock struck, he couldn't concentrate anymore. He wanted to blame it on the dreams, but they didn't interfere with his sleep. He felt as rested when he woke up as he did before, when he wasn't having these dreams. More, even. When he messaged Gaia about it, she confirmed it shouldn't affect his sleep cycle. Apparently, she'd gone to a sleep clinic and there had been nothing unusual, even with her dreams.

I had to make sure it wasn't affecting me negatively, she'd messaged him when he asked why she'd done it. *Would have been a lot harder to swallow if it did.*

So he couldn't blame a lack of sleep. The only thing he had left to blame were his feelings. For Gaia. Feelings that made him want to woo her with beachside dinners and romantic sunsets. He told her things that he'd never told anyone else. And when he stood in front of those sticky notes, reading the key points of her book . . . it felt as if she saw him.

Chris had a decent relationship with his mother, except she relied on him. A lot. There was no father in the picture, so Chris had been the man of the house since he was a kid. It was a lot of responsibility, but he reasoned that it was the least he could do for the woman who birthed him. That reasoning was layered with some guilt, some resentment, and a deep resignation that he was the only person who could help.

It was nearly identical to how Jacob felt about his own family situation. Except there was less guilt and more resentment. More over the last couple of months. He didn't know what had changed, but he didn't want to be responsible for keeping their family together anymore. He wanted his father and brother to get their acts together. And he wanted—

He stopped that thought. There was no point in wanting what he couldn't have. He'd already indulged it too much. And he'd allowed it to spoil his date, which was the worst thing he could have done.

"That was a little broody, wasn't it?" he said as they walked over the narrow pier that led to some restaurants.

"A little broody, a little dark." Her eyes twinkled at him. "Nothing I haven't experienced before."

"I'm done with it," he replied, and offered her his hand.

There was a short moment before she took it, though it felt much longer. But he forgot that as soon as their hands touched. The warmth that shot through his body felt like he was holding a piece of the sun. He had protection from the burning rays of it now, but even he knew that one day, that protection would disappear. He would wear the scars of whatever was happening between him and Gaia for a long time.

He knew it, and he was still touching the damn sun.

"I don't do this very often," she said softly, staring at the ocean, at the blue and pink and purple sky, as they walked. "I don't take drives. I don't get out of the house a lot. If I do, I go to familiar places. Places that feel . . . I don't know . . . safe, I guess."

Her grip tightened on his hand.

"But this is what I miss," she murmured. "The color of the sky after the sun goes down. The sound of waves crashing against the shore."

Two young children ran past them, fast as only that kind of youth allowed. Their shrieks pierced the air, shattering Gaia's quiet contemplation. Jacob forced himself not to smile. He was tempted to, what with Gaia's face adorably rumpled, as if she couldn't quite believe her peace had been interrupted.

He cleared his throat. "You missed the noise, too, which I'm guessing makes you rethink the rest."

She looked at him. At the edges of his mouth as they crept up because he couldn't resist his amusement anymore. She rolled her eyes, but she was smiling.

"I could do without the people," she told him haughtily. "But I've spent a lifetime wishing I could avoid them, and it hasn't done anything to help matters, so I suppose it's fine."

They walked in silence for a moment, heading to the end of the pier where Jacob had booked their dinner. It was the last restaurant in the line of restaurants overlooking the sea. He'd chosen it because it wouldn't get as much foot traffic as the rest of the places. It would be more private, and Gaia would get to avoid the majority of the people she claimed she could do without.

"You've said it before, you know," he said, leading her to the blue building. "That you don't like people. At the party. And then there was something about you not liking the world—" He cut himself off when she stiffened, then decided tonight was a night for throwing caution to the wind. "Don't do that," he urged her. "Don't close up on me. I want . . . I want to know what you're thinking. I want to understand why you feel the way you feel."

He thought she wouldn't reply. Took her silence as an answer. She didn't utter a word when they reached the restaurant and were led to a table on the deck. Candles fluttered on the boundary of the deck, a few more on the tables both inside and outside the restaurant, creating an intimacy he'd wanted but somehow felt wrong now that she was so quiet. Blue paint covered the outside of the building, and from what he could see from their table, the inside was green and white. Stone tiles lined the floors, while stone accented the largest inner wall. Pictures and figures of sea animals were plastered on the other walls, which somehow gave the place both a tacky and classy feel.

The server handed them both menus and disappeared into the restaurant. Gaia didn't look at hers, though she ran a finger along the edge of it.

"I'm thinking," she said, and, quite frankly, it startled him, "that it makes me uneasy that you remember something I told you a month ago. And that you want to know the reasons I do what I do even when I don't want to know them."

He stared, not wanting to interrupt. No, he only wanted to lap up the honesty she was giving him. Heaven only knew why. With each word she said, he lost a layer protecting his heart. Still, he listened. Still, he wanted. More, more, more. He wanted everything.

Panic fluttered deep inside him.

"As for your question," she continued, unaware of his turmoil, "though it technically wasn't a question . . . Yes. I suppose I don't trust the world. Nor do I trust people, but those two are interwoven." She paused. "My parents died when I was two. They had cousins who were contacted about taking me in. They refused. I bounced between foster homes, good and bad ones, and things haven't always been great for me as an adult." Another pause. "The world we live in, objectively, is horrid most days. Social issues, environmental issues, politics . . . None of that tells me I should trust it."

"Yet you write about love." He couldn't help himself, though a lot of what she said stuck with him. Fluttered inside him along with some other suspicions he had about her. "You write about the very thing that makes the world worth living in."

Her mouth lifted. "I should have known when you picked this restaurant"—she gestured to the candles, and the rose he had only now noticed on their table—"that I was dealing with a romantic."

"I'm not a romantic."

She laughed. A surprise, considering the tension of what they were talking about. It wasn't even a sharp laugh, a mocking one. It was genuine, and rolled over his body, *into* his body, somehow soothing the panic.

"It's not an insult, Jake. There's nothing wrong with being romantic."

"Ah, but you didn't call me romantic. You called me *a* romantic, which implies that I romanticize things, and I don't."

"Well, you did just tell me love makes the world go 'round."

"That's not what I said."

"Semantics," she said, challenge gleaming in her eyes.

He opened his mouth to argue, but instead said, "I'm going to continue with my original point, which is that *you* believe love makes the world go 'round. You have to, because that's what your characters believe."

Her snort was all he got in reply because the server returned, asking about drinks. Jacob ordered a bottle of wine for the table after a quick nod of confirmation from Gaia. As soon as the server left, he asked, "You don't believe in what you write?"

"That's not a fair question," she told him. "It's not the right question either. And neither is your assumption that I believe what my characters believe. They're fiction. Their beliefs range from completely idiotic—in which case I'm offended that you think those are my beliefs—to more mature and hopeful than I could ever be. In that case, it's sweet that you think me capable of it."

He didn't know how to respond. She was too quick, too clever. He'd never had trouble getting his point across before. But perhaps this was because it had nothing to do with his point and everything to do with his disappointment. He'd hoped that she would believe in love because—

No. Nope. He wasn't going there.

Not now, not ever.

"I don't believe you're capable of writing something idiotic," he said, moving on from that thought, because *not ever.*

"In my third book, my heroine's a virgin because her mother told her sex was from the devil."

He blinked.

"She grew up in a religious home. The kind where sex was only a means for reproduction."

"Wouldn't that imply—"

"That children are from the devil?" she interrupted. "Yes. Which did heavy things to my poor heroine's psyche. But the point is—believing sex is from the devil is kind of idiotic. I mean that on a basic level. I'm sure there are ways for the devil to use sex." She grimaced. "This conversation is getting weird."

"It's been weird since you started talking about sex."

She laughed, eyes sparkling. "Are you one of those people who believes sex shouldn't be talked about?"

"Not on a date."

"This is a date?" she asked, a flush on her cheeks. But she didn't let him answer. "And to be fair, talking about sex on a date is pretty standard."

"When it's about you and your date having sex, sure. Not when you're talking about fictional characters' beliefs."

The server cleared his throat. They both looked up. The man wore a faintly pained expression, but he said nothing as he poured their wine.

"Are you ready to order?"

"Not yet," he answered when Gaia shook her head. "We'll call you over."

He gave them a stiff nod before walking away. Jacob turned his attention back to Gaia.

"I'm sure he didn't hear anything," Jacob assured her.

"He heard everything," she said with a roll of her eyes. "As if he doesn't think about fictional characters' sex lives."

"It's not exactly normal."

"Please. He probably rooted for the Mother of Dragons to sleep with her nephew."

He angled his head. He hadn't considered the television angle. Or movies. "Touché. Definitely normal."

"You were rooting for the incest, too?"

He chuckled. "I didn't watch the show."

"No?"

"Nope. It was too much of a time investment."

She frowned. "What do you do for fun?"

"Recently? You." He grinned.

"You have not been *doing* me."

"Oh, shit. No, of course not." He winced. "Sorry, that was stupid."

"Yes, it was." But she looked amused. "I get it. You're spending time with me now. What about before? Other women?"

"No time to date," he replied, exceedingly pleased she'd asked. "I spent most of my time working, Gaia. Wooing new clients, re-signing old clients, turning my family's company into something we can be proud of again." He paused. "I would still be doing all that if I hadn't met you."

She didn't answer immediately. He shifted, not liking how the silence made it feel as if he'd revealed too much. To himself, too. Except he already knew that he was spending more time with Gaia than he had with anyone else in years. He'd thought it just that afternoon. But admitting it out loud, to the person shifting the things in his life? It was scary.

"I'm honored," she said simply.

And then it didn't feel so scary at all.

CHAPTER 19

She and Jacob talked about everything during their dinner. It was nice to have a normal conversation with him. Every now and then, they would veer into something unexpectedly deep, like when he told her he was working less because of her. She had no idea what to think about that. Didn't know if it was good or bad; only that it made her feel significant in a way she hadn't before. And, like with that conversation, when something deep came up, they dealt with it swiftly and moved on.

By the time they were eating dessert, they'd circled back around to whether or not she believed in love because she wrote about it.

"Of course I believe it exists," she said, more relaxed than she'd been in a while, in no small part because she was on her third glass of wine. "But in the world I create."

"So not in this world?" Jacob asked, leaning forward.

"I didn't say that."

"You implied it."

"Yes, well . . ." She had no good retort to that. "Okay, fine, I implied it. But only because the world I live in isn't the same as the world I write. The worlds I write . . . They're beautiful. Safe." She sighed contentedly. "Things are hard there, but they always get better by the end. Because that's how I write them."

"There are people in love here, Gaia," Jacob said easily, leaning back in his chair. "And those people think this world is beautiful and safe, too."

"My parents were in love and look where that got them," she said, toasting the point with her wine as if it were something to celebrate.

Jacob shifted, moving his forearms to the table. "That had nothing to do with whether they were in love."

She set her wine down. "Probably not." She snorted. "Hell, I don't even know whether they were in love. But that's the idea I have of them." She went quiet for a moment. "They met at university. He was the teaching assistant and she was the passionate English student who went the extra mile for a higher grade. She annoyed the hell out of him, and she enjoyed doing it. He was too smug, too sure of himself. He needed someone to rub him up the wrong way."

"Until it was the right way."

"Gross! These are my *parents*."

Jacob grinned, not falling for the trap. It made her laugh. He was getting to know her so well. Funny how it didn't seem like such a worrying thing now.

"But yes, the night she graduates, he's at the same party she's gone to, and finally, now that they don't have to be in each other's faces anymore, they take their annoyed-with-one-another energy and turn it into chemistry." She shimmied her shoulders, the scenario warming her. "In their relationship, they don't allow one another to get away with anything. There's still annoyance, but now it's lined with affection. They get married and have a kid." She waved a hand down her body in a dramatic fashion. "And they live happily ever after." Warmth turned into an ache, but she kept her smile on her face, not wanting Jacob to see that sadness. "Of course, in this scenario, they didn't die.

They live. They live and raise their child and we all live happily ever after."

He was watching her closely, clearly not fooled by the smile or the false upbeat tempo of her voice.

"It sounds magical," he commented.

She toasted to that, and drained the glass. When she was done, she reached for the bottle, but stopped when she saw it was already empty. Jacob had stopped after his first glass, which meant her three had been . . . generous.

No wonder she was being so dopey. Revealing her deepest fantasies about her parents. Telling him they would be alive in those fantasies. It was easier to keep those things inside. That way, they couldn't make her feel vulnerable. They couldn't make her desperately want his approval, or his comfort, or his hands, stroking her body to make her forget.

"It sounds," he said slowly, "a lot like Gershon and Terry's story."

She blinked. "What?"

"You heard me."

"Yes, I did. I'm wondering if I have wine stuck in my ears—"

"—why would you have—"

"—because I think you said Gershon and Terry, who were the main characters in my very first published book."

He gave her a look. "You don't have wine stuck in your ears."

She took a moment. "You read my book?"

"I'm *reading* your book. I'm at the part where they're fighting about what they want for their futures now that they've graduated. Personally, I think it's more about the fact that Gershon wants Terry to say she wants him, because he needs that security after a childhood with unstable parents. And Terry is too afraid to say it, because if she admits it, she's putting herself at risk for heartbreak, like her father did every time he fell in love with a new woman." He lifted an eyebrow. "Am I right?"

And at that moment, Gaia didn't care about the fact that they were at a restaurant, in public. She didn't care that she wasn't supposed to let herself feel this way about him. The warmth, the happiness, all of it pooled together in her heart, making Jacob seem like someone she could trust. Like someone she *did* trust.

No, at that moment, she only cared about how sexy it was that he'd read her book.

So she got up, walked over and sat on his lap. Then she kissed him.

It wasn't a chaste kiss either. She opened her mouth as soon as she could, eager to taste those sexy words on his tongue. Since, technically, words didn't have a taste, she only tasted him.

It was no consolation prize.

He tasted like the chocolate dessert he'd eaten, like the mint mocktail he'd drunk. He tasted like a hot summer's night, when lust and desire kicked common sense aside and welcomed temptation. His mouth had opened to hers as soon as she'd asked for entrance with her tongue, as if he was as eager to taste her. She hoped he tasted her need. Her fascination with him. How much she wanted him to touch her and kiss her, this man who read her books and told her that love in a world she'd thought terrible was possible.

His hands tightened at her waist. For the first time, she realized he was touching her, heat simmering underneath her skin right at the point of contact. She didn't want to soothe it; she wanted it to blaze. To spread, with his hands, over her stomach, her breasts, down between her thighs. She wanted him to set her on fire by lingering in the heat at her center, torturing her, teasing her with skills she knew he had.

And if he didn't have them, she didn't care. She would teach him what she liked. And she would learn what he liked.

"Gaia," he whispered as he ended the kiss. His voice was low and hoarse, as if he'd been screaming. So was hers when she whispered back. "What?"

"You moaned."

"What?"

"You moaned," he said again, firmer this time. He pressed a kiss to her lips. It was as chaste as the one he then pressed to her forehead.

"I did not moan."

He smirked. "You did, babe. And while I'm glad I have the skills to: one, make you moan; and two, not make you realize you did, I don't think this public place is where we should be doing this."

Primly, though heaven knew it was too late for that, she got up and pretended not to notice that people were staring at her as she took her seat. He was still smirking at her, which was annoying, but the flush on his cheeks told her he hadn't been as cool during their kiss. To be fair, the fact that he'd called her "babe" without realizing it, she was pretty sure, told her that, too.

But since she was denying that that had happened, or that there had been a responding kick somewhere in the vicinity of her heart when she'd heard the word, she would focus on that flush.

"All this because I read your book?"

"Please," she said, rolling her eyes. "You knew what you were doing when you told me you were reading my book."

"Oh?" he asked, sitting back with folded arms. "And what might that be?"

"Seducing me."

He grinned. "It didn't even occur to me."

She narrowed her eyes, then opened her hands on either side of her body and spoke to the sky. "If he's lying, strike him with lightning, that he might learn the value of truth."

"You're *cursing* me?"

"It's not a curse," she said, scoffing. "It was a bargain."

"Yeah? And what are you giving these powers you're bargaining with"—he circled his index finger in the direction of the sky—"in return for striking me with lightning?"

She shrugged. "We're still negotiating."

"Maybe admitting you believe in love?" he asked casually, though his eyes were sober. "The person who wrote the book I'm reading isn't someone who doesn't believe in love."

She lifted her hand to ask for the bill, but she didn't drop eye contact. "Authors who write horrors don't have to believe in murder. Or supernatural beings. Monsters, evil clowns. And if that rule applies to them, I certainly don't have to believe in love."

"Except you do," he said quietly, all casualness disappearing from his voice, his body.

She shook her head. "Why is this so important to you?"

He licked his lips. Just a quick flicker of his tongue that told her of his hesitation.

"If you don't believe in the love, hope, goodness of this world, Gaia, one day, you'll find a reason not to live in this world at all." His gaze was steady on hers. "And what will stop you from doing that when you have the powers to live in a different reality altogether?"

The question lingered in the air as he paid the bill. He fully expected Gaia to offer to pay, or to pay her half, but she was too distracted to react in any way. He was glad for it, though he had thought about how to navigate the situation if it came to that. He wanted her to feel heard and valued and retain her agency, so he would have let her pay for her half if she wanted to. But still, being able to pay made him feel like this was a date after all. Even if he did seem to have broken the woman he was on the date with.

"It's late," she murmured at his side, pulling the jersey she'd brought with her tighter around herself. She was looking out at the night sky, the dark blue of the ocean. They heard it crash more than they saw it, with city lights only shining in the car lot.

He didn't respond, shoving his hands into his pockets to keep from pulling her into his arms. He wanted to feel her warmth pressed into his body, so he could re-create the feeling he'd had in that restaurant when she kissed him. It had surprised him, that kiss, but in the best possible way. He was so damn turned on that he'd had to stop them, especially after that little moan, though it was the last thing he'd wanted to do. And he knew he was fooling himself if he thought only pulling her into his side would re-create what he'd felt at that moment.

"What time is it?"

He took out his phone and checked. "Ten."

"Ten o'clock? In the evening?" She made a noise of disbelief. "I can't remember the last time I've been out this late."

"Yeah?" he asked, lips curving. "When's bedtime at the old age home?"

"Look at you, making age jokes again."

"To be fair, I haven't made age jokes before tonight."

"Honestly, I find it disgusting," she continued, as if he hadn't spoken. "I'm older than you. Surely that deserves respect?"

"It's only two years."

"If someone you cared about told you you would only be seeing them again in two years, would you say 'it's only two years'?"

"That's not the same thing and you know it."

"Do I—"

She was cut off by . . . Well, he supposed by her feet. She stumbled, not by anything perceivable on the ground, but he was moving before he could even make that connection. He didn't catch her in time, because apparently that kind of smoothness was reserved for the romance novels Gaia wrote. Instead, he ended up stumbling with her. They fell to the ground, but he twisted, managing to keep himself from falling on her. And when they landed, she was partially sprawled on the sand and partially sprawled over his upper body.

Which, he considered, was pretty damn smooth.

Maybe the powers that be knew what they were doing.

"Are you okay?"

"I am so sorry," she huffed in response. "I have no idea what happened. One second I was walking, the next, my foot sank into sand that came from nowhere—"

"You're at the beach."

"*Nowhere*," she repeated. "And I fell."

"It's your age," he said solemnly, completely content to remain under her. "I hear falling is a hazard as you get older."

Close to her now, he could see the lines creasing the skin between her eyebrows. Or could he sense it? It was too dark to see such detail, even though his eyes had adjusted. And he could feel that frown, feel the ripple of amusement and annoyance in her body. He knew before she spoke that she would say something sassy, possibly offensive.

He was so aware of her. Of everything about her, from the little movements, the gestures, her features, to what she would say. To the way her body, soft and warm, curled over his chest. Her breasts were pressed against his side, softer, warmer than the rest of her, though that could have been his imagination. His lust.

Except it didn't feel like simple lust anymore. It was layered with emotions he didn't want to examine, or feel, really. He *wanted* simple lust.

And yet he said, "I like that you're older. Fooling around with an older lady has always been a dream of mine."

Her throaty laugh pushed him a little closer to lust. "You have weird dreams, Jake," she replied affectionately.

"Yeah, I do. Last night, I was washing myself down in a client's backyard and somehow my shirt came off. I would do neither if that were really me. It would be unprofessional."

"You would do exactly that if you were trying to impress your client." She set her chin on his chest, looking up at him. "It's a bit foolish, considering she's already seen you naked, but, of course, you're not allowing yourself to think about *why* you're doing it. To you it's because you're hot, and there's a hose, so it's a simple solution. But as I said, you're a fool." There was a pause. "Also, this isn't you. So technically, I can't say that you're foolish, Jacob Scott, although I do think you can be."

He brushed her hair back with a finger. "To be fair, I think I can be foolish, too."

She snorted, leaning into his hand. He didn't think she realized it, but that small thing made the lust layer with emotion again. It didn't matter. The feeling had already woven its web, and he was caught, despite his protests and reason.

"You make me foolish," he said softly. "I entertained erection jokes the first night we met because you make me foolish."

She laughed. "Please. You can do foolish all by yourself."

He smiled and slid his hand over her neck. At the slight pressure, she came willingly, touching her lips to his in a gentle kiss. Fireworks went off—at the contact of their skin, their mouths—around them as he closed his eyes and slipped his tongue into her mouth.

She gave a needy little moan, and the sound traveled down, settling at the hardness between his legs. He moved, rolling her over so they were farther from the path, farther into the darkness. Once he had her beneath him, he touched her waist. A warning that he wanted to touch more, perhaps, but a selfish one. He loved the feel of her skin there. The slope of it that lay between her breasts and her hips, with its plushness, its warmth.

When she didn't protest, he let his hand spread over her stomach. More softness there, though this kind made him want to trace kisses over her skin. To nip and nuzzle. To taste her. It was, after all, the path from her breasts to her center, and he had no doubt he would savor the taste of each of those, too.

Heady at the thought of it, he drew her closer, slipped his hand beneath her top. He wanted to caress her breasts or the heat between her legs, but they were in public. Hell, he probably shouldn't be doing any of what he'd just done to her. He should definitely not explore, now that he could feel her skin.

"We can't do this here."

If disappointment had a sound, it would be that sigh from her lips. "I know. And my place is an hour away."

"Mine"—he winced—"has my father."

"Hmm."

"I could kick him out?"

She laughed now, and gently took his hand out from under her top, sitting up. "Even if you dared to do that, I doubt he would go without a fight."

He sat up, too. "It's almost as if you know my father."

"Almost," she agreed. They were silent for a few minutes. "We should . . . um . . . We should get going."

"Yeah, of course."

He stood, helped her up, and they walked to the car. Only when they reached the car lot with the lights did he see how she looked.

"You look like you've had a tumble in the sand."

She looked down at the sand clinging to her clothing. "So I do." Her gaze moved to him. "And so do you."

He'd figured as much. He shook off as much as he could, wiped off what he couldn't shake, but still, sand remained. On Gaia, too, he saw.

"Sand is like glitter," she said darkly. "It seems perfectly harmless until you find it in a crack or crevice it shouldn't be in."

"Speaking from experience?"

"Obviously."

"Which crevice did you find glitter in?"

She narrowed her eyes at him. "You'll never know."

CHAPTER 20

Gaia invited him inside because it was almost midnight and she needed to ply him with coffee before he drove back home. Except when she put the kettle on, she prepared two cups of tea. And when she turned to face him, she said, "You can stay here tonight."

Pleasure and surprise took over every feature of his face. It didn't help that the result made him look happy. As if she were Father Christmas and she'd granted him all his Christmas wishes.

But he didn't reply the way she expected him to.

"Thanks. I'm exhausted. Do you mind if I take a shower? I'm worried about sand in places it shouldn't be."

"Go ahead."

And he did. He just *went ahead* and *showered*. She had told him he could stay the night after two hot-as-hell kisses, and he'd responded by asking if he could take a shower.

He'd responded by *asking* if he could take a *shower*.

Was that a code of some kind? Did he want her to take a shower with him? If he did, they were going to have a serious talk about how she wasn't the kind of woman who wanted to fool around in the shower. She had her hair to worry about.

She also took up a decent amount of space, as did he, and they would never fit in a shower, let alone move body parts.

Or was she overthinking this? She was overthinking this.

She walked to the bathroom. Stopped. Walked back.

Because what if she wasn't overthinking it? She was willing to sacrifice her hair for the sake of an orgasm, but that was awfully presumptuous. Though she had a solid foundation for the presumption, what with how two kisses, *kisses*, had been so damn hot she'd nearly turned to ash. If his mouth could reach hers and his fingers could move between her legs, she was pretty sure of that orgasm.

She walked to the bathroom again. Stopped.

Was she really going to do this? Was she really going to walk into the bathroom and fool around with Jacob? What if she'd read the signs wrong? Knowing her brain, this was a strong possibility. Also—what had she been thinking, inviting him to sleep over? Was she really going to have sex with him? Was she really going to sleep with him, a man in the real world?

She didn't have time to answer when the door of the bathroom opened. She'd missed the stop of the shower. And she was halfway to the bathroom, which made it seem like she was on her way to the bathroom. And while yes, she was, he absolutely could not know that.

So she ran, *ran*, back to the kitchen, grabbed the kettle and poured the water into the cups, and was stirring when he stopped in front of her.

"Everything okay?" she asked, pretending to be normal instead of the idiot she was.

"Yeah. But I don't suppose you have something more comfortable for me to wear?"

She looked up. Stopped stirring.

"What is this?"

He lifted his eyebrows. "What?"

"This." She gestured to him. "This . . . this nudity?"

"If I recall correctly, you assured me being topless wasn't nudity."

"Except you're not topless." Her voice had stopped pretending to be normal. It was now at a weird, high pitch that she didn't know could come from her. "I can see your legs."

He bit his lip. She narrowed her eyes.

He was enjoying this. Which meant he knew exactly what he had been doing when he'd walked out of the bathroom with only that towel on. He wanted her to react this way.

And, if she was being fair, she understood it.

She made the fictional version of him naked whenever she could. Purposefully, despite what she told him, because she remembered what he looked like when he'd come out of the shower the night she met him. But in the dreams, he didn't have this magnetism. He was playing Chris, after all, and Chris wasn't Jacob. He wasn't the man she'd felt drawn to from the day they met. That lick of desire in her belly, the way her body wanted to cling to his. It proved what she'd been saying to Jacob all along; they weren't the characters they played at night.

For the first time since she said it, she believed it. And understood what Jacob meant when he said that if she didn't like the real world, she would live in her fictional worlds.

That's exactly what she had been doing for the last twelve years.

Damn it. She had been perfectly content ignoring that she was doing that. Or pretending she wasn't. She hadn't known any better, so she *could* be content. But she did know better now. She could see that she was doing it. More disturbingly, she could see that her fictional worlds couldn't compare to the real world. Nothing she had ever dreamt could compare to what she felt with Jacob.

When he touched her, electricity sparked. It had only buzzed in her dreams. His kisses were like sinking into a pit of lava; they were hot pools with her heroes. His laugh was more enjoyable; the anticipation more intense. And the heartbreak, when it eventually came, would be so much worse, too.

She turned around, shutting her eyes. Waves of panic swelled in her chest, thickened her throat, burned her eyes.

"Gaia?" His voice was closer than before, and lacked all of the teasing lilts it had had then, too. "Are you okay?"

"Fine," she managed to say. "I'm fine. I . . ." Pure determination had her clearing her throat, turning around, plastering a smile on her face. "I'll check for you, okay? If I have something, I mean."

She walked past him, ignoring his weak call after her. Instead of going to her bedroom though, she went to the bathroom. It was the only door in her home with a lock. She locked it, and caught the sob before it could come. She closed her eyes, pressed a hand to her chest, and told herself to breathe. But she was breathing in the steam from when Jake had showered, and somehow, despite using her soap, her shampoo, she could still smell him. That unique Jacob scent that made her knees weak and smelled so much better than what she had created for Chris.

She put the water on for the shower in time to hide the sound of her next sob. But she wasn't sure it was a sob. It sounded more like catching the breath she'd lost. She sucked in another, and another, and when it didn't help, she stripped off her clothes and stood under the water.

It gave her something else to think about. She could focus on the water hitting her skin, the steady stream of it beating against her body. The air she let into her lungs was filled with steam, but it didn't add to the panic in the same way it had earlier. Slowly, she reached for her soap, and when that didn't kill her, she began to wash herself. The steady movements and routine of it calmed her mind, had her heart slowing down, and finally, she could think through the last fifteen minutes.

She'd overreacted. It happened occasionally. It had happened many times before. This was her adjusting. She always needed time to adjust. To new foster homes, which had been hard because often, as soon as she adjusted, she wouldn't be there anymore. She had to adjust when she left foster care. She knew she was leaving to a better life, but she was also leaving behind all she knew. It had taken a while for her to get used to her new life, her freedom.

Then it had been university, the flat she rented. The part-time job she had at the bookstore after she sold her first book; when, by her tenth, she could afford to write full-time; when she bought her own place. And through all of those changes, she'd had books. Since she'd left foster care, she had her gift.

It had taken time to figure her gift out, too, but she had. So the way she'd reacted when Jacob suddenly had access to her dreams was normal. Her reaction now? Realizing that this world, with its tragedy and neglect and instability, offered more to her than her fictional worlds? Also normal. Her fictional world had been the most solid thing in her life for twelve years, after all.

She shut the water off, and took a deep breath. Before realizing that Jacob had used the only towel in the bathroom.

"Crap," she muttered, looking around for an alternative. But there was only the clothing she'd taken off. The clothing that still had sand on it, and there was no way she was going to give the sand the opportunity to sneak into one of the many rolls of her body. Not again.

She sighed, got onto the bathroom mat, jumping in small little movements to keep it under her feet. She unlocked the door and peeked out.

"Jake?" she called out.

"Yeah."

Startled, she looked down to where the voice had come from. Jacob was sitting against the wall opposite the bathroom.

"What's going on?" she asked carefully.

"I was waiting for you."

"I can see that. You're on my floor though. Still naked, I'm assuming, under"—she tilted her head—"is that my couch's throw?"

"It is." He winced. "It's longer than the towel. I didn't want to give you an eyeful if you came out. I'm wearing my underwear," he added quickly. "I shook it out very thoroughly outside before I put it on. Your neighbors really don't give a damn about you, do they?" A frown she hadn't noticed until now deepened on his face. "I was a naked man shaking out my underwear on your porch and no one cared."

"As much as I'd like to indulge this conversation, I'm naked, and wet, and I need a towel. Can you get me one?" He didn't reply, only stared at her dumbly, nerves apparently forgotten, and she sighed. "Once you stop malfunctioning over the fact that I said I'm naked and wet."

He blinked. "Sorry, what do you need?"

She huffed out a laugh, which she couldn't quite believe. She'd been hyperventilating only minutes before. "A towel, please. You'll find it in the cupboard of my en suite."

"You have an en suite? Why did you use this one?"

"The en suite only has a bathtub." When he kept frowning, Gaia said, "Jake, the towel."

"Oh, yeah, right."

He stood, and her attention shifted to his chest. It was so strong and firm and *strong*. She wanted to run her hands along the planes of his muscles, press her fingers into the grooves between those planes. When he turned and walked to her bedroom, it confirmed what she'd seen that night he'd stripped at the beach: his back was as promising as his front. More so. What was it about a strong back that turned her on? She didn't know, didn't care, only kept staring at it before he disappeared into her bedroom.

Then she gave herself a pep talk because she was on an emotional roller-coaster and she needed to get her act together.

Get your act together.

That was all the pep she had.

He returned shortly with a towel, which she grabbed with a quick thank-you before shutting the door again. Part of her wanted to lock it, but she knew Jake wouldn't come inside. She wrapped the towel around herself, bracing for his comments about her in a towel when she opened the door. But he wasn't there anymore. Something clanked in the kitchen, and with an odd feeling of relief that he hadn't left, she hurried into her bedroom. She dressed, found a pair of track pants that Seth had given her once when she'd gotten her period at his place. She'd never given it back—figured if he'd given it to her, he probably knew she wouldn't—and with an oversized T-shirt, she went back to the kitchen.

"Will these work?"

He looked up from where he was apparently making them more tea. She blinked, as if her eyes wanted a photograph of a half-naked man making tea in her kitchen. She couldn't blame them.

"Yeah, that's perfect. Are those . . . Why do those look like Seth's pants?"

"They were once Seth's, a long time ago. Now they belong to me."

He smiled, but it wasn't entirely genuine. "I thought people only did that to their boyfriends."

"I've never had a real boyfriend, so I had to settle for best friend."

He nodded and handed her the cup of tea. "I'll go change."

She sipped as she waited for him to come back, the liquid scalding her tongue in the way she'd learned to enjoy. He was back in less time than she thought he needed. The pants fit him fine. The T-shirt, however, hugged his body in a very disturbing way.

"Whose is this?" he asked.

"Mine. Although I'm totally fine if you want to keep it. It looks better on you anyway."

He rolled his eyes, though she swore she could see the tug at his lips.

"Your living room looks somewhat habitable again. Do you want to sit there?"

"Sure."

She followed him to the couch and set her tea down on the table at the same time he set down his. For a long while after, they sat in silence. Eventually, Jacob asked, "Are you okay?"

"I'm fine."

He waited a beat before he replied. "I thought we were past the 'lying to each other about how we are' stage."

They were, even if she didn't want to think about what those stages meant. "I had a moment. In the bathroom."

"Why?"

"Because I wanted to come into the bathroom with you." It wasn't the whole truth, but at least it wasn't a lie. "I was contemplating it, even though I've never . . ."

She caught herself before she said it. But then, she didn't have to say it. He understood. She saw it in the way he widened his eyes.

"Not outside of my dreams, anyway," she added softly. She might as well. She had already exposed herself.

"You've . . . made love in a dream but not in real life?"

There was mainly curiosity in his tone, but she heard the faint judgment. She might have been projecting.

"It's not that I didn't *want* to. I've never had a boyfriend. The men I dated lost interest before we got to a point where I felt comfortable." She shrugged. "Then I lost interest in dating, and that was it."

He took some time to respond. "You write about love and sex though. You experience it in your dreams. It wasn't just 'it.'"

"I thought we already established what I write and what I believe aren't wholly linked?"

"Except you also believe in giving your readers a better world than the one we live in," he said. If she had known he would use her words from the night they met against her, she wouldn't have said them. "Unless," he continued slowly, "you're really giving *yourself* a better world to live in?"

She didn't care for that question. Didn't care for the answer either, which she had only now figured out for herself. But she had questions of her own. Like why he kept bringing up how she lived in her fictional worlds.

She lived in them because she had no choice. It was dictated by an ability she had been *given*. She hadn't asked for it, but she had accepted it. Was it so wrong that she used it to become a better author? That it taught her about what she wanted to experience in the world? That it helped her see what her readers deserved? And what was so wrong with it if she preferred that world?

You don't prefer it when it comes to Jacob.

Ignoring the thought, and his question that led to the thought, she said, "I've written books with sex in them, and I've written books without sex in them. It took both kinds to teach me . . ." She exhaled. "I started reading romance pretty young. When I was eleven or twelve. Long before I should have been. No one stopped me, but no one explained that the romances I was reading . . . they came from a different time. It took me a while to figure out the love I wanted to write and experience didn't look like the love I read in those books."

"But you wanted to experience that love?"

She studied him. Saw that he wasn't trying to trap her into admitting anything. He was genuinely asking. She had no idea why, didn't dare speculate, so she answered him.

"Yes. Of course." She paused. "Maybe it was wrong of me to imply that I didn't believe in love. I do. Of course I do. I believe that love can exist and that it can be beautiful. But I'm not . . . I'm not sure it exists for *me*. And that's okay," she said quickly when he opened his mouth. "I get to experience it in my dreams. It was probably the universe's way of balancing the scales."

"Or you're using it as an excuse not to face the real issues you have."

She shook her head. "You have no idea what you're talking about."

"I do, actually," he said. "I've been doing the same thing with my work."

"That's not the same thing."

"No, it's not," he agreed. "I chose to avoid my issues the good old-fashioned way. You get to use magic. It's infinitely cooler. And infinitely more dangerous." He didn't give her a chance to reply. "You get to use your dreams to ignore the moments you have in the shower. To not interact with people. To stay in your house whenever you feel the need to hide. You get to use them to not face the shit being in the foster system gave you, and you get to call it magic."

She stood. It was abrupt, and it startled him, but it didn't matter. She needed to protect herself from the raw feeling in her body. Standing somehow made her feel like she was doing that.

"Gaia, I'm sorry. I shouldn't have—"

"We should get some sleep."

"We should talk about this."

"I don't know what more I can say."

He looked at her for the longest time. Then he said, "What happens if you don't have your dreams to run away to any-more?"

She walked away without answering.

CHAPTER 21

Jacob stared at his team. He was sure he looked as dumb-founded as each of them.

"They didn't like it," Charity said, stunned. "Not one single idea. Not one of the *ten* ideas we spent *weeks* brainstorming and researching and developing. That's only happened—" She broke off with a furtive glance in Jacob's direction.

He didn't need her to finish that sentence anyway. He knew what she was saying. A client hadn't been this unhappy with their pitch since the last years of his father's management. Sure, there were clients who wanted changes—some comprehensive, some mere suggestions—but rarely did they flat-out refuse any of the pitches. Especially if those ideas had gotten the client to sign with them in the first place.

Frankly, he didn't know what to make of it. But he couldn't tell his staff that.

He mustered as much authority and positivity as he could, and gave them a pep talk. After, when they all left looking less deflated, he couldn't remember a word of what he'd said. He went to his office, started working through his emails. It was important that the company not see him unravel because a client hadn't liked their pitch. For everyone's sake, his own included, he needed to keep working.

He pushed through lunch, kept working until dinner. Hell, he kept working until the last of his people went home. He locked up and grabbed takeout for dinner. It was after nine when he got home.

He found his father waiting for him in the kitchen.

"How did it go?" Keenan asked, eyes sharp despite the fatigue in almost every other part of his body.

"Hi, Dad," Jacob said. "How was my day, you ask? It was pretty crap. The client didn't like any of the pitches. He wants something entirely new."

"What happened?" his father said after a moment.

"What do you mean, what happened?" Jacob asked sourly. "I just told you."

"I meant, why didn't he like it?"

"I don't know."

"You should know. That's the point of running the company. You should know what went wrong and what went right."

"Is that how you ran things, Dad? Because I remember something different." His words were met with silence. He closed his eyes. "I'm sorry, I shouldn't have—"

He broke off when his father pushed out of his chair and walked to his bedroom. The door closed firmly; not quite a slam, but close enough. Jacob exhaled, though it did nothing to calm his anger. At his father for acting like a child. Or a manager, pointing out where *Jacob* had made mistakes. But not like a father. Consoling or comforting. Hell, he would have been happy with supportive.

And while all of that was true, the person he was most angry with was himself.

He hadn't allowed himself to think about it while he was at work. He didn't know where that would lead, and he needed to show his company that he was strong. That he could handle setbacks. That they all could. Especially since they weren't the reason the pitches had failed. He was. If he hadn't been so distracted the past month, the past weeks, he could have done more research. Offered more insight. Or *done* something, damn it, that would have made this day more successful.

It didn't help that the object of his distraction still occupied his mind. He only saw her in dreams since that night he'd slept over. Things had been tense because of their conversation; that hadn't changed the next morning. Or the following week. The book progressed as per usual, but there was a distance he couldn't wrap his head around. Was it because of what he was feeling about the real Gaia? Or was she somehow writing that distance into the book? He didn't know and it pissed him off. How could he argue that the real world was better when even he couldn't distinguish between what was real and what was fiction?

Was it worth it anyway? Their relationship, if they could call it that, came at a cost. His success, his career, his relationship with his father. His sanity, since he was questioning all of it. The echo of it reverberated in his head, mocking him.

Cursing silently, he heated his cold meal, already knowing it would taste like cardboard. He took the food to his bedroom and switched on the television. He chose a rerun of an old show he liked, needing the comfort. For hours, he resisted sleep. But at one in the morning, he couldn't resist anymore.

He faded into the dream.

"You're infuriating!"

"And *you* work for *me*!" Jade snapped. "If I want to choose a new color to paint the walls with, I can choose a new color to paint the walls with."

"Yeah, you can. Hell, choose ten colors. But don't do it when I'm halfway through the project."

"You," Jade snarled, "*work* for me. You do exactly what I want you to do."

"You're a pain in the ass."

"Who's paying you?"

"You know what?" Jacob said, because he'd watched this fight long enough and he was pissed enough to make some changes. "Stuff this. Paint the damn wall yourself."

Jade blinked, and just like that, he saw Gaia.

"What are you doing?" she said.

"I'm leaving."

"Yeah, I can see that. Why?"

"You think you can treat me this way and expect me to stay?"

Her eyes widened. "You don't have to stay. Hell, I've been waiting for you to go the moment you first walked into my life."

They weren't talking as Chris and Jade anymore. He didn't care.

"That's what you don't get. I *have* to stay. I have no choice."

"You always have a choice."

"No, I don't," he disagreed. "I have to see you when I go to bed at night. I think about you during the day. You've forced me to think about how much I hate my job and everything it represents. You draw me away from my job so easily, and then I fail. The company and my father . . . and her. I fail *my mother*." His voice broke at the end, but he ignored it. "I don't have a choice when it comes to you, damn it."

Her lips parted, and suddenly he noticed how pink they were. As if she was wearing makeup. In fact, she looked pretty amazing. Her hair was tied up, pinned to the top of her head with loose tendrils floating around her face. Her white dress was beautiful against her brown skin, a star in a dark night. Thick gold hoops dangled from her ears, matching a simple gold necklace that dipped to the start of her breasts.

"Where are you going?" he asked.

"What?"

"You look nice. You don't look nice to talk to me."

"Oh." She flicked her tongue between her lips. "I have a date."

"What?"

"A date. With a man."

"Another man, you mean."

She made a face. "As opposed to who? You?" She snorted. "You've blamed me for all your problems and you expect me to see you as the man I need to give significance to in my life?"

"*Yes.*"

Jealousy—irrational jealousy—had him stalking forward. How could he feel jealous of a man who didn't exist? How could he hate the idea of Gaia playing the part of her heroine with another man when she was doing just that—playing a part? It wasn't real, none of this was.

Except in that very moment, he realized it didn't matter that it wasn't real. The real and the fictional had blended for them. It had the moment he got sucked into her dreams. If he couldn't tell the difference between what he felt and what Chris felt; between what Jade felt and Gaia felt, it was because he wasn't meant to. There were too many similarities, too much of them here.

Had Gaia planned it that way? He had no idea. But it didn't matter.

"You're ridiculous," she snapped.

"I'm not ridiculous," he retorted. "I'm jealous. Stupidly jealous of you dating some other man."

"You're—"

"It's me," he interrupted, stopping centimeters from her. "I'm meant for you. You're meant for me. That's why I can't detangle you from my life, from my problems."

She blinked rapidly, her mouth opening and closing. "So what?" she asked, but her voice was weak. "Do I let you blame me for every painful thing you're going through?"

"Keep doing what you're doing. Challenge me. Swear at me. Fight with me." His heart was beating so damn fast. "Then kiss me, make love with me. Make me realize why I'm being foolish."

"You really think I'm going to kiss the same mouth that insulted me?" she asked indignantly. But her eyes had already dipped to his lips, and when they lifted, desire had joined the annoyance and frustration.

"Yes," he said, and closed the space between them.

Her hands were already reaching for him when she said, "Damn it," and pulled his head to hers.

Their mouths slammed together without grace, but with much satisfaction. A head-on collision that didn't bring pain or tragedy, but desire and pleasure. Their tongues found one another instantly, tangling, teasing, devouring as he ran his hands down her body, over her butt and discovered her dress was shorter than it looked.

"You were wearing this dress for him?" he asked, pulling back.

Her lipstick smudged, a flush deeper than blush streaking her cheeks, she glared at him. "No, you idiot. I was wearing this dress for you. So you'd think it's for him and go insane with jealousy."

"It worked."

"It did until you stopped kissing me."

Grinning, he kissed her again, his hands below the curve of her butt, content with gripping the flesh there. No—that was a lie. He would never be content with touching only one part of her. Unless it was all he was being offered, which wasn't the case now. He cupped her butt cheeks, groaning at the feel of the soft, rounded flesh. Groaning when squeezing it brought her closer to him, to his hardness, and she let out a throaty moan of approval.

Without thinking about it he lifted her, and her legs wrapped around his waist. It gave him greater access to her heat, and now he was moaning, adjusting her so that that heat was poised over where he needed it to be.

When it didn't work, he walked until he found a wall, and pressed her against it.

"Unfair," she said, words breathless. "You know this is a thing for me."

"Isn't that the point?"

"It is," she replied, with a vaguely impressed look on her face. "I'm insulted you didn't consider that."

"Put your mouth to better use than talking."

Would he die because of this woman? Possibly. But it would be worth it.

He pressed his lips to her neck, to the pulse that was beating erratically. Erotically, since he knew he was the reason for it. She angled for him, giving him greater access to the gloriously smooth skin. He kissed his way down the slope of it, stopping as she caught her breath. He used his tongue, grazed her with his teeth, and he felt her skin turn to gooseflesh. Easing her down against the wall, he waited for her feet to touch the ground before he lifted his hands to her neck.

He wanted to feel the tiny bumps of her skin. Bumps that he'd caused. He wanted to trail his hands over every part of her. He started at her neck, down, over her shoulders. He took the straps of her dress with him, unintentionally, though if he *had* thought about it, it would have been intentional.

Especially if he'd known she was wearing that.

"What is this?"

"A bra."

He traced the curves of plump flesh visible above the material of what she called a bra. His fingers moved lightly, reverently, because her breasts damn well deserved it. He hadn't paid them the proper respect that night at the party, and he would make up for it.

"This isn't a bra."

"It's strapless bra," she corrected, "which I know you know exists."

"It isn't a bra," he said deliberately, lowering to kiss the mounds he'd traced, before lifting his head again, "it's a castle, housing royalty."

Her eyes softened, then crinkled. She let out a hoarse laugh. "You are so corny."

Unoffended, he said, "Yeah, I am. Doesn't make it any less true though."

"They're just breasts."

"Just breasts?" He scoffed. "Please. For one, they look like this." He nodded his head in their direction. Then, because he couldn't resist, he cupped them.

"I'm waiting for two," she said softly, "because I suspect it's going to mean taking the bra off, and I'd really like that."

His eyes fluttered up, and the vulnerability he saw there had him leaning in for another kiss. This one was slow, lazy, as if he had nothing to do but kiss her. As if the most important thing was kissing her. For all intents and purposes, that was true.

With one hand, he reached behind her and slowly, clumsily, undid each hook of her bra. Then he looked at her breasts. Allowed his eyes to feast before his hands did. His mouth.

"Two," he said, touching her right breast, "they make you feel."

He slid a thumb over her nipple. She shivered. The vibration fluttered through him, and his hips ground against hers in response. He lowered his head, drawing the peak into his mouth. She slid a leg around his waist, drawing him closer, hands braced on his shoulders.

"It's not them," she rasped, her hands now moving to his head. "It's you. You make me feel."

He lifted his head at that. If he thought she'd been vulnerable before, when she was asking him to look at her, this meant she was stripped bare. It had nothing to do with her being partially naked in his arms, and everything to do with her confession.

It was a declaration of her feelings. More than he thought she would allow herself to say. But her eyes were wide, open. With desire, and something deeper. Something more meaningful. Trust. He knew she didn't afford it to everyone. Hell, she didn't afford it to *anyone*. Not even to Seth, not entirely. If the words she'd said earlier—*I've been waiting for you to go the moment you first walked into my life*—were any indication, she expected people to leave. And according to her, Seth had. She didn't trust her best friend enough to think that he would come back.

She didn't trust Jake enough to expect him not to leave. Yet here she was. Offering a declaration of her feelings. And he knew it was significant. For her. And for him.

He cupped her face, lay a gentle kiss on her lips. He was about to murmur her name, but he couldn't. And he remembered this was a dream, her book. He knew that the lines were blurred now, with them, between fiction and reality. He could accept it—if she understood that. He didn't think she did. She trusted her fictional worlds more than she did reality. She could be vulnerable here more than she could be in reality.

And he couldn't trust *her* here if that was the case.

"If you really believe that," he said softly, "say it to me."

She frowned. "What do you mean? I said it to you."

"No, you didn't."

He gave her a moment. Lifted the straps of her dress back over her shoulders, not wanting her to feel more exposed once she realized what he meant. It took her a few minutes, but her face tightened, and he took it as a sign.

He stepped back with a curt nod. "I'll wait until you do."

CHAPTER 22

Stupid. Stupid, stupid, stupid. That's what she was. *Stupid.*

Gaia thought it for days after her dream with Jacob. She had fallen for his smooth words and emotions that night. She should have known better. She wrote men who trapped women with smooth words and emotions all the time. Yes, it was usually for their mutual benefit. It added to the happily ever after. Eventually. Which made her even madder that she'd stepped right into Jake's trap.

She knew he was the romance-hero type. From the moment he'd aimed that lazy smile at her, shirtless, at Seth's party. But what had she done? Fallen for his charm. Fallen for his kisses and his tongue grazing her nipples and damn it, even the thought of it turned her on.

The very worst part of it all was that it worked for her book. When she reread the scene that night, the fact that Chris didn't accept Jade's decision to repaint the half-painted house an entirely different color worked. If he walked out, he wouldn't finish the job and have the money to help his mother. Jade would point that out, mention that after sleeping with his last possible client, now this, it seemed like he didn't *want* to help his mother. Was he sabotaging himself? And that would lead to a realization that he didn't want the pressure his mother put on him anymore.

And Jade's irrationality would lead to a confession of her own mother coming to visit, and the pressure she felt there, too. Jade and Chris would bond, and contentious feelings would slide into common ground. Friendship. And from there, it would be easier to show her readers the progression of love.

It worked, damn it. *Damn* it. Damn *him*.

And then there was this.

She looked around at the large conference center. The ceiling was high, the wallpaper on the wall a disturbing gray color, but she barely noticed those things. There were too many other distractions. Tables in rows from one side of the room to the other, interspersed with banners advertising the authors those banners belonged to. There were stacks of books piled on most tables, pens and bookmarks and other swag strewn out next to the books. Brown boxes were visible everywhere. Empty ones because authors had already packed out their books, full ones because they hadn't yet, or were expecting more fans than she could even conceptualize.

Her heart was skipping, but it had been since she'd gotten the reminder from her agent about the event. Everything else had been planned months ago, and a lot had happened in those months. It wasn't that everything that had happened made her forget about the book signing; more that they'd pushed it to the back of her mind, and thus her list of things to worry about. Then her agent had gotten into contact about something innocuous regarding the event, asked if she was okay with everything, and brought it to the top of things to worry about.

The only upside was that she wasn't being consumed with the relationships in her life anymore.

She bit her lip, so hard she thought she might break the skin. She hated this. She'd agreed to do the signing because things like this never happened for her. She was a South African author with an American publisher. Moreover, she was a South African *romance* author with an American publisher. Unless she went to conferences overseas, readers didn't know who she was.

But this event was the first South African romance signing event. It was organized by the local romance writers' organization, which she was a part of, though she wasn't really active. But she'd gotten a special email from the organization's chairperson, telling her about the event for traditionally published and self-published authors, asking her to attend, and she couldn't say no. Literally—she had a hard time saying no. So she contacted her agent about the books, and she contacted the publisher, who enthusiastically agreed that this might up her profile in her home country.

She didn't think it would mean much to her sales. Most of that came from the American market. And Germany, whenever she was translated. But upping her profile anywhere made sense to publishers. She agreed in theory. Until she was standing there, alone, because she had isolated her best friend; she couldn't make the emotional declaration her kind-of boyfriend was asking for; and she had no one else in her life.

She swallowed, and tried not to think about that. Instead, she thought about the younger Gaia. She would have loved to know something like this was happening. Would she have attended then? An event with lots of people, involving speaking to strangers, even if those strangers were the authors she loved. Confessing that she admired them and wanted them to sign her books? Debatable. But she would have *wanted* to attend, which was as important.

Probably.

The doors were opening in fifteen minutes. She took a deep breath. Gave herself a talking to.

You just have to smile and say thank you.

If anyone comes.

Of course someone is going to come.

Of course *sounds overconfident.*

She stopped the pep talk then, because the voices in her brain were arguing with one another and that wasn't helping matters. Least of all her sanity, which she would need if she were trying to convince herself she was steady enough to deal with this.

She went over everything again, trying to distract herself.

Her publisher had had her books delivered two days before, so she was fine where that was concerned. Her most recent two-book series—each stand-alone—were stacked in two piles on the table in front of her. She'd remembered to bring a table-cloth, which was white, making the brown-skinned models on the cover stand out. She took pleasure in it in the same way she did the banner with the cover of the latest book in the series on it. She hadn't seen books like that when she was growing up. Young Gaia damn well would have appreciated that.

She'd had little chocolates, wrapped with the series covers, as her swag, along with some candles that had her name and slogan on them. *Diverse romance with laughter and heart.* She'd come up with it herself, and while it might not have been the most original, she was quite fond of it.

Someone called out that they were ready to open the doors, and she stopped thinking about it. She focused on breathing—*in, out, in, out*—even as people walked in, past her, to other booths. There weren't many of them, to be fair. It was the first event, and she doubted a nonprofit organization could afford a comprehensive marketing campaign. Most people seemed to be going to people they knew, anyway. Family members or friends, she supposed. Which explained why her table was still empty while others weren't.

She pulled out her phone, brought up Jacob's number. Was she feeling insecure enough to call him?

"Hey," a voice said.

A voice *in front of her* said.

She looked up. "Gemma."

Warmth unfurled inside her for no reason other than the fact that someone was there. It had nothing to do with the woman standing in front of her, cute as a button in a green summer dress and sandals, hair long and sleek over her shoulder. Gemma was smiling, brightness exuding from her as if she *were* a summer's day, and it didn't make Gaia happy at all. Not one bit.

"Hey! I heard about this online. Well, when I was looking you up online, there was a social media link that told me about this event and I thought, hey, that sounds like fun! So here I am." She looked around. "This is great."

"Is it?" Gaia asked, not bothering to address anything else Gemma said. She wasn't entirely sure how to respond, and even if she did, they'd already spoken about the stalking thing. She could hardly get uptight about it.

"Yeah! I mean, I've never been to one of these before, but it looks great."

"I've never been to one of these before either, so I can neither confirm nor deny that."

"You haven't?" Gemma blinked. "But you're an author. This is your life."

"No, my life is convincing myself to write when I don't feel like writing, spending a lot of time avoiding writing, and then complaining that I don't have enough time to write when deadlines come along." Gaia grinned at the surprise on Gemma's face. "It's part of the job. I don't make the rules."

"It kind of sounds like you do," Gemma said with a smile. "But that makes it fun."

Before Gaia could say anything else, the large bearded man from the café stopped behind Gemma. He didn't offer her a hello in anything other than the barest of nods, then kept skulking behind Gemma as if he were standing in for her shadow.

"Can you sign my books for me?" Gemma asked, rummaging through her handbag as if he wasn't standing so close to her.

"I bought all of them, as you know, and I started at the beginning, so you can just sign the first."

"Oh, okay. Yeah, of course." She sat down, pulled out her pen. But her eyes kept going to the man. She couldn't ignore it anymore. "Hey—do you know there's a man standing really close behind you?"

Gemma looked behind her, head tilted up as if she knew the exact height of said man.

Interesting.

"Yes." She hesitated for a moment. "This is Levi. He looks big and scary because he is big and scary. He also doesn't believe in smiling, or personal space." She looked back at Gaia with a smile that seemed fake, but Gaia couldn't quite tell. "He's fine though."

"So you keep saying."

"Hmm. Well, will you sign my book?"

Gemma pushed the book forward, but it wasn't the book she'd told Gaia she wanted signed. Quickly, she put it back, went back into her handbag, and pulled out another. Again, the wrong one.

"How many books of mine do you have in there?" Gaia asked, curious.

"Er . . . a few."

Levi snorted. Gemma ignored him. Again, Gaia wondered about their dynamic.

"I'm assuming that your . . . partner's snort is because you have more than a few."

"Oh, no, he's being annoying." Gemma waved a hand. "Signing this one would be really great."

She slammed a book on the table, harder than either of them expected, and they both jumped.

"I'm sorry! I—"

"Gemma," Gaia said, staring at the book. "This still isn't the right book."

"Right. Okay, hang on."

"I'll sign them all," she said with a laugh. "Give them all to me and I'll sign them."

"Yeah?" Gemma gave her such a happy smile Gaia could swear her teeth asked her why she never smiled like that. "Thank you!"

Gemma looked at Levi, squealed, adding a little bop of her shoulders to the squeal, and his lips curved. It wasn't quite a smile, but it was as close to one as Gaia had seen on him. Did it hurt him, physically, to show his teeth? And how could he resist Gemma when she was such a breath of fresh air? In a world that pretty much sucked all around, Gemma didn't seem to be affected by it. And she shared that unaffectedness with everyone, including surly men and strange—and possibly surly—women.

"Why don't you go get some coffee or something?" Gaia asked, watching as Gemma stacked the books on top of one another in piles of five. There would be six piles by the end, and it impressed Gaia that Gemma had managed to fit all of that in one purse. Vaguely, she realized she should be impressed that she'd written all those books, too.

What a strange thought.

"It's going to take some time to get through these," she continued, "and there's a coffee store on the floor beneath this one."

"I thought— Yeah, sure." Gemma looked oddly disappointed. "Do you want anything?"

"Um." It took her a second to get over the surprise. "No, thank you. I don't want to put you out."

"You wouldn't be," Gemma assured her. "Let me do this for you. Please."

It came out like a plea, and she couldn't exactly say no to that. Though she didn't understand Gemma's motivations at all. Why would it be important to buy her a coffee?

"A red cappuccino, please." She reached down for her handbag. "I can give you enough cash for—"

"Oh, no, please don't. I have enough." Gemma hooked her

arm into Levi's. "Come on, darling," she all but purred, "let's go get some coffee."

Gaia could swear she was winding him up, but Levi gave no indication of it. Just let Gemma drag him down the aisle to where the doors were.

"So weird," she muttered, watching them, but shook her head and started signing.

She was so engrossed by the task, writing short notes in each book, which she thought Gemma might enjoy, that she didn't notice anyone was in front of her until someone cleared their throat. She looked up.

Her eyes widened as she took in the short line.

"This is really big of you."

"Shut up."

Jacob smirked at that reply, but decided shutting his mouth was the best option. He wouldn't admit it to his brother, but he was glad Seth had invited him over. Because, of course, Seth didn't want to come to the house when their father was there. Probably a good thing, since he would have questions about the fact that Jacob and Keenan weren't talking.

Jacob was finding it a little hard to talk to his father after that dream with Gaia. He'd said things that night he couldn't forget—and he'd tried to—and it played in his mind over and over again.

Did he really hate his job? Was he tired of his relationship with his family? What would happen if he tapped out of both? He was too afraid to answer the questions, so he pretended that they didn't exist. Except they wouldn't be ignored, and kept popping into his mind at the oddest times. He had no one to speak to about it. The only person he could speak to about it was only contacting him through dreams, which had gone on fairly uneventfully since the last one where he'd had her up against the wall.

His father must have sensed he was still in a mood because

he didn't try to talk to him either. Of course, it was entirely possible that Keenan was still annoyed with Jacob for snapping at him. Possible, and likely. And since Jacob had no desire to smooth things over as he usually did, they weren't communicating at all.

He had little to no desire to explain that to Seth either.

When he got to Seth's place though, his brother asked him to go with him to a book signing. Gaia's book signing. Which was weird, because Gaia wasn't the kind of author to do signings. But apparently, Gaia had told Seth about it months ago, begged him to go with her, and he'd put it in his calendar.

"I don't know if she still wants me there," Seth said tersely, "but I know she's probably nervous as hell. I figure if I take you with me, it'll be a sort of olive branch."

"You want to use me as an olive branch?"

"Yes." Seth narrowed his eyes. "Don't make this a thing."

"This is a pleasant change of pace," he replied, ignoring Seth's warning.

"What part of 'don't make this a thing' do you not understand?"

Jacob lifted his hands. "Fine. I'll go with you."

"That's oddly less reassuring."

He shrugged, and kept his opinion to himself all the way to the venue.

The truth was, he was glad to have a reason to see Gaia again. He'd had to keep himself from driving to her house and finishing what they started in that dream. But he needed her to come to him. It hurt him more than he liked that she hadn't, but it had only been a few days. She needed time to adjust. He understood that. Only, understanding didn't make something any easier to handle.

He wanted Gaia, needed her, and she didn't quite feel the same way.

Wasn't that a hell of a thing?

The venue wasn't very busy when they arrived, though Seth explained it wouldn't be.

"She told me it was the first romance-author signing in Cape Town, and not to expect much." Seth smiled fondly. "I told her I never expect much when it comes to her."

"Exactly as supportive as *I* expected you to be," Jacob commented.

Seth sighed. "No one's giving me friend-of-the-year prizes. I get it."

"You do?"

"Yeah, asshole," Seth said without heat. "Why the hell do you think I'm bringing you? To make amends for being a dick."

Jacob was actually proud of his brother for coming to that conclusion. He strongly suspected Seth had had help from Lizzy, but he wasn't going to mess with Seth's moment of growth.

Or maybe he was.

"Gonna be hard for her to forgive you if you keep acting like a dick."

"I just said—"

He stopped when Jacob took his arm, drawing him to the side, and said, "Look, I realize this is . . . a kind of role reversal. Me, warning you about Gaia. Or bringing up anything like this at all, I guess." He didn't dwell on it. "But Gaia and I . . . We have something, Seth."

Seth's expression hardened, but he only said, "What are you saying?"

"I'm saying . . . I'm saying don't start acting like a dick again. Don't hurt her"—he lingered, despite knowing it was cruel—"again."

Seth swore. A few women looked over at them, their faces offended.

"My initial reaction," Seth said slowly, ignoring them, "is to ask you why, out of every woman in the world, you would choose Gaia. But since I already had that reaction, and it put me in a situation where I haven't spoken to my best friend of the last twelve years in over a month, I'm going to go with my second reaction." His jaw clenched. "You better know what you're doing. If you hurt her, I'll hurt you."

"Now, now," Jacob said, exceedingly pleasant, "if I took that approach with you, you'd be somewhere in a ditch."

"You're an asshole."

"Yeah, but I'm not wrong."

Seth glowered, but after a moment, he deflated, as if the anger slipped out with his sigh. "I don't like this dynamic."

Jacob laughed. "I do. If I'd known this is what being a self-righteous prick is like, I would have done it ages ago." Seth rolled his eyes, but he didn't disagree. Jacob tried not to be too satisfied about it. Instead, he focused on Seth's other words. "I appreciate that. The support for our relationship, I guess. Whatever. Just . . . thank you."

Seth studied him. "I'm not going to say it's a pleasure. It wasn't."

Jacob laughed again. "Don't worry about it. I think swallowing your pride hurt you enough today. That's good enough for me."

Seth grunted, and they went back to looking for Gaia. They found her a few minutes later, toward the end of the first row of authors. She was talking to three girls, who stood in front of the table, crowding it. She laughed with them, smiled, but even from where Jacob was, he could see she wasn't comfortable. When the girls left, another woman stepped forward, then another. There had been a line, he realized, of people trying to get her autograph. Not a long line—there weren't any people there now—but enough that he paused. Touched Seth's elbow so they could watch.

He had no idea why he'd done it beyond that feeling inside him. Instinct, perhaps. But he knew she would need a minute. When the last person left her, Gaia sagged. Not enough to make her look unapproachable; but enough for anyone who knew her to want to offer comfort.

They watched as she took a deep breath, then another, and another, before she dipped her head in a nod that he thought was meant for herself.

"She does this," Seth murmured. "With people. She doesn't really talk to them. And when she does . . ." He didn't finish the sentence, the evidence of what she did right in front of them. "It's why I wanted her to come to the party. I thought if it was a trusted environment, she would engage and it wouldn't make her feel this way."

"It's not the environment," Jacob replied. "It's people. She struggles because she doesn't trust them."

Seth's abrupt turn toward Jacob was the only indication of his surprise. "She told you that?"

"Pretty much." He paused. "Although she didn't have to."

Seth didn't reply. They waited a few more beats, then slowly walked toward Gaia's table.

Doubt weighed down Jacob's every step. Was he right to accompany Seth, or was he being selfish? He wanted to see her so badly, but he also didn't want to pressure her. It was worse that he was doing it here, in a space she would already feel pressured in.

On the other hand, he wanted to support her. If this was hard for her, and it clearly was, he wanted her to know he was there. Through the easy and tough stuff, he wasn't going anywhere. He needed her to know he was there because he needed her to trust him. And the people around her. The world.

No, that was pushing it. So maybe just the people who cared about her.

With an unsteady breath, he kept walking.

She didn't notice them, her head dipped in copies of books she was signing. She'd put a book on the second-to-last pile when she glanced up. She reached for the first book of the last pile, then looked up again. Her gaze narrowed on him and Seth. Seth sucked in his breath while Jacob released his.

Seth didn't look at him as he said, "She's only a person. We shouldn't be this afraid of her."

"Yeah, but she's our person. In different ways," he clarified, "but still ours. Fear's a reasonable response."

He could almost hear Seth roll his eyes. "We're bonding over my best friend. Delightful."

"It's been a while since we bonded over anything," Jacob said quietly, his heart skipping at those words. "I wouldn't call it delightful, but it isn't the worst thing in the world."

Before either of them could say anything else, Gaia tilted her head. "Are you two going to talk to me, or just stare?"

It was the fire she used on them in private. An indication of a level of trust Jacob was eager to accept. He smiled, but let Seth take the lead. He would have his chance after all this, he knew with certainty.

His brother walked forward, until he stood in front of the table. Jacob hung back.

"Hey," Seth started. "I thought . . . Well, I remembered . . . today."

It bordered on pathetic, but Jacob understood. It must have been hard for Seth, this awkwardness. He was usually so easy. Around people, new situations.

It was likely why he didn't completely understand Gaia. How could someone with such ease understand the anxieties of someone who didn't trust people? How could someone who was so sure of their place in the world understand the constant fear, the constant uncertainty of someone who worried their place would be snatched away? Who expected people to hurt them?

But Jacob could see how it affected Gaia. With each inter-action, in reality and dreams, he understood her more. He saw her more, too. A fact she didn't like because he saw what she was avoiding. Those "moments" she kept having, the way she struggled with people and the world . . . There was something deeper there.

She had thought he couldn't hear her sobs over the sound of running water, through the bathroom door, that night he'd stayed over, but he could. And he was helpless, so helpless, to do anything to make her feel better.

Yes, her issues were deeper, he thought again. But she didn't want to face it, though he knew she was aware of it. How could she not be? She tried so damn hard to understand what her readers needed. She cared about social issues, wrote stories about love that was nuanced and representative. He had finished her first book. It blew him away. And now, starting her second, he could see the care. The intention.

She was aware of more things than he even thought about. She must be aware of mental health. And if she wasn't, it must have been purposeful. Avoidance, as he'd thought. Or perhaps denial.

He wasn't one to judge since he'd spent most of his adulthood doing the same. He was still doing it, even though now, he knew he was unhappy. With his family and his job. And to change things, he would have to disrupt the life he knew. It might mean he no longer had *any* family or job; not just ones that made him unhappy. And would he be going against his mother's wishes if he did? Would his family break up and the company decline? Was his happiness worth even considering it?

"You came," Gaia said, breaking into his thoughts. The fact that he'd thought so much—too much—without that interruption told him how long it had taken her to respond to Seth.

Seth shrugged.

"That's it?" Jacob muttered, hoping only Seth could hear but doubting it.

Gaia merely lifted her eyebrows at him and turned to look at Seth. "Yes, Seth. Is that it?"

Seth exhaled roughly. "Is this how this is going to be? You two ganging up on me?" Jacob opened his mouth to caution his brother, but Seth continued before he had a chance. "That wasn't what I meant to say." Pause. "Would you buy it was a joke? A fun moment of banter?"

"No," Gaia and Jacob said at the same time.

"Fine." He exhaled again. "We need to talk. Properly. I need to . . . to apologize."

Gaia studied him. "Yeah, you do. And so do I." She silenced Jacob's protest with a look. "It's enough that you're here, Seth," she added softly. "It's enough for now."

They shared a look Jacob felt embarrassed seeing, full of relief and intimacy. The embarrassment came at the ripple of jealousy witnessing the look brought. He didn't like it, but it did make him wonder if Seth's anger at seeing him and Gaia together at the party had come from something similar. Gaia was *his* friend, and Jacob had taken that from him.

But that sounded stupid, and quickly put his own jealousy into perspective. Human beings didn't have a finite amount of any feeling. Simply because she shared something special with Seth didn't mean what she and Jacob shared wasn't special.

He would have to tell Seth that.

Before anyone else could speak, a couple joined them, the woman plopping a takeaway coffee cup right in front of Gaia.

"Sorry it took so long, but Levi said you would probably need time to sign the books. I told him it was just a signature. Then we argued about that for a while and then we came here." The woman grinned, then turned to Jacob and Seth. "Oh, it's you. Nice to see you again."

It took Jacob a second to realize she was addressing him. When he did, he remembered that she had been the one donating the books that night at the bookstore. Which also meant she was the one who'd admitted to stalking Gaia.

His gaze slipped to the man behind her. Tall, bulky, brooding, her companion looked much more menacing than she did. They were in a relationship, if Jacob recalled accurately what Gaia had told him. He didn't trust the man. There was something . . . off about him. This woman could easily be a distraction for Gaia, and when she least expected it, the man would strike.

"Who are you?" Jacob asked him, his voice lower than he intended.

He only got an unaffected stare in return. The woman spoke up.

"Oh, we haven't really introduced ourselves, have we? I'm Gemma, this is Levi. We're . . . a thing," she said with a wave of her hand. Jacob swore he saw Levi's eyes sparkle at that. But sparkling wasn't exactly the word Jacob would use to describe Levi or anything about him. He dismissed it. "And you are . . . ?" Gemma asked.

"Jacob," he said when Gemma prompted him. "And this is my brother, Seth. We're friends of Gaia's."

"Yeah?" Gemma smiled. If Levi was using her to distract Gaia, he was a smart man. If the "joy" emotion could be contained in a person, she would be it. "That's awesome."

"I must have missed how you two know Gaia," Seth said smoothly.

"Oh." Gemma's eyes widened, and she turned to Gaia, who was watching everything in silence. "I'm a fan. Of Gaia's." She pointed to the stacks of books in front of Gaia. "These are mine. Because I'm a fan."

Jacob's eyes didn't leave Gaia's face. Her expression was closed, but her eyes . . . said something. He wasn't quite sure what, and he wished they were alone so he could ask. He would run a finger down her face as she told him, then over that collarbone. It was exposed under the loose jersey she wore over a dress he was sure was strapless. It was simple and black, that dress, and ran down to her ankles, which he could see under the table. The jersey was open at the front, in a muted pink that matched the necklace and earrings Gaia wore. Her hair was spiraling in curls around her face, unadorned with makeup, highlighting every perfection and flaw of her face.

Damn it, she was beautiful. Breathtaking. And he wanted her to be his so much he was imagining seducing her while she told him all her secrets.

Heaven help him.

"I haven't got to the last pile yet," Gaia said slowly, "but I'll do them now and you can get going if you want."

Gemma blinked. Again, and again, as if Gaia's perfectly reasonable response had upset her. Levi stepped closer to her, and Gemma leaned back into his space, though Jacob didn't think either of them realized it.

He met Gaia's eyes.

She tilted her head, as if to say, *This is weird, right?*

He nodded.

Her lips curved.

So did his.

And for a few seconds, they were half smiling at one another.

Seth nudged him in the ribs. Jacob pulled his gaze from Gaia's, but didn't look at his brother. Instead, he waited to see how Gaia would play it.

"Yes, of course. We'll leave." Gemma smiled again, though it was decidedly dimmed. "Because I'm just a fan, and this is a signing, and there are other people here you need to talk to."

Levi's expression turned pained, but he didn't say anything.

"Yeah, lots of people. All of them standing in line for me, as you can see."

There was no one in line for her except them, and Gaia's expression was soft as she looked at Gemma. It was strange seeing it, knowing that they'd only met a few times. But there was a connection there, and Gaia's sarcastic tone—her second nature—proved it.

"You can stay if you want," Gaia said. "All of you"—her expression became . . . well, he wasn't quite sure what to call it, but it was both precious and alarming—"um . . . all of you can stay."

Including him and Seth.

Before Seth could respond though, Jacob said, "You have a ride home?"

She blinked. "Yeah. I have my car here."

"Cool. We'll see you some other time."

Seth looked at him. Jacob gave him a warning look. Seth sighed.

"If you have company already, we don't need to be here," Seth said.

Blunt with the people who he cared about, as usual, his brother.

But Gaia merely said, "Thank you for coming."

Seth nodded, Jacob nodded, then they were walking to the door.

"That was . . . weird."

"Yeah, it was," Jacob agreed.

"Why the hell would you leave her alone with those weirdos?"

"We're not going to. We'll give them space, but we'll be downstairs, having lunch, drinking coffee, until the day ends, and we'll make sure she gets to her car okay."

Seth gave him a sly look. "I like the way you think."

"So does she."

Seth snorted. They walked into the elevator. As the doors closed, Seth said, "Is it me, or do they kind of look alike?"

Jacob considered. "No," he said slowly. "It's not you."

CHAPTER 23

Gaia knew she had shadows, but honestly, she didn't mind it. They kept their distance, thinking themselves covert, she was sure. She would make fun of them later. Right now, she was tired. All peopled out, and a little overwhelmed by the day, if she was honest.

She hadn't expected anyone to come. Gemma had been a nice surprise. Their conversation after Seth and Jacob had left had been nice, too. Gemma seemed to be a genuine, if somewhat strange, fan. Her boyfriend was less pleasant, but he supported Gemma, in slow, subtle ways. Gaia couldn't begrudge Gemma that, despite the unconventionality of their relationship. She'd had other fans, too, throughout the day. Not that many, though she hadn't expected it, knowing where her market was. But it was nice to speak to readers, no matter how few, and the cherry on top was Jacob and Seth. Her shadows. Two men who frustrated her, but had wiggled their way deep into her heart.

She didn't realize Seth would remember the event. They'd had the conversation months ago. He'd told her he was proud of her for doing something outside her comfort zone and promised to be there. Despite everything that happened between them, he'd been there.

It choked her up. Reminded her of that moment when Gemma, Seth, and Jacob—and Levi, if she counted him— stood in front of her and she invited them to stay. She had never thought she would have that kind of support. She still couldn't quite believe it. Almost as much as she couldn't believe that Jacob and Seth had come together.

Tears pricked at her eyes. She swallowed. Turned the radio up. Tried to sing along. But it didn't help. She still felt emotional, the idea of people pitching in for her, for *her*, clawing at her heart, her tear ducts, demanding she cry.

She bit her lip hard, hoping the pain would keep that from happening. It didn't. She needed a better distraction. She needed *not* to remember how she felt when she saw those four faces together. She was afraid she would begin to trust it.

So, distraction.

She came up with the plan fairly quickly, which might have explained its idiocy. It made her smile though. Turned her fatigue into a giddiness that was probably *because* of the fatigue. And still, she pulled her car into the lot of a sex shop close to her house.

She'd never actually been inside. She would never risk the embarrassment of seeing someone she knew.

There were many problems with that logic. One was that she shouldn't be embarrassed to go into a sex shop. Another was that she didn't actually know anyone. Besides the two people she had purposefully led there—which, now that she thought about it, pointed out another logical flaw—there was no one she could possibly bump into.

Eh—she was in it now. She might as well see it through.

She waited for their car to round the corner before getting out. She pretended not to notice them as she walked through the doors. She waited, but they didn't follow her in. Minutes passed as she stood near the doorway, examining the animal masks they had in a glass cabinet.

Right, she thought after a while. They weren't coming in. Good to know her plan had worked so perfectly.

"May I help you?"

She jumped. Whirled around. There was a cute blond girl looking at her. Her eyes were blue, skin pale, makeup perfectly done, and she looked all of thirteen. Which probably wasn't accurate. They don't let thirteen-year-olds work in sex shops.

"No. No, thank you. I'm only . . . looking."

"Of course." The woman smiled. So pleasantly, so innocently, that Gaia had to stomp down the urge to carry her out of the shop. "Shout if you need anything." She paused. "We're having a sale on vibrators, by the way. Twenty percent off, plus a Not Your Mama's lube for free."

"Not Your Mama's," Gaia repeated. "That's the name of the lube? Or is it not the kind of lube mothers use?"

The smile turned more genuine. "If it was the latter, it would be incorrect. I believe it's the preferred brand my mother uses."

"Oh?" Okay, they were sharing personal anecdotes about lube now. "Well, it must work then. If she's, um, using it."

"I think so. Do you want me to ask her? She's right upstairs. This is a family business."

What would it be like to be so open about sex with a parent? With anyone, really. Or were people usually this open? Was she the problem?

"No, no. No, you don't have to do that."

"Are you sure?"

"Very. But thank you so much for offering. It's the extra mile that makes this place so popular."

As if proving it, three men walked into the store. They went in separate directions almost immediately, keeping their heads down, and Gaia didn't keep watching them to allow them their privacy.

"No problem. Honestly, it's rare to have this long a conversation with a client anyway. Most of the people who come here want to be left alone to do their thing." She smiled at Gaia again. "Shout if you need me." With a quick wave, she walked back to the counter.

Gaia nearly sagged with relief—maybe she *was* the problem—before she realized she would be leaning against the animal mask cabinet if she did. She swallowed and walked as discreetly as possible deeper into the store. It was a labyrinth dedicated to sexual pleasure. Objects she'd had no idea existed were encased in glass cabinets; costumes she had not considered erotic—but clearly were in the proper context—hung from the walls; and somehow, despite the dawn of the internet, there were hundreds of DVDs.

Some were for sale, others to rent, and she hoped for everyone's sake that the rental copies were handled properly.

Her characters never used sex toys in her sex scenes. She didn't have anything against them, but she didn't have any experience with them. Of course, she could have had her characters experiment with toys. She'd had them do so with sex, which she'd then experienced in her dreams. If she did so with sex toys, she'd have experienced that in her dreams, too. But experiencing things—sex—in dreams wasn't as simple as it once had been. Now, she could only think that sex toys required trust. More strongly than with vanilla sex—at least she had the lingo down—though again, that perception might have been specific to her.

It *was* specific to her. And she only felt it because she had ripped off the Band-Aid with regular sex. Well, not ripped. More slowly peeled off the Band-Aid, testing whether it would hurt. Then, it had come down to trust, too. Even though she only played the heroine of her books in her dreams, she had had to trust her heroes before she felt comfortable enough to handle sex with them. Anything new in that regard would require her to trust them even more, hence the fact that sex toys hadn't occurred to her.

Because even in her dreams, in the world she created, she held back, apparently.

Huh.

She was too tired to think about the implications of it. In fact, her need for distraction had drained her in a way she hadn't expected. She wanted to leave, but she felt as if she would be disappointing the blonde if she didn't buy anything. So she grabbed a vibrator—good heavens—and accepted the free lube. Then she put the bag in her handbag and walked out.

Right into her two men.

"What were you doing in there?" Seth asked. "You took forever."

She pursed her lips. "It's none of your concern."

"You went there while we were following you," Seth countered. "Obviously, it's our concern."

"You're going to need to watch that level of entitlement," she warned. "It's not a good look. Also, how was I supposed to know you were following me?"

"We weren't being particularly discreet about it."

She shrugged. "There was a lot to consider inside."

"Yeah?" Jacob said, speaking for the first time.

The word was imbued with a world of emotion. Amusement, interest, lust. She looked at him, standing there in his black T-shirt and easy smile, and her stomach flipped. Then something a little lower flipped and asked her why the hell she wasn't sleeping with him.

"Yeah," Gaia confirmed with a small smile.

"Oh, this is torture," Seth groaned.

"Why don't you go home, Seth?" Jacob suggested, still looking at Gaia. "I'll get a lift home with Gaia."

Seth didn't reply for a moment. "Your car's at my place."

"I'll take him to get it tomorrow," Gaia said brightly, dragging her eyes from Jacob. "Would that work?"

Seth opened his mouth and closed it again, countless times.

With each, Gaia had to try harder not to smile. Especially when Seth shook his shoulders, his head, as if trying to get the idea of them going to her place to play with sex toys out of his head.

"Fine," he bit out. "It's fine."

Gaia didn't bother to hide her smile. She leaned forward and brushed a kiss on Seth's cheek. "That's very big of you. Well done."

Seth took in her expression, Jacob's, and his shoulders sagged. "You were messing with me."

"Yeah," she said, at the same time Jacob said, "No."

"Not funny." But Seth smiled. "Okay, you've proved your point. Let's go home, Jake."

"Oh, no, Jake's still coming with me," Gaia said. "That part was true."

Seth stared. "What part was you messing with me then?"

She angled her head. Looked at Jake. Shrugged. "Not sure." She laughed when Seth swore. "It'll all be perfectly above-board," she told Seth. "I promise."

But she squeezed her handbag under her arm, letting the bag the vibrator was in rustle. And Jacob said, "Don't make promises you can't keep."

Seth swore again; this time, it was directed at both of them.

She laughed again, gave him another kiss, and said, "I didn't think you would come today. But you did and . . . I have . . . feelings about that."

"Sure, sure," he grumbled, but he squeezed her hand. And watched them as they went to her car, waving them off.

CHAPTER 24

Seth waved at them. His brother had actually *waved* at them as they drove off together, after strongly implying they were going to have sex. With toys. Jacob was fairly certain he was malfunctioning at the thought. He could only imagine how Seth was feeling.

Probably not as excited as Jacob.

Gaia said nothing as she drove them back to her house. Nothing about going to that sex shop, which he was fairly certain had been to wind them up, and nothing about insisting he come home with her. He had been playing around when he'd suggested it, but then she'd said she wanted him to come and he'd felt . . . Well, it wasn't only the sex toy that was making him feel as if he were malfunctioning.

When they got to her house, she opened the door and let him in, before locking it. He waited for her to give any indication of what she expected him to do, but she only leaned against the door, eyeing him tiredly.

"That was some day," she said in a voice that reflected her expression.

"I can imagine." He stepped forward. "I didn't think I'd ever see you at a signing." He paused. "Doesn't seem like your kind of thing."

"It isn't. Hence the fact that my feet don't really feel like they can move from this spot." As if proving it, she sagged down against the door until her butt hit the ground. "This is fine, right? You don't mind talking like this?"

He studied her, and realized she was in no state to talk. He didn't respond, instead walking into her bedroom, into the bathroom she'd said only had a bathtub, and began to run the water. She had a trove of bath things in one corner. He read the labels, put some of those things into the water , and tested the temperature. Hot, but not scalding. Satisfied, he went back to the door. Her eyes were closed, and she looked so helpless, so fatigued, that his heart turned in his chest. Gently, he lowered and picked her up. Her eyes instantly opened, her body tensing, until she saw it was him and sagged into his chest. Damn if that didn't make his heart turn, too.

"I was only resting my eyes," she said to him.

"I know," he replied, kissing her head. He couldn't resist.

"I don't ever go to bed this early."

He chuckled. "Liar."

A faint vibration against his body told him she was laughing, too. "Fine. I do, if the occasion calls for it."

"Is the occasion every night?"

She gave a delicate little snort. "I do not sleep at seven p.m. every night."

"It's eight."

"Is it?" There was a pause. "Well, eight's an entirely different story."

I adore you.

The words were on the tip of his tongue, demanding he say them. But it wouldn't be fair. She was vulnerable, tired. If he said it, her defenses would come back up, and she wouldn't feel safe. And he wanted that for her. He wanted her to feel safe and respected and cared for. *He* wanted to do that for her. Even though it threatened his own safety. Which, to be fair, had been an illusion for the longest time. He had convinced himself he was content with his life. He wasn't. He wanted more. He wanted her.

He was a goner and there was nothing he could do about it.

"I drew you a bath," he said, setting her on her feet. He didn't move until she was steady. Even then.

"That's sweet." She offered him a sweet smile of her own. "Are you going to bathe me?"

Fire—hot because it was always simmering in his veins when he was with her—flared. "I don't think that would be a good idea."

"Probably not," she agreed. But she shrugged off the jersey from her shoulders, revealing the smooth skin beneath it.

The dress was indeed strapless, held up by firm breasts that he'd had in his mouth in both real and fictional worlds. His mouth watered, as if remembering their taste, but he clung to every inch of his control. There was no benefit in indulging this.

Well, there would be *some* benefit. But it would be temporary. Short term. He needed to focus on the long term.

Yes, that was a good reason not to think about her breasts.

"You know," she said, her voice husky, "that sex shop made me realize I haven't written a sex scene in my book yet." She took off her necklace, her earrings, and set them on the windowsill behind her. "I know it makes me a fool. I mean, look at you. You deserve sex. I deserve sex with you." She leaned down to take off her shoes, throwing them to the side. "And I know you know what you're doing. I'm trying not to think too hard about how"—she gave him a lazy smile—"but I should be benefiting from this. From you."

He swallowed. "I don't believe I've ever said anything to deny that."

She turned her back to him. "Would you undo my zip, please?"

He hadn't realized a simple request could kill him. He hadn't thought a back could kill him. Yet here he was, being asked to undo a zipper, staring at her back, and he thought he might be dead.

Her shoulders sloped gracefully, her back curved elegantly, and they both called for him to kiss their skin. Stepping closer, he pressed his lips to the nape of her neck, to the place before her right shoulder began, and another, to the area above her collarbone. He couldn't resist the temptation, and when she made a breathy sound, arching her neck for him, he kissed along the same trail. This time, he lingered, slipped his tongue over each place, tasting her skin.

"This," she said softly. "There should be more of this."

But there hadn't been, he thought, and knew she had a reason for it. He undid the zip and turned around before he could see any more.

"You're unzipped. I'm . . . I'm going to give you some privacy."

"Stay," came the quiet command.

He was helpless not to obey. Instead, he closed his eyes. Prayed for strength. Her dress rustled against the floor, there was a snapping sound that made him vaguely concerned, before the water lapped and she let out a groan.

"I'm decent," she said after a few minutes. "There are enough bubbles here that you won't see anything."

He turned. Told himself he was a fool to believe bubbles could protect him from her. Because her sitting in a bathtub, bubbles covering everything beneath the water's surface, was still torturously sensual. For him; with her. It felt as if she had been designed to turn him on. Everything she did, everything she was, was a constant test of his self-control.

He sighed.

She gave him a look. "What's that for?"

"You," he said without a beat.

"I didn't do anything."

"Beyond this, you mean." He gestured toward her in the bathtub.

She studied him from hooded eyes, and nodded to the door. "You're free to go." She waited, as if daring him to. When he didn't move, she continued, "There's a chair in the kitchen if you'd like to stay."

He snorted, but kept standing. She pursed her lips at the strange tension jumping between them. A mixture of the tension of things unsaid, things undone, and everything that had been said and done. He watched her as she watched him. As he felt her eyes see everything he didn't want her to.

That he was unhappy with his life.

That he was too happy around her.

That he adored her. Maybe more.

Then she kicked, splashing water on him and all over the floor. Mostly the floor.

He quirked a brow. "Not your best moment."

"You're probably right," she said. "But if I did what I wanted to do, which is get out of this tub and use you as my towel, you'd sigh at me again, and I don't think I can bear it."

"Instead, you're just going to short-circuit my brain by putting that image into it?"

She frowned. "What do you— Oh. I didn't mean it that way. I meant . . . You know what? Doesn't matter. Your way sounds more interesting."

He didn't reply for a moment. "It would be." He paused. "Why are you avoiding it?"

Any playfulness that might have been in the air got sucked into the tension still between them. She lowered into the water until her chin was submerged. Straightened again, the water lapping against the skin above her breasts. Another temptation he had to resist. He kept his eyes on her face.

"I'm scared."

He hadn't expected the candid answer.

"You know that already," she said, half smiling, though her

tone was almost sad. "You know I'm afraid of the world." There was a long silence. "But I'm afraid of . . . of you. Of this, us." Another pause. "I feel things I've never felt before. Not even in my books." Her voice had dropped to a whisper. "And what happens if you realize you don't want me? This? Us?" Her eyes, open and so disarming. "I don't think I can take another person, especially one I care about, not . . . wanting me."

The admission was raw. Like a beast, it scraped him raw, too. He swallowed, took a breath, stuffed his hands into his pockets; all of it to gain some measure of control over his emotions. It didn't matter. In the end, he dropped to his knees in front of her. He took her hand. Placed it over his heart.

"You scare me, too. You . . . you make me think about what I want. And I'm not talking about only you, Gaia. I'm talking about for my life. My family. It's terrifying." He took another breath. "But one thing I know is you. I will always want you. I know that because I've wanted you every day since I saw you at that party. Before the party," he admitted. "I was a kid, but even then, I knew you were special. And I wanted you."

She gripped his T-shirt where he'd placed her hand, then pressed it flat again. "See, it's this," she said shakily. "This smoothness, that makes you so dangerous."

"I thought it was my dashing good looks."

"That, too." She gave him a small smile. It faded. "Did you still want me when you found out about the magic?" Only the tiniest flicker of emotion in her eyes. "Do you still want me with the magic?"

"I . . . needed time with the magic." He frowned. "I needed time to fully accept it, I guess, but that's more about the entire world as I know it being different to what I thought it was." He brought her hand to his lips. "You're the only reason I'm willing to accept it at all."

"I'm sorry," she whispered. "You're experiencing it because of me, and I'm sorry."

"Don't be."

"I'm not done yet." She swallowed. "I'm relieved. I'm relieved that you're experiencing it, because it means it hasn't been in my head for the last twelve years. I'm not . . . I'm not delusional. I was relatively sure," she added quickly, "but getting undeniable confirmation . . . I'm glad for it. And I'm sorry about that most."

He gave himself a moment. Met her eyes. "Don't be sorry," he repeated. "After I got through the shock, I thought about how glad I am that I get to share the magic with you. That you don't have to deal with it alone anymore. What you just told me makes me feel more strongly about that."

She was studying him, which was how he got to see her eyes fill. She dipped her head back, lips curved into a smile.

"I had no chance with you," she said, looking at him again. A tear slipped down her face, and he wiped it away with his thumb. She lifted her hands to his wrist, grasping it, before turning to press a kiss to his palm. "No chance at all."

He knew it then. Knew it in that moment that he was in love with her. No—he'd known it before. Long before, and had been avoiding it. But seeing her naked in front of him, in every sense of the word, made him acknowledge it.

"Tell me," she said, and his heart stopped. "Tell me about what you want for your life."

She didn't mean she wanted him to tell her he loved her. Good. Because he didn't want to tell her. Not yet. Not until he knew what he wanted to do about it. Because acknowledging it, as it turned out, didn't do shit to help him process it.

"This," he said, taking the cloth that lay across the bathtub and dipping it into the water. "To come home with you after a long day and do this." He slid the cloth over her back, ignoring the way his body was reacting to her slight arch.

"You know that wasn't what I was talking about," she said gently.

He didn't respond for a while, only dipped the cloth into the water again. This time, he slid it over her front. Their eyes met as the cloth traveled lower now, over each breast, down, over her belly. He parted her thighs with it, but didn't touch her core, only the sensitive skin of her inner thigh, her outer thigh. He shifted so he could reach her feet, lifting them out of the water and pressing his fingers into the muscles there. She let out a little moan of gratitude, again when he did the next foot. When he lowered it back into the water, she was looking at him from hooded eyes.

"This is a distraction." Her voice was low and hoarse and seductive. And he knew that she didn't mean them, or what they'd done, or what they might do. She meant now, when he didn't want to answer her question.

He rose to his feet. Her eyes dipped, heat flaring when she saw the evidence of his distraction.

"I'll make tea."

The words were abrupt, mainly because his body was asking for more, telling him to sate the hunger in her eyes. He left before he could.

She was aching. Physically, because he had seduced her. He was torn about it, about their conversation, but he couldn't seem to resist touching her. And he *had* touched her. Everywhere except the most private part of her, and she had no idea whether that was to save her sanity or make her lose it.

But the real ache was emotional. The longing she felt to have him and that life he'd outlined for them. But could she trust it? She trusted him, and that was still something she was coming to terms with. Whatever was happening between them though . . . That was something else entirely. Or was it?

It didn't matter. Her priority now was to get him to talk. She wanted him to confide in her. If he did, maybe it would take away the power whatever he wasn't saying had over him.

She went to her bedroom, pulled on a long-sleeved sweat-shirt that dropped to her knees, and went to find him.

He was stirring a teaspoon in a cup of tea, his handsome features knitted into a tight expression her fingers itched to soothe. She stood there a long time, looking at him. His broad shoulders that held the burdens of the world; that muscular chest that housed his big, overworked heart; the arms that lifted her when she was too tired to get up from the floor; the powerful legs that carried around all the responsibilities the rest of his body had.

Her heart caved—simply *caved*—at the overwhelming emotion of looking at him. Of loving him.

No.

It was a silent, pointless cry of protest. And of no use to her now, when she was trying to get him to trust her.

"It meant a lot to me," she said, interrupting the stirring that had gone on much too long, "when you said you were glad you could experience the magic with me. So I wouldn't go through it alone." She didn't have to repeat it when it had happened minutes ago. "Let me share your magic with you, Jake."

He looked down at the mugs. "I don't have magic."

"You're wrong." He lifted his chin at that. "You're wrong," she said again. "Your magic is your ability to care. For all of us, even when we don't deserve you." She gave him a moment. "You've taken so much responsibility for the last eight years. And now you're feeling guilty because you don't want to anymore. You don't have to feel guilty."

"My mom asked me to take care of them," he rasped. "Before she died, she asked me to take care of them. Of course I should feel guilty if I don't want to do that."

"No," she disagreed, moving forward so she could touch him. Comfort him. "You took care of them, Jake. But at the cost of yourself. Of your happiness." She paused. "At the cost of their independence."

He stiffened beneath her touch, though she'd only managed to lay a hand on his.

"You're saying I made them dependent on me?"

"Maybe." She forced herself to speak through the tightness in her throat. She didn't like even the thought of conflict with him. "Or maybe they've made themselves dependent on you. Either way, it's costing you. And changing that isn't something you need to feel guilty about."

He snorted, as if he didn't agree, but he didn't say anything. Instead, he handed her the tea. She took a second, then tilted her head toward her bedroom before walking there. He followed, as she'd wordlessly asked him to. They set the mugs on the bedside cabinets, and she went to the curtains to open them.

The window looked out onto her small garden. There was only space for one large tree, a chair, and a flower bed, but it brought her an immense amount of joy. She stared at it for a moment, remembering all the things she had once dreamed of and now had. With no small amount of pleasure blooming in her chest, she walked to the bed.

He was already sitting there, watching her. She curled her legs under her, grabbed her mug, and drank. Closed her eyes as the heat settled in her belly. Then she spoke.

"I dreamt of this life when I was a kid. Having my own space, drinking my own tea, owning more than a bag of clothing." She sipped again. "I never told anyone those dreams. I didn't have anyone, for one, but even if I had . . . I wouldn't have said anything. Because they were my dreams, and the only thing I had for myself." She exhaled, the air heavy with the memories. "I also felt stupid for having them. Stupid for having dreams, for wanting things, when it didn't seem possible that they would come true."

"But they did," he said a little hoarsely.

"They did," she agreed. "And it took me a while to realize they weren't stupid. I wasn't stupid for wanting things. I had to actually get them to realize that, and I wish . . . I wish I'd realized it long before then, so I could have enjoyed the hope that came with having dreams. Sometimes, that hope is as important as the things you want."

The silence was long and tense, but she waited it out. She waited for him because she knew he would do the same for her. He *did* the same for her. And when she was in a dark place, he reached out for her. Helped her. She could see the darkness around him now, and she wanted to reach for him. To help him.

But only because he had done the same for her. It had nothing to do with the feelings she was still stubbornly ignoring.

"I want them to figure their shit out." He spoke so quietly she had to strain to hear him. "Seth and my father. I don't want to be the middleman anymore."

She didn't comment, afraid he would stop if she did.

"I want my father to care about us beyond the business." His voice broke, and she set her tea down and shifted closer to him. He looked at her, expression broken, but grateful at that little show of comfort. "I know that's not entirely possible because he doesn't know how to care about us beyond giving us material things. It was like that before Mom died. After . . . it got a lot worse. We barely talk except about the business. I know that's how he shows his love, I know that, but it makes me feel . . ."

He trailed off.

"Trapped," he finally said, closing his eyes. "It makes me feel trapped in the business because if I don't run it, what will we talk about? Will the family break completely, like it almost had when Seth refused to take over? Will the business fail, like it had under my dad, if I leave?"

More fears poured out of his mouth. About the business, about his family. He wanted them both to succeed, and he was worried they wouldn't without him. But he was tired. Tired of trying so hard at both things. It didn't feel the way it had at the beginning, when he'd been desperate to fix what his mother's death had broken. Then, it had felt like a purpose. A way for him to deal with his own grief.

Over time, that grief had faded. He missed his mother desperately, but she was gone, and life had gone on. He wanted his life to go on, at least, but everything in his life seemed to want to hold him back. Keep him from moving forward into happiness. As if grief was his punishment for loving someone who died, and he didn't deserve redemption from it.

"And then you came along," he said softly. "You distracted me from working so much. I'd lost touch with myself and what I wanted, and in my distraction, I finally realized all this." He lifted a shoulder. "You have a job you love so damn much you manifested magical powers to help you get better at it."

"I don't think that's how it worked."

"Yeah, but you don't know," he said cheekily, "so my theory works."

She laughed lightly and lifted a hand to play with his hair.

"I want more for my life than what I have, Gaia. I want so much more, and I can't have it."

"That's bull," she told him gently, but firmly. "You can have it. You deserve to have it."

"How?"

The helplessness had her stilling. "By being brave. By trusting yourself to know what's best for you. Not what you *think* is best for you, but what actually is. No," she said when he was about to argue, "you know. Everything you told me proves that you know."

"You make it sound easy."

"It's not." She shifted and he opened his arm, welcoming her into his embrace. Damn if it didn't make her feel special, warm, *loved*. "I know it's not. But it's worth it."

They sat like that for a long time. Her lids began to feel heavy, and she closed her eyes, but she heard him say, "I wanted to be a graphic designer. To be a part of my dad's company in that way, but to still do what I wanted to do. I used to love it."

He didn't speak again, and she wanted to comfort him, to

say something, but she couldn't form the words, she was so tired. Then he was moving her toward the center of the bed. She mumbled a sleepy protest when he left her side; the covers gently tugged out from under her body in answer. Some time later, he lay beside her again as the weight of the blanket settled over them. She snuggled into his side, felt her body relax against his when his arms drew her in close. She had never felt safer in her life, not even in her books.

The thought stayed with her as she fell asleep.

CHAPTER 25

Gaia woke up when light poured in through her windows. She'd forgotten to draw the curtains, which explained the unreasonable warmth she also felt. It was summer, the sun was already up, and—

No, she realized. The warmth had absolutely nothing to do with it being summer, with the sun, or with the curtains. It was because she was in bed with Jake, tucked in under his arm as they'd fallen asleep the night before. She didn't know if they hadn't moved during the evening, or if they had, but had come back to this.

He still wore his T-shirt, but had taken off his jeans. She knew because his leg was pressed against hers, skin against skin. She didn't think about it too much as she reached to rest a hand on his chest. But she stopped. If she did this, he might wake up, and did she want him to wake up and smell her morning breath?

No, she did not.

Slowly she untangled herself, went to the bathroom and brushed her teeth. She used the toilet. Washed her face. Stared at herself in the mirror. Her hair wasn't great, but it rarely was in the morning, despite the satin pillowcases she slept on. She fluffed it as much as she could without wetting it and alerting him that she tried to look good for when he woke. Then she returned to the bedroom, slipping into bed.

He shifted when she did, and she turned to her side, hoping he wouldn't wake up. His arm lifted over her, his body slotting in behind her, and he pulled her in until there was no space between them.

Her skin turned into gooseflesh, heat rushing into her body, into her core, when she felt the erection pressed against her backside. His fingers ran down her arm, shifting to her stomach. She felt the heat of it on her skin as acutely as she did the heat of desire inside her. Slowly, he ran his hand over her hip, under the sweatshirt she wore, making his way back up her stomach until he got to the underside of her breast.

"Morning," he rumbled into her ear.

She trembled. *Trembled.*

Traitor, she mentally told her thirsty body.

"Hi," she said in a voice that was much calmer than that tremble suggested. "I was wondering if you were going to say anything at all, or if you were just going to touch me."

"Not just touch."

He proved the words by pressing a kiss into her neck. It was the same thing he had done the day before, when he'd taken off her dress. It was as erotic now as it was then. More now, considering where his hand was.

"Just because you woke up in my bed doesn't mean you have a right to my body," she said slyly. He stilled, but she continued. "You have a right to my body because I *want* you to touch me."

With that, she covered his hand and lifted it until they were both cupping her breast. His hips shifted against her, an instinct to satisfy the desire, she knew. Knew because she had immediately arched, as if somehow, rubbing her butt against him would ease the prickling between her thighs.

He squeezed her breast lightly, as if testing its weight, before his fingers moved to her nipple. Her hand moved with him. Almost without her realizing it at first; then, because there was something powerful and pleasurable in feeling him tease her in such an immediate way.

Then his hand was moving until it was on top of hers, guiding her fingers to where his had been.

"Touch," he whispered, and she did, taking her nipple between her fingers and squeezing it, brushing it with her thumb over that spot she knew was directly connected to her center.

He moved his hand, a slow descent that would lead to madness—or less dramatically, consequences she wasn't sure she was ready for. She stilled, but he growled at her not to stop, and she obeyed. Kept teasing her breast as his hand slipped into her underwear, his finger instantly finding the part of her she desperately needed him to touch.

"Like this?" he asked as he circled, as she circled, as she felt heat and moisture pool between her thighs.

"Yes," she choked out, then cried out, when he bit into her neck. "Lower," she said then, wanting to feel his fingers playing between her legs. Bucking when he did as she asked, expertly tracing her most sensitive skin. His finger dipped inside her, only enough to bring her wetness with it as he went back to tease, and she let out a little huff of air. A protest.

"You want more?"

She swallowed. Yes, she did. She wanted more of him, of what he was doing to her. She wanted him to make her scream, to do things to her that her heroes did to their heroines, to her. But this was already more pleasurable than anything she'd experienced in her dreams. It was real, and real came with emotions and awareness that weren't there in her dreams. Both seemed worth the risk, worth the pleasure, but they terrified her. His question terrified her. If he was asking, she was giving permission, and she would have to take responsibility for partaking in whatever they were about to do.

It was the entire point of consent, and for the first time, she realized how damn scary something she'd written for years was.

"Gaia," Jacob said softly. When she didn't answer, his hand slipped out from between her thighs, gripping the hand that had stilled at her breast at the question.

"Gaia," he said again, this time flipping her onto her back.

His hair was rumpled from sleep, his face flushed from what they were doing, and she could still feel his hardness pressed into her side. But patience won out over desire as he looked at her, his hand gripping hers tightly where they now rested below her breast.

"You don't have to do anything you don't want to."

"I . . . I want to. I'm just . . ."

"I know," he said, pressing a kiss to her lips. "I know."

There was no judgment in that tone. He knew she was scared and he respected it. He wouldn't push, wouldn't do anything she wasn't comfortable with, because he cared about her. The way he was looking at her felt like perhaps he more than simply cared about her.

It filled her heart, but filled the well of terror she kept inside her, too. Currently that well was full to the brim with the realization that she more than simply cared about Jacob. Now, it overflowed.

But she would clean it up later. Or drown in it. Whatever. But she wanted to show him how much his patience meant to her. His respect.

She ran her free hand down his chest, slowly, so slowly, her eyes never leaving his. His body tensed beneath her touch, his lips parted for what she knew was a protest, but she shook her head. He didn't have to tell her she didn't have to do this. She knew that. Knew he didn't expect it from her either. But she wanted to touch him. To show him she understood this physical intimacy was tied to their feelings for one another. Deep, terrifying feelings that they couldn't talk about, but perhaps could show to one another.

She pulled down the briefs he wore, left side, then right, and gave him a moment to shimmy it down his legs. Then she gripped him. Lightly, firmly, getting used to the smooth hard skin. It pulsed in her hand, and she tightened her hold, before bringing her lips inches from his.

"This is the last thing I should be noticing right now," he said, eyes glazed with desire, "but how does your breath smell so good in the morning?"

Surprise courted laughter from her lips, but she pressed them together. "I woke up like this," she said, then moved her hand. Otherwise, he might have got distracted by something equally irrelevant next.

He groaned. Brought his hand out from under her shirt to peel the blankets away. To watch her tease him. It was a heady sensation, coupled with a layer of embarrassment that he was watching her. She wondered if the embarrassment would go away, if the power would override it. That didn't make her feel any less sure she wanted to make him feel the way he'd made her feel moments ago though. If that meant dealing with some embarrassment, so be it.

"You're thinking," he said, breathlessly. "What are you thinking?"

"Who says I'm thinking?"

"I do."

He leaned forward and kissed her hungrily. She stopped moving her hand, caught in the kiss. She hadn't thought she'd want to kiss anyone first thing in the morning, but she didn't care with Jacob. The added benefit was that her mouthwash was strong enough she couldn't entirely taste the morning on him. She almost smiled, but deepened the kiss instead. He groaned, pulling at her sweatshirt. They succeeded in lifting it up to her shoulders, before they had to pull apart.

She took off the shirt, but kept on her underwear. He pulled off his shirt despite the fact that she wasn't naked and he was, and didn't seem disturbed by it a single bit. Her eyes swept over his body, over that brown skin that looked like the gods had blended it using sunshine and nature, over the muscles it covered, the hardness that lay over his stomach.

"You're gorgeous," she breathed.

He smiled, his eyes hungry, and she realized he'd been looking at her, too. He came to her then, and she lowered onto her back, letting his eyes feast on her body. His fingers skimmed her neck, her collarbone, breasts. Rested on her stomach.

"Will you be okay with me touching you again?" he asked.

"I . . . yes."

"Gaia—"

"Only if you let me touch you, too."

He studied her as if she were a model and he an artist, as if he was scanning her for details, for any sign of something that couldn't be seen without that level of study.

He was searching for any sign of uncertainty.

"Do it," she commanded quietly, but no less emphatically. "Make me scream and let me do the same for you."

"You don't have to—"

"This," she said, resting a hand on his stomach, "is how we start. I want to . . . do all of it with you. Someday." She swallowed. "Today, I'm ready for this." She pushed his hand lower. "I'm ready."

With one last sweeping look, he pressed his lips to hers, let his fingers move between her legs, and made her scream. And when she was done, she pushed him on his back and did the same for him.

CHAPTER 26

The doorbell rang approximately twenty-three minutes after they left the bed.

Not that Jacob was counting or anything. It wasn't like what they'd done in that bed had changed his whole damn life.

It wasn't like *she* had changed his whole damn life.

"Can you answer that?" she asked. "You're already wearing clothes and I still have to get dressed."

He drew her into his arms and reached for the corniest line he could find. "You don't *have* to get dressed."

She snorted, but placed her hands on his chest. "As impressive as you are, I need food."

She pressed a kiss to his lips, lingered, and he growled in approval. The doorbell rang again.

With a sigh, she pulled back. "Can you answer it?"

"Sure." She was asking him to answer her door as if it were normal. As if they were in a relationship and she trusted him to answer her door. "But if it's Seth, and he guesses what happened and kills me, I expect you to be in mourning for an appropriate amount of time."

Her laugh followed him to the door. He was smiling when he opened it, but it quickly froze.

"Gemma?"

Gemma's eyes widened, but she cleared her throat. "Hi, Jacob. I didn't realize you would be here."

He frowned. How did she know where Gaia lived? Gaia wasn't the type to give out her address, even if she did seem to like Gemma. Unusually. He didn't like the situation. Gemma had admitted to stalking Gaia. She appeared in places where Gaia was. Now this? It was all suspicious and maybe he needed to get involved.

He closed the door behind him. "You want to see Gaia?"

"Yes." Gemma offered him a tentative smile. "Is she home?"

"How do you know where she lives?" he countered.

"I . . . um . . ." She swallowed. "Look, I only need a second, okay? Is she inside?" She lifted to her toes to peek over Jacob's shoulder, as if he were hiding Gaia behind him.

"Gemma," he said, edging forward. She took a step back. He stopped, realizing what it must have felt like to see him advance. "You told Gaia you're stalking her, right? Forgive me if I'm a little concerned that you're now showing up at her house. It was bad enough that you showed up at the café. And the signing."

Gemma's head dipped, causing her hair to fall forward in a curtain covering her face. Was it purposeful? So he wouldn't see her expression? Except then she lifted her head, and he saw more than he was prepared for. A vulnerability that was so deep, so raw, it reminded him of Gaia when she'd kicked Seth out of her house all those weeks ago.

It . . . reminded him of Gaia.

"I have to tell her something. I should have told her at the café, the signing, but if I don't do it now—"

"Is there a problem?"

Levi lumbered out of the shadows, standing behind Gemma, though he'd positioned himself so that if need be, he could shield her. Jacob had no intention of creating that need. His morning had been pretty good up until this point, and he wasn't going to spoil it by getting into a fight.

Unless, of course, he had to.

"No," Gemma said. "No problem. We should . . . we should come back at another time."

She turned. Levi's eyes dropped and scanned her face, her body. He said, "No."

"What?"

"We're not leaving," he said gently. It was the first time Jacob had heard that tone come from the man. Hell, it was the most Levi had ever said in his presence. Levi directed his next words to Jacob. "Can she see Gaia?"

"No," he replied easily. "I'm not letting someone see Gaia who's admitted to stalking her. Not in her home."

Levi aimed a level look at him. "You really think she's going to hurt Gaia? She's a literal piece of sunshine." It sounded like a compliment, but Jacob wasn't sure. Gemma didn't look sure either. "She just wants to speak with her."

Jacob waited a beat. "Tell me. If someone pitched up at several of the places Gemma was at, claiming to stalk her, then showed up at her home, would you give them access to her?"

The hesitation was all he needed to smirk. And the door opened behind him.

"What's going on?" Gaia asked, stopping next to him. "Gemma? What are you doing here?"

She wore a white dress that fell to her feet, as if worshipping the sparkling sandals crowning her toes. Her hair was wet, pushed back by a white hairband, curling all around her face. It was a simple look that punched him in the gut. She was beautiful. Too beautiful. And the morning they'd spent together—the night, too, when they'd shared all those things with one another—told him she wanted him as much as he wanted her.

She was his.

"I'm your sister," Gemma blurted out, stunning the thought right out of his head. "Your biological sister, I mean. I don't know if you have any foster sisters you still keep in touch with."

There was a long stretch of silence that Gemma seemed to take as a sign to continue her bombshell reveal.

"I know that sounds like a lie, but we're sisters. We were both put into Angel's Care foster house when we were two. I . . . I was adopted," Gemma said, the stutter the only sign of uncertainty in her entire explanation. "And my parents didn't take you. I didn't know and I'm sorry. I'm so sorry."

It wasn't clear what Gemma was apologizing for. Telling Gaia all this in the way that she had? For being adopted? For her parents not telling her about Gaia? He didn't particularly care. Not when Gaia's chest was moving faster than he liked; not when her expression was contorted in confusion and . . .

And pain.

"How do we know this is true?" Jacob asked, reaching for Gaia's hand. It was cold. She didn't grip it back. His heart thudded.

"I have papers. Documents." She reached in her handbag, but Levi stepped forward and handed her a file. "You can have it," Gemma said. "All of it."

She offered the file to Gaia, but Gaia didn't take it. She looked at Jacob, beseechingly, and he took the file from Gemma, scanned through the documents. And it was all there. Birth certificates, the foster home's documentation, Gemma's adoption papers. As he sifted through them, something dropped to the floor. Before he could reach for it, Gaia picked it up. Made a strangled noise in her throat and handed him the picture before he could ask.

It was of two little girls, one curved around the other in sleep. They looked remarkably like Gaia and Gemma; one had curls, the other's hair straight; the features all the same, down to their facial expressions.

"And I have this," Gemma said, lifting her hand and twirling a ring with a blue stone in it around her middle finger. "You have a pendant from this set, don't you? It was our mother's, and—"

Gemma stopped talking when Gaia walked back into the house and slammed the door behind her. There was another silence, this one as tense as when Gemma had made the announcement, though somehow more fragile. That was because of Gemma. Her face crumpled, swiftly and completely, as if someone had taken a sheet of paper and crushed it in their hand.

"It's a lot to process," Levi said quietly, his focus entirely on Gemma. "You have to give her time."

Gemma let out a small breath, gave a small nod. "Of course."

But the devastation lingered on her face, and she turned away from Jacob, from Levi, and walked toward a car Jacob only now noticed in the driveway.

"It's a lot," Levi said again, this time to Jacob. He didn't quite understand why until Levi nodded his head at the door before turning around. He was telling Jacob to go check on Gaia.

Jacob prepared to do that. But before he could open the door, he hesitated. He had no idea why or for how long. It was selfish, but he was afraid of what he would find in there.

They'd finally made some progress in their relationship. And not subtle shifts in the way they felt about or spoke to one another. *Real* progress. Delicate progress. The kind that needed to be nurtured between the people in a relationship for some time before it was ready for the world. For bullshit like this.

He wanted to bang his head against the door. It probably wouldn't knock the frustration out of him—or the shame that this was what he was thinking about instead of going to check on her—but it would feel damn good. Gritting his teeth, he went inside the house.

And found Gaia sitting perfectly calm at the kitchen table.

Her heart was thudding. Her throat felt tight. There was a pounding in her ears; white spots in her eyes.

Gaia merely breathed.

Deep, steady, measured breaths.

Inhale, exhale. One, two, three, four, five, in. One, two, three, four, five, out.

When Jacob walked through the door, she was feeling okay. Brittle, but okay.

"Don't stare at me," she said, pushing her chair out. "I'm fine."

"That's ironic, since I'm not."

"Do you want a cup of tea?"

She didn't wait for the answer. Having a task would give her something to do. Something to focus on. And tea had become the unofficial mascot of her and Jacob's relationship.

Besides, it was the perfect antidote to that tight throat. She had enough experience to know that if she drank it, the heat would burrow a tunnel—

"Gaia," Jacob said, gently taking her hand as she reached for the tea canister. "I don't want a cup of tea."

"That's fine." She pulled against his grip. She couldn't handle him touching her. It brought flashes of memory from the night before, from that morning. From when things were good. If she thought about how far it was from that right now . . . She didn't want him to touch her. And he stopped doing so. "I need a cup," she said, offering him a smile she thought might make her look like she was preparing to murder someone.

"Then let me make it."

"No, it's fine."

"You need a moment to—"

"It's fine. I don't need a moment to anything. I'm fine. I just want to make this cup of tea."

"Baby—"

"I'm fine," she snapped, slamming her hands against the counter. The cup fell to the floor. She felt as if it had crashed inside her, the pieces of it slamming against her chest, sending shards of glass into her heart.

The pain was sharp and oddly specific. Or perhaps not odd

if they were shards that had pierced certain parts of her heart. But the cup hadn't crashed inside her. Her heart was breaking from something else entirely. And maybe it was because of what Gemma had said. Maybe it was because she couldn't understand it all, and she hated that Jacob was there, watching her, expecting her to break.

She didn't want to break in front of him. It felt too personal to show him that side of her. Yet she didn't think she had much choice in the matter. Her heart beating, her throat constricting, her ears pounding, her eyes blinding . . . All of the symptoms were much harder to control now. Her lungs weren't working again, the assholes, and her trick to breathe was nearly impossible if she simply *couldn't* breathe.

Distraction, she thought. Distraction.

She should pick up the glass on the floor.

It was a good idea until she tried to drop to her knees and was kept from doing so by strong arms.

"I'll do it," Jacob's voice murmured into her ear. Or he might have said it. She couldn't hear all that well through the pounding.

"I broke it. I want to fix it."

"You tried to kneel in the glass."

"I was fixing it."

"Okay—Hey!" he said when she tried to break free of his arms. "What are you doing?"

"Fixing it!"

"Gaia—Shit, you're strong."

"Yeah, I am." She stopped struggling and faced him. "I am strong. I can handle this. I'm not going to fall apart and—"

She broke off when tears heated her eyes. When the water content in her body was betraying her as if it cared about Jacob more than it did her. And sure, maybe that water had some allegiance to him after this morning in bed, but it was still *her* water. She should have its loyalty all to herself.

She was losing it. Damn it.

She stepped out of his embrace. Clasped her hands behind her so he wouldn't see her shaking. But he saw. She knew he saw because his expression pooled with sympathy. Understanding. It as good as melted all her defenses, and she let out one loud sob before he pulled her back into his arms.

But she wasn't crying. The sob was her gasping for air. A desperate attempt at seeking it. It was as if her body knew she was no longer keeping things together. Her brain struggled against it, against the rawness of it all, but it had no sway over her now. Logic rarely did when she felt like this.

She pushed Jacob away, bending and resting her hands on her knees as the gasps came.

"Gaia?" he asked, carefully, though the alarm was clear.

She didn't reply, only stepped back now, one, two steps, until she was out of the kitchen and in front of the door. Then she dropped. To the floor, on her knees, to her side. She curled into a ball as she had done that week when she'd stayed in her bedroom, trying to figure out how Jacob had gotten access to her safe space.

It was ironic that again, he saw her in her safe space. The home she had created after years of not having one. *She* had given him access. *She* was allowing him to see her curled up, struggling for breath, for her *dignity*. It wasn't entirely a choice, but it was humiliating, and she shut her eyes when that idea tightened her lungs even more.

She couldn't stop the tears that came. That poured down her face as she broke before him. But breaking implied that there would be pieces after. If there were pieces, she could put herself back together again. It wouldn't be perfect, of course, but it would still work. That wasn't the case here.

She wasn't breaking but disintegrating. Disappearing. She preferred it. Disappearing would mean she wouldn't feel so overwhelmed, so inept, so completely unable to get ahold of herself even when she tried to.

Sobs, inhalations, exhalations, tears, those haunting thoughts. They mangled together, shrouding her in a darkness she hadn't ever allowed in. It had courted her throughout her years in foster care. She had no idea how she'd resisted, but she had. Even when she'd learned her family didn't want her. Even when she'd realized no one would. It had made a play for her hand when she found out about her magic. When she wondered if people could always sense that she was different than them, and that's why she had no friends, and she was never adopted.

She'd refused then, but today it had pulled out all the stops. It had done a damn grand gesture. How could she resist that?

She couldn't.

She didn't know how long she lay on the floor. Was barely aware of it when Jacob scooped her into his arms, putting her on the bed they'd done such wonderful things in that morning. It was a light, those memories, but it was so far away. She would have to reach out through the darkness and she . . . she couldn't.

Voices sounded in her house an indiscriminate amount of time later. She thought she'd imagined it until Seth's face appeared in front of her.

"Gaia," he said, his voice a rasp of concern.

She didn't say anything, didn't even move when he took off his jacket and curled himself around her. She turned, the crying starting again, though this time it felt more manageable. It felt real, not a distant haze of overwhelming emotion. It felt like *she* was crying; not someone else.

"I have a sister. A sister. Family."

Seth's only response was to hold her tighter. Thoughts, more coherent now, stumbled into her head.

She had family. Her entire life, someone—a sister; a *twin* sister—had existed and Gaia hadn't known. How was that possible? How had the social worker told her about the family who hadn't wanted her, but didn't tell her *this*?

In all fairness, the social worker hadn't even wanted to tell her that. Gaia had insisted. It was after the third foster home, when she was old enough to understand the concept of family. More importantly, she'd understood she didn't want to depend on people who, to her mind, could give her up on a whim. But there was no other choice. Her parents had died, the only other family she had had been contacted and they didn't want her. Her last option was to be adopted.

She hadn't asked about siblings. Why would she? Though wasn't that the kind of information they should have given her? It didn't matter anymore. It wouldn't change that she had a sister; they had been separated; Gemma had been adopted and she hadn't been; and she had no idea how she was supposed to feel. She had a *sister*? How could she understand why her sister's adoptive parents thought *separating* them would be a good idea?

Anger slithered into her heart, her lungs. It hardened the unsteady beating; commanding her erratic breathing. The tears stopped. She pushed against Seth's chest and he moved away, his eyes sweeping over her as she stood. For the first time, she noticed Jacob standing in the doorway. He was watching her with an unreadable expression. She avoided his gaze. She couldn't look at him, knowing what he'd seen. What he'd witnessed. She wanted to push it out of her mind entirely.

Without a word to either brother, she went to the bathroom in the hallway, stripped off her clothes and took a shower. It was short and cold, and brought her back into her body. She didn't look in the mirror when she was done, afraid of what she would see, but wrapped a towel around her and returned to her room. To both brothers waiting for her.

"Can I have some privacy?" she asked to no one in particular. Seth left, but Jacob lingered in her doorway. As if he was afraid to leave her alone.

"Jake." Seth's voice sounded from behind him. "Come on."

Jacob ignored him. Instead, he stepped forward and closed the door behind him. Gaia waited for a minute, but when he didn't seem inclined to speak, she started to get dressed. There was nothing erotic about it. None of the teasing she would have done if he hadn't seen her at her most vulnerable. Rather, it was a blur of shimmying underwear up her legs under the towel, turning around to put her bra on, getting the first piece of clothing she could find onto her body, then facing him.

"What?" she asked flatly.

Jacob's expression hardened, but not in the way she expected. She expected it to be less . . . confusing. Anger that she was speaking to him this way when he'd done nothing wrong.

But this . . . this looked like resolve. Like a crystallization of emotion she couldn't identify—or didn't want to.

"You're pushing me away," he said.

"No."

"Bullshit. But you know that already, don't you?" His voice was like the hardness she expected. Except it felt dangerously like a casing for his hurt. "You knew that the moment you wouldn't let me comfort you when you were—"

He broke off with a ragged breath. Her heart stuttered in protest, but she ignored it.

"*You* called Seth," she pointed out woodenly.

"Because for an hour, you wouldn't say anything. Not one single thing."

An hour? It couldn't have been.

Could it?

"I was desperate," he continued. "I wanted you to come back from wherever you'd"— the pause he took felt like the longest one in existence—"gone."

She shook her head—her heart—so she could stop thinking about how vulnerable he looked and get over his words. She reminded both body parts that he'd *seen* her. He'd seen her in the worst possible light and he would never be able to see her differently again. When he looked at her, he would see the woman broken on the floor, crying without tears, gasping for breath.

She couldn't live with the man she loved looking at her and

seeing that. She wanted him to see her sensuality, her intelligence, her strength. She wanted him to see the best of her and he wouldn't be able to. It was already in his eyes.

"I'm sorry," she said softly. "I'm fine now."

"No, you're not."

"I will be."

"I know that. You have . . . you have us to help you."

She was shaking her head before he could finish. "I'm not interested in your help. I'm not . . . a charity case. I'm not broken. I'm . . . I'm fine. I'm strong. I will get through this."

He gave her an incredulous look. "No one said you were broken. No one said you weren't strong. But . . . even strong people need help, Gaia. There's nothing wrong with that."

"So you'll be telling Seth and your father the truth then? You'll turn to them for help?"

She hated herself for saying it. For using what he'd told her the night before against him. But her brain finally seemed to be listening to her. No more pandering to Jacob's vulnerability. She would use it instead. Use it to make him go away so she could lick her wounds in private.

His face shuttered closed. "Seth's right outside this door," he warned. "Don't do this. Don't . . . don't say anything more."

She would. She would say more and have Seth hear it.

No, her heart said. And she remembered what she'd written in her book. When Jade had replied to Chris's assertion that her body wanted him, she'd told him her head and heart had an equal say. Gaia's heart was more powerful now. And it kept her from making a mistake she would never be able to forgive herself for.

And then Jacob said—no, *begged*—"Please," and she knew she'd already crossed the line into eternal damnation.

CHAPTER 27

It was all falling apart and he could do nothing about it. He could see it on Gaia's face. He could hear it in his own voice as he begged her not to talk about things he wasn't ready to talk to his brother about yet. And then again when realization rippled over her face. In the guilt, the regret, the pain that followed.

They were over before they'd even really begun.

"I'm sorry," she said, her voice the sound of bad news over the phone. "I shouldn't have . . . Oh, no," she moaned. "I'm sorry."

He kept himself from reaching out to her. Mentally at first, but when that felt tenuous, he put his hands in his pockets. "I'll go."

She made a strangled sound, but she didn't try to stop him. And though he saw it clearly, called her out on it—thought, at first, he wouldn't fall for it—he let her push him away.

What choice did he have? He wouldn't force her to be with him if that wasn't what she wanted. Which seemed to be the case, despite that morning, and the night before. And the past months, damn it, that they built something so special. Now, it was broken. Not because she was broken—he would give anything to make her see she wasn't; he *had* given everything—but because she didn't want him. She didn't want his comfort or his reassurances or *him*. There was nothing he could do about that.

It might kill him. Knowing she was going through something and not being there for her. He would remember the way she looked curled into a ball on the floor, gasping for air, for the rest of his life. The empty expression on her face as he carried her to her bed would haunt him every time he closed his eyes.

He felt so helpless. Then, when she hadn't responded to his questions, to his touches. Now, when she didn't want him to remind her that what happened wasn't her entirely. It was a part of her, a part that needed to be addressed, yes, but only a part. There were so many other parts, and all of them made her the woman he loved. The woman he would gladly do anything for.

But she didn't feel the same way.

"You need help, Gaia," he said because he couldn't walk away without saying it. And because what did he have to lose? "I think . . . I think you had a panic attack. I think you've been having them for a while."

"No." She shook her head. "No," she said again, but something devastating was crossing her face. Her final "no" came out on a sob, but she pressed her hand over her mouth, as if she could take it back somehow.

He didn't acknowledge the urge he had to comfort her—what would be the point?—but said, "There's nothing wrong with getting help."

Then he opened the door and walked out. He found Seth in the living room, pacing the length of the floor. The house was small enough that Jacob had no doubt Seth had heard what happened in Gaia's bedroom. He nodded his head in her direction before heading to the front door.

"Are you okay?" Seth asked before he could open it.

"Yeah," he replied without turning around. "I always am."

He shut the door behind him, heading for his car. It took him a minute to realize it was still at Seth's house. He called a taxi, got his car, and drove home. All of it was a blur. Except when he got to the house. He found his father in the kitchen.

When he saw Jacob, Keenan stood. "Where the hell have you been?"

"Out."

"You didn't let me know."

"I was distracted."

"By some girl?"

"Do you really want to know?" he countered.

A deep frown etched itself into the skin between Keenan's brows. "None of my business who you like, boy."

Which was true. But his anger told him it *was* his father's business, in the most basic of ways. Keenan was his father, for heaven's sake. The only parent he had left. Shouldn't Keenan *want* to know who Jacob liked?

"You could pretend," Jacob said softly, the anger still there, but muted, as if realizing the words were more important. "To be interested in my life."

"I asked where you were."

"Did you ask that because you were interested?"

Keenan shifted. "Sure."

Now the anger disappeared completely, leaving only confusion. "What aren't you telling me, Dad?"

Keenan's jaw tightened. He put his hands on his hips. Dropped them. Then folded his arms. "Your brother called last night."

"What?" Jacob asked. "Why?"

"Well, now, he . . . er . . . he wanted to . . . share"—each word seemed to be a delicate move in a high-risk surgery—"that you might be feeling . . . uncomfortable . . . about . . . dating." Keenan cleared his throat. He looked like he wanted to be anywhere but there.

"He said that, huh?" Bastard. "And what do you think I'm uncomfortable with?"

"Well," his father said again, "that's the thing. I don't care. That you're dating an older woman, I mean."

Jacob did not see that coming.

He took a second to calibrate.

"Seth told you this?"

Keenan nodded.

Jacob didn't know how to reply. Had his brother decided to play a prank? Was Seth paying him back for the sex toy thing with Gaia? Why else would Seth, after years of contacting his father only on special occasions, decide to breach the gap with this shit? Unless . . .

Unless, Seth had really thought it would be uncomfortable for Jacob to tell his father about Gaia. Or not uncomfortable; difficult. And it was. Less because of who he was in a relationship with—an older woman, really?—and more because of what the relationship meant: the company was no longer his top priority.

The more he thought about it, the more it made sense. Yeah, the age thing might have been payback, but telling Keenan Jacob was dating someone? Not only was it helping Jacob to broach a topic with his father he wouldn't have otherwise, it was an acknowledgment of his relationship with Gaia. No, not acknowledgment—acceptance. And it made sense if he thought about the Seth who'd asked Jacob to accompany him to Gaia's book signing. *That* Seth wanted to make amends; maybe this was the first step toward Seth making amends with their father, too.

It was significant, but it was also for another time. Now, he had to deal with his father.

"I'm dating someone two years older, so technically, he's right." His father didn't need to know Jacob's use of the present tense was generous. "Why do you think Seth told you about my personal life?"

Keenan blinked. "You and I don't really talk about that kind of stuff."

"And you and Seth do?"

"I thought . . . maybe it was because she was older . . ."

"You and Seth haven't spoken about much in years, but he called you today because I'm dating an older woman?" Jacob didn't give his father a chance to reply. "No, Dad. He called you because he knew I wouldn't tell you about it. And that you wouldn't ask, because you *haven't* shown an interest in anything in my life outside of the company since Mom died. Maybe even before."

Jacob surprised himself with that. And since he couldn't retract the words—he would never admit it, but for a brief second, he'd fantasized about grabbing them out from the air where they lingered between him and his father—he continued.

"I haven't dated anyone of any age in the last eight years. Not seriously, anyway. I haven't had the time. I was too busy saving the company and keeping you and Seth from breaking the family apart."

There it was. Succinct and to the point. At least he was burning down everything in a flash fire and not letting the burn linger.

His father didn't reply. He only stared at Jacob with an expression Jacob couldn't read. When no words came even minutes later, Jacob left the kitchen. *Stupid*, his brain whispered. Over and over again because he *was* stupid for thinking something would change because he'd spoken up.

Would it be the same for Gaia? He hoped not. He hoped she talked to someone, anyone, about what she was going through. He hoped they would be more understanding than his father. That they would give her the support she needed as she faced whatever she needed to.

He trusted Seth would offer some of that. His brother's face had been grim when Jacob opened the door for him at Gaia's. It had twisted into something fiercely loyal and concerned when he'd gone to her in her bed. His quality as a brother might be debatable, but the man who held Gaia as she sobbed would be good to her.

Jacob didn't have any of those qualities. He was too busy fixing things he'd had no hand in breaking. But then, stepping in *to* fix them might have contributed to how broken they were now.

It took him some time, the realizations coming with a tangle of other thoughts he had to wade through to get to the core of his family issues.

He might not have broken the family company or his family, but he had broken something in himself. Didn't that matter? Didn't he matter? It seemed like such a long time ago, but he had once been excited about his life. The possibilities of his career. The hope of having his own family.

Those had been his dreams. Working for his father's company, but having a life outside of it. Then his mother had died and things had fallen apart and he'd told himself it was temporary. Pressing pause on what he wanted for his life was supposed to be temporary. But it hadn't been. It had been eight years and nothing had changed. Because *he* hadn't changed. And he hadn't expected his father and brother to, either. It was as much his fault as it was theirs.

But that would stop now. If his specialty was fixing things, he would fix this.

He would fix his life.

"Is the sitting here and not saying or doing anything going to continue for much longer?" Seth asked her later that night. "I need to prepare myself if it is."

He had stubbornly refused to leave after Jacob left. She thought the not saying or doing anything would tell him how she felt about that, but no. He remained. Doing annoying things like bringing her tea, making her toast, and occasionally asking her silly questions.

Who did he think he was, asking her if she was okay or prodding her about what she said or did?

"Your best friend," Seth answered, and she realized she'd asked those questions out loud. Oops. "I used to be the only person in your life who would." He sighed. "The good old days."

He was sitting next to her on the bed, fully clothed. She had managed to get him to take off his shoes by growling at him when he'd tried to put them down on her covers.

"Now you have my brother, who's apparently fallen for you or something equally disgusting"—her stomach flipped—"and my girlfriend, who's texted me a million times to check on you. She also told me to apologize for her not making it to your signing yesterday. There was an emergency with payroll or something." He waved a hand. "And then, there's the sister you apparently have."

She swore, but the sound was muffled under the pillow she put on her head to drown him out when he said the word *sister*.

"I know you heard me," Seth said, taking the pillow out of her hands. "You have people who care about you. More than simply me. I'm here as a representative of that body."

She grabbed her other pillow and hit him with it.

"Hey!" he exclaimed, stretching out a hand to protect from another hit. "What was that for?"

"It made me feel better."

He rolled his eyes. "I can't believe I missed you."

Her heart squeezed. "I can't believe it either." She paused. "I mean that literally."

He nodded, as if she'd told him something particularly mundane. "I know you do." Not mundane then. She'd said something he already knew. "I've been friends with you for twelve years. I know you in ways you've never shared with me."

There was a long silence as she figured out how she felt about that. As he gave her the time to.

"I know you expect me to stop being your friend," he said eventually, in a solemn voice that sounded nothing like his usual snarkiness and sarcasm. "I know that when I was trying to figure out how I felt about you and Jake, you were telling yourself 'I told you so.' It haunted me the entire time we didn't speak, but I needed to . . . I don't know. I needed to figure out how I felt about two people I've been trying to help for as long as I can remember, not needing me. Just each other."

Her head whipped toward him. "What? That's ridiculous."

"I realize that," he said with a small smile. "It took me some time, and a kick in the butt from Lizzy, but I saw that I was being . . . selfish. Which I tend to be in relationships, I've been told."

"She's not wrong."

He snorted. Neither of them said anything for a while.

"I hope she told you that wanting to help the people you care about is a pretty unselfish desire, too," she said.

"There was some of that," he admitted. "But it only came later." He paused. "I need to be needed. That's the shit I discovered when I started going to therapy last month."

She tried not to show her surprise. "That's . . . impressive."

"Hmm," he replied, not sounding entirely convinced. "Apparently, I inherited my father's desire to be needed. Like my mom needed him, I mean." He waited a beat. "When she died, he didn't feel that anymore. He didn't care about the business needing him, or his kids. The same way I didn't . . . ." He trailed off with an exhale. "The same way I didn't care about him needing me. Or Jake. I needed to be needed in a *specific* way. I don't know much more about that right now. I guess I'll figure it out in other sessions." He crossed his arms. "I'm still at the acknowledging-I'm-wrong-and-trying-to-do-better stage."

She let his obvious tension mix with silence. Waited for it to dilute his tension. When he glanced at her, she said, "I'm proud of you."

His mouth lifted. "Thanks. But it's okay if . . . if you're angry at me. For being a dick and not talking to you while I discovered this."

She sighed. "I was angry. Mostly because it hurt." She lifted a shoulder, though they were lying down. "It did feel like what I was waiting for, for twelve years. For you to leave. I thought I'd prepared myself for it, but it hurt, and I couldn't . . . I didn't know what to do about it. So I left it alone. The time we didn't talk was just as much my fault as yours."

He reached down and squeezed her hand. "You've always been more mature than me."

"I know."

His mouth lifted. "Doesn't excuse my behavior."

"No," she agreed.

The half smile turned into a genuine one. Then it faded, his grip on her hand becoming tighter. "You should be angry with me about more than that."

"Why?"

"Because"—he broke off with a sharp exhale—"I let you need me."

"I don't know what that means."

"It means that I knew for a long time that you had anxiety problems—panic attacks when things got overwhelming—and I did nothing about it because it meant that you needed me."

Well.

That was all she could think for a good solid minute.

Well, well, well.

What the hell did that mean anyway?

It's a distraction so you don't have to think about what he said.

Oh, great. Her brain was back online. The logical software had apparently updated, which meant she had to process what Seth said. What Jacob had said earlier.

"Is this because Jacob told me I had a panic attack? He doesn't know what he's talking about."

"That's not true," Seth disagreed. "He knows what he saw. He knew it when he came to find you all those weeks ago." She was about to protest when he said, "*You* know it, too. But you haven't faced it, and no one in your life's forced you to. I cannot tell you how much it gets me that he's spent less than two months with you, but he could pinpoint it *and* have the courage to tell you the truth."

"It isn't a contest," she said tersely.

"No, of course not," Seth replied quickly. "Of course not. I just meant . . . Gaia, I should have said something the first time I noticed you were struggling. Instead, I let you call me, I came over with food, and we didn't talk about it. It's happened enough times for me to know we've established a pattern. Jake got us out of that. And now I'm telling you that you struggle with anxiety."

"No, I don't."

But it was a lie. She knew it was a lie long before Seth began listing the signs.

"You don't like spending time with people—"

"—that has nothing to do with anxiety—"

"—because people stress you out. You stay at home—"

"—I *work* from home—"

"—and rarely leave because new spaces freak you out. You don't like change"—she had no argument there—"conflict situations are difficult, social situations are a challenge. When you face any of these situations you struggle to breathe, or to sleep, or to get out of bed. These are things *I've* noticed. Things you've allowed me to notice. I'm sure there are others that you don't tell me about."

Not really, she wanted to say. Then her brain said, *What about the life you prefer to live in your books because it's easier to be there than in the real world?* And it dared to continue, *What about how you only feel truly safe in those books? Not counting Jacob's arms, of course.*

"Traitor," she murmured.

"It's the truth," Seth replied.

"I wasn't talking to you."

"There's no one else here."

"Yeah, but you broke my brain. It's pointing out how all my little quirks sound a lot like . . ."

She didn't finish her sentence. She couldn't bring herself to say the word. If she said it, it would be harder to deny. And everything that day had already been so damn hard. She could give herself a break. She deserved to give herself a break, at least from this.

"So. I have a sister."

Seth gave her a look, but indulged her. "Plot twist."

"I hate them."

CHAPTER 28

Over the next week, Jacob began to analyze the business to identify its strengths and weaknesses. He had done it before, after he took over the company. And a couple of times after that, to evaluate the business. But in recent years, with the success of things, he hadn't had to. And even if he had, he wouldn't have done it in the way he was doing now: to figure out whether he was still needed.

He wanted to do it properly, thoroughly. He noted where his presence was requested, tried to figure out if it was necessary or merely a luxury because he'd made himself available in that way. He outlined what his daily routine looked like, divided the tasks into what were his responsibilities and what he'd made his responsibilities. He evaluated every conversation, every email. Identified key employees, wrote up their strengths and weaknesses. At the end of it, he had a thick folder of information on what was needed in his job. And a presentation for why he was no longer the best person to do it.

All of this happened in between preparing the new presentation for their challenging client. It had actually provided the perfect opportunity to see how his people coped in a crisis. He pulled some new people into the group, had some rough conversations with those he pulled off the project, and watched them theorize. He offered his expertise when asked—if he kept working there, he would still be able to do that, so he didn't mind—but mainly encouraged them to do it themselves.

He invited his father to attend the presentation. Keenan agreed. It was the first thing they'd said to one another since what Jacob had said in the kitchen a week ago. It wasn't that Jacob was avoiding Keenan. He was just busy. He left early in the morning; returned late at night. And it suited him while he figured out how to deal with this entire situation. With his father, with Seth. While he tried to forget about Gaia.

The presentation was part of his plan. If he could show his father that the people Jacob had hired could thrive with difficult clients, it should be easier to convince him that the company didn't need Jacob. But if they didn't thrive—if they didn't get it right this time either—it would set him back. He wasn't sure if his faith in his employees was that strong, or if he was that desperate to start his new life. Either way, the entire pitch meeting was an exercise in control.

Controlling his breathing, his facial expressions, his responses to the idiotic comments the client made. He was making sure he didn't look at his father to see if there were any clues to Keenan's feelings about the meeting. And he was struggling against the curse words that were on the tip of his tongue when their client once again dismissed all their ideas.

"Is this going to be a problem, Jacob?" Dean Sherman said in front of the entire room. In front of Sherman's own team, in front of Jacob's, in front of Keenan. "There seems to be some kind of misalignment and I'm struggling to see a compromise at this point."

Jacob didn't reply immediately. He was too busy noticing how none of Dean's team members looked at him. It was the purposefully shifty feel of it that had him suspicious. That, and a gut instinct.

"No," Jacob said, "you wouldn't see a compromise."

"Excuse me?"

"You don't want to work with us." It was simple now that Jacob saw the truth. "You're thinking about the counteroffer you got when you tried to drive down our prices. Or maybe you're not. Maybe you're thinking about how you're not happy with how I refused to compromise on that."

"I don't know what kind of business this is, but if this is the way you talk to clients, then maybe we shouldn't be in business together."

"Maybe." Jacob stood. "Why don't we discuss this further in my office?"

He didn't look at the rest of the room as he strode out. The resulting meeting was as tense as he expected. But he didn't want to work with someone who didn't engage with the ideas his employees spent time developing, and their business spent money on producing. He could handle complete dismissal once, but twice? After adopting ideas *their* company had suggested? After working with *their* point person on said ideas? Dean Sherman's business wasn't operating in good faith and Jacob wouldn't see his own people's creativity and motivation destroyed for Dean's selfish purposes.

He sat in his office for a long time after Dean left. A knock on the door forced him to look up.

"Yeah, I know," he told his father.

Keenan walked in. "What do you know?"

"The meeting was a disaster, I was unprofessional, and you're disappointed."

Keenan closed the door behind him and settled in the chair opposite Jacob's. He gave Jacob a look that made him feel uneasy.

"The meeting was a disaster, you were unprofessional, and I'm disappointed. *But*"— Keenan interrupted the snark before it fell out of Jacob's mouth—"it wasn't a disaster because of you or any of the people who work here. Your unprofessionalism was only in response to Sherman's, and it was necessary. You had to see the way your people's chins lifted the moment you stood up for them. They needed to hear it, and you said it. And I am disappointed," Keenan powered on, a boat with its engine running even though they'd reached the dock, "that I haven't said how damn proud of you I am."

None of it was what Jacob expected. A suspicious lump grew in his throat, a strange burning pricked his eyes. He didn't say anything, only blinked. His father took it as a sign to continue. Or maybe he continued because the engine was still running, and once it turned off, it would stay off forever.

"I'm proud of what you did to clean up my mess, son." There was the shortest pause. "It shouldn't have been at the expense of your life."

"I—" He stopped himself from denying it. It was the truth after all. "Thank you."

His father nodded. "It shouldn't have been your responsibility. Not this, or my relationship with your brother."

"I had to," he said. "You asked Seth to help. You were angry that he didn't. He was angry that you even asked. And Mom—"

"She should have never asked you to step in between us."

He felt the surprise go off like a bomb inside him. "You knew?"

Keenan nodded mournfully. "Heard her before she died. Didn't stop her because I wanted her to die in peace." His father's lips trembled, but he was speaking again. "I asked Seth to help with the business because it was one way I thought I could bond with him. Make things easier between us. Keep us together like your mother wanted." He lifted a shoulder. "I didn't stop to think about whether he wanted to do it, and I was bitter with grief when he said no. I was just . . . bitter." He took a breath. "And then you stepped in and things were easier. I didn't have to try. I stopped trying, and when I realized it . . . guilt made it so I didn't start again."

"Guilt?" Jacob asked, not stunned enough by his father's words to let him get off easy. "Or pride?"

"Both," Keenan answered after a long time. "Both."

Jacob didn't need more words to know how much this took from his father. He didn't need anything more to know it was progress. It wasn't an apology; he doubted his father was capable of one. But it was an acknowledgment of mistakes, and that was a form of apology, too. It was better, wasn't it, if his father tried to rectify those mistakes?

The question was then whether his father *would* try to rectify his mistakes.

He didn't give himself a chance to think about it.

"I don't want to do it anymore."

"What?" came the careful, measured answer.

"This. This job." Jacob paused. "You and Seth."

His father didn't reply as quickly this time. Then he said, "Let's talk about it."

And Jacob's world shifted.

Gaia hadn't spoken with Jacob for two weeks, but she saw him in her dreams.

She couldn't stop writing, despite everything. She needed her stories now more than ever. The comfort of putting words onto the page, of getting lost in the purpose of writing a novel. Getting lost in the words themselves. The familiarity of routine was a good way to deal with all the unexpected things that had happened in her life the past few weeks. Or so the numerous articles she'd read online said.

She had done a lot of reading on anxiety. At first, it was intimidating. Anxiety disorder was a mental illness. If she admitted to having a disorder, she would be admitting to being mentally ill. There was nothing wrong with being mentally ill. She knew that, deep in her core, and would go to battle with anyone who said otherwise. But it was different accepting that *she* was mentally ill.

Besides, it was such a weird concept. Or was the weird part that she now had a name for it? For those things her body went through? The way she struggled to breathe sometimes. The rapid beating of her heart at the slightest discomfort. How her brain went on and on, like a hamster on a wheel.

It was weird that she now knew her habits weren't habits, but symptoms of an anxiety disorder. She didn't need an official diagnosis—though she would get one when she was ready—when she said yes to every item on the "do I have anxiety" on-line questionnaire. Or when her gut told her that was the case. Or when she had panic attacks. Honest-to-goodness panic attacks.

She had thought those panic attacks were simply her way of processing. They probably were, but they didn't have to be.

Her life didn't have to be filled with anxiety and panic.

Funny how she had never even *considered* that was a possibility.

Hell, she hadn't considered she had an anxiety problem at all. She had never used *anxious* to describe a state of feeling for herself—or her characters, for that matter. As someone as widely read as her, as someone who made it her mission to know about all kinds of social issues, her ignorance on this matter stunned her. But it was a deliberate ignorance. Avoidance. Or denial. She must have known, at least subconsciously. And she didn't know how to feel about it.

It was a lot. Grappling with all of it was a lot. She needed time. To understand it, or at the very least, to wrap her head around it. Then she would go see a professional. Once she did that, she could face the fact that Gemma was . . . her sister. The documentation still lay on her kitchen table, untouched. She worked around it or ignored it. Gemma, mercifully, stayed away. Maybe she could sense Gaia needed space.

Which she did. She needed space and time. And routine. And, though she couldn't bring herself to say it out loud, Jacob.

Maybe that was why she poured herself into this book more

than any other. She delved into the relationships between her main characters and their parents. She focused especially on the thread between Chris and his mother. About responsibility and love, and the balance between the two. She got so much writing done in two weeks that she'd reached the post–emotional climax portion of the book.

Jade and Chris had fought about the pressure Chris was putting on her to confront her mother about what the woman expected from Jade. Jade said she would do it once Chris put up boundaries with his mother. They said things that hurt one another, especially when it turned out the things plaguing the relationship with their mothers were almost identical to what they were doing with one another. Neither of them needed to deal with those issues in a relationship they *chose* when they had to deal with them in relationships they didn't choose. So they went their separate ways.

It was always difficult to write the emotional climax. This one hit Gaia particularly hard. Probably because she put so much of herself into it. Probably because things weren't great between her and Jacob. She had pushed him away in real life— there was no point in denying it—and now, Chris and Jade were doing the same thing with one another.

Living it twice felt cruel. Worse yet was that *she* had been the only one doing the pushing with Jacob, unlike her characters. It was more noticeable in her dreams because of it. Jacob must have noticed it, too. But if he did, he said nothing.

In fact, he didn't engage with the dream at all. There was no flash of him in Chris. It was as if Jacob were merely a puppet for Gaia's words.

She didn't let the desperation of that derail her. She was tempted to. Many times, she wanted to write something that she knew would illicit a response from him.

But if she thought breaking things off twice was cruel, she could only imagine how he felt. It must have contributed to why he didn't respond. And she couldn't bear to punish him because he was trying to protect himself. He had every right to.

Which was why when she got a message from him two days into writing the post–emotional climax scenes, she understood.

Stop. Please.

She stared at the words. Traced them over her screen. Her phone asked if she wanted to copy the text.

"No," she murmured. "I don't have to."

It was already repeating in her head, like a terrible song she couldn't stop hearing.

Okay.

She sent her reply and switched off her phone.

The song echoed in the sudden emptiness in her heart, her head.

Her soul.

When she cried this time, it had nothing to do with panic or anxiety or the fact that she had a sister she never knew about. It was because she had been stupid enough to lose the man who had made her feel special. Who cared enough about her to come look for her when she didn't reply. Who embraced her magic as best he could because he wanted to share the burden with her. He visited her, took her out, cared about her despite all of her quirks. Her insecurities. Her anxieties.

And because she realized now that through all of those anxieties—about people, about being in new spaces, about change—not once, not *once*, had she been anxious about Jacob.

CHAPTER 29

"Shit. Shit, shit, *shit*."

"Get a grip," Seth told her, annoyance adding an edge to his voice.

"I can't get a grip," Gaia snapped back. "I'm nervous. *Shit*."

Seth rolled his eyes and reached out a hand to Lizzy. She took it, smiling up at him, and some of Gaia's tension eased at the affection. They were better now, Seth and Lizzy, after everything that had happened. It made them ridiculously sweet, annoyingly close, but she only felt that way because she didn't have her own person.

But if everything went well, she would.

"You owe me," Seth said, not for the first time. "And I'm going to choose a day when you least expect it to collect."

"You're being very intense and I don't need that energy right now," Gaia replied.

"Would you like me to call Jake and tell him the truth?"

Lizzy elbowed him before Gaia could reply. "Cut it out. She told you she was nervous. Let's get out of her hair and let her be nervous alone."

"This is our house, woman. I can stay as long as I want."

He silenced Lizzy's retort with a hard kiss to her lips. She was laughing when he drew back. Gaia made a face. "Please leave. You two are disgusting."

Seth smirked. "I forgot my wallet. Give me a second."

As soon as he left, Lizzy said, "It'll be fine, you know. He adores you."

Gaia hoped her smile reflected Lizzy's confidence. "I hope so."

"I've seen his face whenever Seth brings you up. You have nothing to worry about."

Except she did. Because she'd screwed up possibly the best thing in her life because she had been too scared to trust it. *Him.*

"Thank you."

Lizzy smiled, and Gaia realized it wasn't only Seth's relationship with her that had improved. Gaia had Lizzy in her corner now, too. She had gone from having no one, to having a best friend, a man she loved, a new friend, and . . . and a sister. A wave of emotion washed over her, just as it had that moment at the book signing. It was overwhelming and terrifying. She was learning that most things for her were.

But *these* things? Support, love, family? They were good things. She didn't have to be terrified of good things.

"Hey—this is random, but I've always wanted to ask you about your sheets."

Lizzy lifted her eyebrows, amusement tugging the corners of her mouth up. Before she could prod, Seth came back.

"Did I hear you ask Lizzy about sheets?" he asked.

"Yeah. I was asking where I could find new ones if things with Jacob and me go well."

Seth swore, and both Lizzy and Gaia laughed.

"Come on," Lizzy said, tucking her arm into Seth's. "We can scrub that picture out of your mind with lots of alcohol at dinner. Let us know how it goes," she directed at Gaia. "If you can pull yourself away."

With a wink, she dragged a groaning Seth out the door. And then Gaia was alone. She looked around the flat. It looked the same as it had the night she and Jacob met except the furniture was back in its place. It felt significant. The venue, and the fact that she wanted to meet him here. Significant and sneaky. She wasn't sure he would come if she told him she wanted to speak to him. She didn't think she would have the courage to say what she needed to say if he didn't.

She settled on the couch, opened the book she had once read during a dream, and waited. She knew the details of Seth and Lizzy's décor intimately, and nothing about the book, by the time the knock on the door came. She pressed a button, and the recording Seth had made—with protest—played.

"Come inside, dear brother."

She rolled her eyes. She hadn't been able to convince Seth to sound more natural than that.

She pretended to be reading when Jacob walked in.

"Dear brother?" he said. "When the hell did you start—"

He'd seen her.

She put up a finger. "Hang on. I have twenty more pages to read."

Slyly, she looked at him. Felt an almost physical knock at how good he looked. At how much she had missed him in the last two weeks.

"I couldn't resist, sorry."

He shoved his hands into his pockets. "Where's Seth?"

"Not here."

"I heard him—" He broke off when she played the recording. Eyebrows lifted. "You had him record that?"

"I did."

"And he . . . did?"

"He's still dealing with some guilt."

"Apparently, if he's tricking me into seeing you."

"To be fair, I did most of the tricking." She stood. "He wasn't thrilled with this plan."

"The one where he tricks me into coming over for dinner, but really, it's to see the woman who broke my heart? I wonder why he felt that way."

Oh. He was pissed.

Did you expect he would fall to his knees in gratitude that you're here?

It would have been nice, she mentally told that contrary voice in her head. Then she told herself to focus.

"I'm sorry. I was afraid . . . I was afraid you wouldn't come if I asked to speak with you."

He didn't say anything. Her heart complained at the rudeness. Or was it merely lamenting that he didn't seem happy to see her? To hear her out?

"I wanted to do this in a book," she blurted. Might as well. "I resisted, actually, for a week after you asked me to stop. I . . . I wanted to respect your wishes. But I wanted to do this in a book. Tell you I'm sorry and that I know I have . . . issues."

Still, that silence.

"I don't trust people. The world. I'm terrified of being rejected again and getting hurt and feeling alone. And falling for you has exacerbated all of those fears. Being rejected and hurt by *you* would leave me feeling much lonelier than anything else in my life has. Saying all of that . . . It would have been easier in a dream."

He didn't speak, but she had run out of steam, so she didn't say anything else. She waited, hoping for any sign that he hadn't stopped caring for her.

"You've had a lot of that in your life," he said eventually. She almost cried with relief. "The rejection and hurt and loneliness. Why is it worse with me?"

Would nothing in this conversation be easy?

"I didn't know them. My parents, my family." She bit her lip. "The foster care system was designed on the foundation of rejection and hurt and loneliness. It wasn't personal."

"This is?"

Screw it.

"I . . . I love you, Jake. It's pretty damn personal."

His expression changed by only a fraction. But that fraction was a softening. It was all she needed.

"I hated that you saw me that way." She didn't bother clarifying. He knew what she meant. He would hear it in her broken voice, too. "How could you love someone like that?"

"Gaia—"

"It was easier to push you away than deal with you looking at me and seeing that. That . . . that *person* who couldn't get her shit together. Who couldn't—" She broke off when her eyes prickled. "If I didn't see that, I wouldn't be reminded that I had a problem." She paused. "I've been running away from that problem for longer than I can remember. I just . . . I keep *running*. You know that." She didn't wait for his confirmation. "But I ran from you, too, and I've never regretted anything more in my life."

She didn't bother wiping the tears.

"So now I've stopped running. I'm facing it. No more having hard conversations in dreams. No more taking refuge in my dreams." She took a breath. "And I hope—I *hope*—I didn't mess things up so badly that you won't take me back."

Again, silence covered them. It coated the hope in her chest, stifling it, and another tear ran down her cheek.

"It's okay," she rasped. "It's okay if you don't feel the same—"

It happened so quickly. One second he was standing, watching her, his chest rising and falling in a quick, unsteady rhythm. Then his lips were on hers.

She opened her mouth. She didn't know if it was to welcome his tongue or to cry out in relief. She didn't care. She wrapped her arms around him, tears streaming down her face at his warmth, his familiarity.

"Baby," he said, moving back, cupping her face. "Stop crying."

"I am. I did."

He chuckled, wiping at the tears that kept coming. "I love you, but I'm not sure I want to taste what's coming out of your nose."

She laughed, but then her brain replayed his words. "You love me?"

"Duh," he said gently. "Everything you've told me I already knew, Gaia. But you needed to know it, too. You needed to . . . decide what you wanted. Whether you wanted to trust me."

"I do. I do trust you."

"I know." Tenderly, he kissed her. "I know this was hard for you. I . . . I appreciate it. I appreciate that you love me and are facing it. More importantly, I'm so damn proud you love yourself enough to face it."

She leaned her forehead against his chest, as if by doing so, his heartfelt words would seep into her mind. She hadn't thought about it that way, but facing her anxiety *was* a form of self-love. She needed to accept every part of herself. That meant acknowledging every part of herself. It meant asking for help when she needed it. She deserved to love herself. She deserved to be loved, too. And she would learn how to love herself—and to accept the love those around her offered.

"You've inspired me," he said close to her ear. "I changed my life because of you."

She leaned back. "You changed your life?"

"Seth didn't tell you?" he asked.

"We haven't spoken about you, really. We thought it for the best."

"He really has grown, hasn't he?" Jacob shook his head. "I guess it means I can tell you the good news myself." He smiled so brightly she almost blinked. "You're looking at a freshly appointed graphic designer at Scott Brand Solutions."

"You were demoted?"

"Yes, indeed."

She laughed at the giddy reply. "Your dream," she said, realizing it. "You have your dream job now, don't you?"

"Yeah."

"That's pretty damn impressive." She got a grin in reply. She hated to ask the next question, but she needed to know. "How did your father take it?"

"It was his idea."

"Oh. Wow." She paused. "We have a lot to catch up on, don't we?"

"Yes." He lifted her then, without warning. Her legs automatically wrapped around his waist. "We have time."

She rested her forehead on his. "Yes." It came out in a whisper. It was all she could manage. "Yes, we do."

Their kiss this time was slower, deeper, more meaningful than anything else they'd shared. They lowered to the couch, but he pulled away.

"I see you, Gaia," he said, eyes sweeping over her face in a way that told her he did. "I see *all* of you, every part. Not only the good, or the bad, but everything. I see the parts you like about yourself and the parts you don't. And I love them all. I just . . . I love *you*."

It took her a moment to work through the emotion. To fight off the tears.

"I was right about you," she whispered. "That night we met, I thought you were too damn charming for your own good."

"I thought it was dopey."

"It's both," she said. "And I love that about you. I love you."

He pressed a gentle kiss to her lips. When he pulled away, he said, "Should we take this to the bedroom? I want to give Seth something to be angry about. This whole therapy thing has turned him into a pretty decent brother and I'd like to see how far that goes."

Laughing, she pulled his head back down.

Epilogue

"I don't think I'm going to like it if I don't live this dream with you."

"I can't base a hero on you again," Gaia said, slipping under the covers and curling into Jacob's side. His heart filled at the simple thing.

"Who says?"

She laughed. "I think my agent and editor would have something to say about it."

"They haven't even read the last book yet."

"You can't stop moving forward because the industry is slow."

"Which is your way of saying the book you started today is going to have a new hero who looks nothing like me and you're going to make out with him."

She didn't even have the decency to pretend to think about it. "Pretty much, yeah."

He laughed and pulled her in closer, only vaguely upset by the idea of her making out with someone else. The fictional world of her dreams wasn't the real world after all. And the real world had been pretty damn amazing in the last month for both him and Gaia. He could see the slight shifts in her behavior that proved she no longer preferred fiction to reality. Even if he hadn't had the benefit of her saying it to him.

Still, she said it.

Having her at his side made the more complicated things in his life easier to handle.

The adjustment at work that wasn't going as smoothly as he'd hoped. The changed roles in his family that were complicated, too. Yes, his father was trying. Seth was trying. But they were still alike, and Jacob stepping back from playing mediator—something both of them had agreed to in the aftermath of that conversation he'd had with his father—hadn't changed that fact. Tension tended to visit and linger when they were together.

But Jacob didn't expect miracles. Trying was okay. And since his relationships with both his father and Seth were getting better, he couldn't complain. The responsibility his mother had placed on him had been shared between him, his father, and Seth, and the weight it had lifted from him, allowed him to enjoy life.

He had a job that gave him time *to* have a life he enjoyed. He was spending every second of that time with the woman he loved.

"Let's sleep and get this over with," he said with a mostly fake grumble.

He'd kind of enjoyed experiencing the happily ever after between Chris and Jade. It was more rewarding because of the entire journey he'd been through with them. He would have liked to go through it again—as Gaia's boyfriend this time; it might have made things more interesting—but he thought that maybe that book was meant to bring them together. And now that they were, there was no reason for him to be in another one.

All of this assumed he wouldn't be in her dreams again, of course. He didn't know why he was so sure of that assumption.

Perhaps because it ended up being true. When he woke up the next morning, he had no recollection of the dream.

"Hey," he said, nuzzling Gaia's neck to wake her. "Stop kissing other men and come back to me."

She opened her eyes with a moan. It could have been in protest, or because his hand was currently making its way to her breast.

"Isn't this better than a dream?" he asked, teasing her nipple.

Her body froze. "No."

"No?" He frowned, hand stilling. "I think you're supposed to lie and tell me it is so I can continue believing I'm better than the heroes in your dreams."

"No," she said again, flopping onto her back. "There was no dream, Jake. There was . . . nothing. There was *nothing*."

"Didn't you write yesterday?"

"Yes."

She wrote again that day, and the next, and the next, but each night came and there was no dream. Jacob tried to prepare her to accept it. Tried to prepare himself for if she needed him. And she would. This was a big change, and changes were hard for her, big or small.

But on the fourth night as they went to bed, Gaia said, "I think I know why the dreams stopped."

"You do?"

"I think . . . I think they stopped because I found my happily ever after in real life." She cupped his face. "I think the point of it all was to find you, my hero. That's why you were in my dreams with me. After true love's kiss, or whatever. The universe, or whoever controls this, was giving me a sign. You're my hero."

He studied her. "You don't sound upset."

"I'm not *not* upset. But this . . . It's a good thing, right? It went away, and I think I'll always miss it, and I guess maybe it'll even take time to grieve it, but it went away because it knows I'm happy. And safe." She dropped her hand to take his. "It's a good thing, Jake. It's a . . . it's a magical thing."

"I love you," he said, amazed by her remarkable strength. By her steady growth.

"Show me," she whispered.

And he did.

"Is this seat taken?"

Gemma lifted her head, the *no* on her lips. She knew the coffee shop was full, but she wasn't in the mood to talk to anyone. It made her feel guilty, but she needed some time to herself, away from her home.

The home she had shared with Levi for such a long time, she didn't know how it would feel without him.

But she might find out how it felt sooner than she was prepared for.

"You don't have to say yes. I would have hated it if someone asked me, too."

Gemma stared. It was Gaia. It was her sister. Her freaking *sister* was asking her if she could sit with her and Gemma was saying nothing.

"Yes," she said, not caring how eager it sounded. "Yes, yes, of course."

Gaia sat down. "Thanks."

"You don't have to . . ." She trailed off. What was the use of small talk when her sister was sitting across from her? "How did you know I was here?"

"Levi." Gaia frowned. "He's still very weird, but I guess I'm okay with it since he obviously cares about you."

Except he's a ghost who might be disappearing soon.

She thought it best not to say those words. Pretending he was her boyfriend was bad enough.

"I'm sorry it's taken me so long to find you." Gaia got right to the point. "I needed time to deal with some stuff. I'll probably need more time with this, too, but I figured . . . Well, I figured we should at least . . . talk."

"Okay," Gemma said. She didn't think Gaia wanted to jump right into the crappy stuff though. She cleared her throat. "How was your evening?"

Back to small talk then. She would have chided herself, but Gaia smiled.

"Not as magical as I expected."

"Is that . . . a sex thing? Because if it is, that's super disappointing. Jacob looked like he knows how to treat a vagina and—"

"Gemma," Gaia said with a laugh. "It wasn't about sex. And—I can't believe I'm saying this—but Jacob's knowledge of the vagina is fine. More than fine."

"Good," Gemma breathed. "Life's too short to be with someone who doesn't know what to do. Or doesn't at least try."

"Agreed."

There was a short pause.

"What did you mean? With the magical."

"Nothing," Gaia said, shaking her head. "It's nothing."

But something about the way she said it . . .

No, it couldn't be. Gemma had learned the hard way that magic wasn't real for other people. Besides, did magic even describe her abilities? She could see ghosts. That was more supernatural than magical.

But—

"Are you talking about real magic, Gaia?" she asked, curiosity winning out over her desire not to scare her sister away. She would blame the nerves and pretend to faint if this didn't work out. Delicately, she would knock her head and claim not to remember anything.

A sound plan, she decided.

"Real magic doesn't exist, Gemma."

"Of course it doesn't," she agreed.

But Gaia said the words without emotion. Coolly, calmly, as if—

As if she was lying.

Gemma smiled. "And do you feel the same way about ghosts?"

ACKNOWLEDGMENTS

I've been lucky to work with an incredible team on this book.

Thank you to my agent, Courtney Miller-Callihan, for loving the idea of a magical contemporary romance, even though it was a first from me, and a gamble to take to publishers. To Esi Sogah and Norma Perez-Hernandez, for reading this book and seeing its potential, and working so hard to turn it into something I'm so incredibly proud of. (As a side note, they were also thrilled to hear about my pregnancy, even though it put this book on pause for some time. I will always send baby pictures as a thank you, even when you don't ask for them.) To the entire Kensington team for working so hard on making this book a success: I appreciate each and every one of you.

I wrote and edited a good portion of this book while I was pregnant with twins during a pandemic, and it was not easy. I could not have done it without my support system. Thank you to my husband, who assured me I could back out at any point and focus on growing babies, and he'd handle the professional fallout. (He didn't say this explicitly, but I know that's what he meant when he told me it was okay to go take a nap.) To all my friends and family—thank you all for caring about me during such a difficult time. To Olivia Dade, Talia Hibbert, Jenni

Fletcher and Kate Clayborn, for always being so supportive and candid. I can't tell you how much it means. To Nick from The Infinite Limits of Love blog, for always supporting me and being such a kind friend, and to every single reviewer and reader who has taken a chance on my books and shared them with others, I cannot thank you enough.

When I decided to write this book, I was doing it for purely selfish reasons. Like Gaia, writing is an outlet for me, and I was going through a particularly tough time in terms of anxiety then. So, I wrote about a romance author who escaped into her books, made that part literal, and gave myself the freedom to imagine what life could be if I became the heroine of my own books.

At the end of the process, I realized that this book had become much more important than simply an outlet. It was a love letter to romance, the genre that has brought me joy and hope during even the darkest of moments. It was also a representation of anxiety in the way I've experienced it: as a part of my life, not the entirety of it. I dearly hope readers who share this disorder with me will see that as well, and understand that the love, hope and laughter of this book is their right. Not only in fiction and dreams, but in real life.

Lastly, to my dear babies, I love you. Everything I do is for you.

Don't miss Gemma's story

A GHOST IN SHINING ARMOR,

coming soon from

Therese Beharrie

and

Zebra Books

Connect with U(s)

Visit us online at
KensingtonBooks.com
to read more from your favorite authors, see books
by series, view reading group guides, and more.

Join us on social media

for sneak peeks, chances to win books and prize packs,
and to share your thoughts with other readers.

facebook.com/kensingtonpublishing
twitter.com/kensingtonbooks

Tell us what you think!

To share your thoughts, submit a review,
or sign up for our eNewsletters, please visit:
KensingtonBooks.com/TellUs.